THE OLD JOKE

REINA JAMES lives in Sussex with her husband. Her deb
This Time of Dying, was shortlisted for the C
Writers' Prize and was awar'
McKitterick Priz

The
Old Joke

REINA JAMES

Portobello
BOOKS

Published by Portobello Books Ltd 2009

Portobello Books Ltd
Twelve Addison Avenue
Holland Park
London W11 4QR

A CIP catalogue record is available from the British Library

9 8 7 6 5 4 3 2 1

ISBN 978 1 84627 194 6

www.portobellobooks.com

Designed by Richard Marston
Typeset in Electra by Avon DataSet Ltd, Bidford on Avon, Warwickshire
Printed in the UK by CPI William Clowes Beccles NR34 7TL

One

I'm waiting to pay for the paper when I hear an old woman in the queue behind me… 'And this ridiculous nonsense with children. I mean, we all watched Punch and Judy, didn't we? And nobody in our generation ever hit anybody or used a gun.' I turn to see if she looks as stupid as she sounds. She catches my eye and there's a tiny flicker of recognition – an expression I've got used to over the years – but before she can say anything, the assistant's taken my money and I'm out on the pavement and walking away. It's windy here in Muswell Hill, a leaf-launching October wind. I push on, a little colder than I expected to be in my thick jumper. There's one more item on the list: a book on dry gardens that I ordered last week. It's in. I buy it and go home, thinking about the woman and what I could have said.

Leslie's at the front door before I'm up the path. 'Guess what, Missus!' he says. 'Charlie's just rung! *You've got a job!*' Charlie used to be my agent. Leslie's my husband. 'Here.' He holds out the phone. 'Ring him back. I said you'd ring him straightaway.'

'What do you mean? What job?'

'He didn't say.'

'Didn't you ask?'

'Course I asked. It's good money, that's all he said. He wants to tell you himself. Go on, ring him.' Leslie now has the phone in one hand and the phone book in the other. He approaches me with both, twinkling like the glamorous assistant proffering the saw.

'But I don't want a job.'

'You don't know what it is yet.'

'I don't care what it is. I don't want it.' I take off my coat and drop it over the bannister.

'Find out what it is. Just for me.'

'I'll find out, that's all.'

Charlie answers straightaway. 'No need for me to ask how Leslie's doing,' he says when we've exchanged greetings, 'I've already heard. Listen, you'll need to meet the client for an interview tomorrow but as far as I can tell it's sewn up. It's an ad for some pill or other. Something to do with brains, staying young – er – you know…'

'I don't want to do this, Charlie—'

'…They love you. They're kids but they know your work. It'll be three thousand for a day's filming and then repeats. They're buying you lunch after. Twelve-thirty for the meeting – off Piccadilly.' He gives me the address and the producer's name, and I try to tell him that I won't turn up but he isn't listening. He repeats the address to make sure and I write it on the pad this time. After all these years, Charlie's still overriding me. He says, 'We'll speak tomorrow afternoon. God bless.'

I put the phone down and give Leslie the facts. He's delighted. 'You never know where this might lead, Mim! This could be the start of God knows what!' Leslie lives in a fan-shaped universe where every road branches out to innumerable other roads and each of those to more. For the rest of the day, he persuades, I resist and then, predictably, I surrender. I have to admit, I'm curious. Why me? I decide that I'll go to the interview and then turn down whatever I'm offered.

The endless speculation begins. What is this pill? Why have they chosen me? What do I wear? Do I present myself as I am, or as I imagine they might want me to be? We sketch out the worst possible ad as we're making dinner: an old woman's sitting in a hat and coat with two cats at her feet. She's dowdy, hopeless, frozen stiff and ready for the abattoir. 'I'm sixty-five,' she says, 'but I can't think straight.' Then she's on her bed, still in the coat but there's a blanket over her and the cats are lying doggo on the floor beside her. They're all dying of hypothermia. An ambulance arrives and she's carried out on a stretcher with a cat under each arm. Now she's in a hospital bed and being attended to by a woman with a clipboard. After a short but fruitful conversation, they hold hands. Last scene: the old woman's wearing jeans and a T-shirt. The room is elegant, there are books everywhere – Rimbaud, Bertrand Russell – the cats are ecstatic, there's a cafetière on the table and biscuits – no, says Leslie, baklava on a plate. The voice-over's jolly: 'Bing-Bong for Brains! Get a PhD in one-two-three!'

Then Charlie rings to say that they can't do lunch after all, some problem with another client, and the time's been changed to five o'clock. The *worst* time: no seats on the tube and I won't get home until seven at the earliest. So what's new? They're indifferent to my needs. If I want to go to the interview, I'll do as I'm told.

We decide that I should look sharp so I wear a black suit, jet earrings and enough make-up to cope with strong lighting. Leslie walks me to the station and waves me off at the barrier.

'Knock 'em stupid, my darling,' he says, rather too loudly.

The office turns out to be a recording studio. There's a huge television blaring out the news and a breakfast-bar affair with piles of crockery, a couple of coffee percolators, boxes of various teas, a basket of croissants, bowls of fruit, biscuits and chocolate bars. Have I got off at the wrong floor? Is this the *canteen*? I announce myself at reception. I'm asked to wait. There's a vast, blue L-shaped sofa, so deep that I'll only be able to leave it with help, like a sack being dragged from a cargo hold. As I'm about to perch on the corner, a young woman approaches me and puts out her hand.

'Miss Shaw?' She's pretty, she's young and there's absolutely nobody behind her smile. 'Please follow me,' she says. She's in four-inch heels and I'm in low court shoes; we travel the corridors together, a high-stepping pony and its peasant master. We reach the interview room in silence and she opens the door, standing with her arm outstretched to usher me in. There are four men inside, young, groomed – three of them bank clerks, if you were casting. The fourth is painterly, rather too deliberately so. They rise to their feet simultaneously. The painter speaks, pushing his dark hair behind his ears.

'My name's Antonio, I'm directing. Thank you so much for coming. It's an honour to meet you.' Then he tells me the names of his chums – the clients – which I forget immediately, we all shake hands and everybody sits down. 'We're doing a campaign aimed at the elderly,' he says, leaning forward with his elbow on his knee. The hair flops forward, he pushes it back. I want to cut the whole lot off and be done with it. 'We're hoping that you might be one of our frontline celebrities.'

He doesn't ask me to read. I don't ask to see the script. They're

4

giving me the once-over, checking to see if I can follow a conversation without dozing off. I can see in his eyes that he knows I was famous at some point before he was born and therefore equivalent to the Spitfire. How do I feel about being asked to represent 'the elderly' by this young man? I want to tell him that 'the elderly' is not a single organism, that he knows nothing and that he has no idea what I know. Neither is 'the young' a useful category, although I have to admit that I'm finding it impossible to differentiate between the bank clerks. Antonio smiles at me. He's anxious, I can see that now, and I'm immediately disarmed. 'I hope you don't mind,' he says, 'but we need a photograph of you, just for the records. May I?' He pulls out a camera and waits for my response.

I say, 'Of course. Where would you like me?'

'You can stay there if you like.'

'Is your family from Spain?' It's a non sequitur but I need to make conversation; I feel very exposed in front of these young men. Do I mug or look serious? They're all staring at me. I decide to smile.

'My father. He's from Seville.'

'Really? That's a beautiful place. And your mother?'

'My mother comes from Kent. Dover, I believe.' He checks the image, takes another and then puts away the camera. I can see that it's time to get down to business.

'So?' I say.

He opens the laptop on the table at his side and taps away at the keys, then turns it slightly so that I can get a better view. 'This is our idea. I hope it amuses you.'

It's my face. It's my posing face, as it was fifty years ago. I haven't seen this photograph for a long time but as one of my 'selves', it's vivid – my compliment to Rita Hayworth. I'm gorgeous, with that curious opalescent glow that film photographers whistle up, making silk out of the light. As I watch, my face begins to melt, small upheavals shift my cheeks and lips, my hair shortens, the picture settles into a still from my final film, *The Curfew*, in 1968. Not quite stopping traffic any more but still a star. The fur coat's turned into a mac and the lighting's a little harsher, that's all.

Antonio points at the screen. I'm melting again. Now it has no reference points, this metamorphosis, it's moving like maggots in a bucket, stopping every four or five seconds to show how it believes me to have aged. The final image is obviously meant to be me. It's hideous.

'We freeze it there – of course we'll do the sequence again when we get a proper photograph – and then it, *you*, tell us a bit about your life and how you feel about the product.' Antonio turns the screen away and I look at a point in the middle distance, trying to gather my thoughts. There's a shuffling on the sofa and the bank clerks lean forward, as a man.

'It must have been a bit of a shock, seeing yourself,' one of them ventures. 'You know, so long ago.'

Even the other clerks can see that this is a tremendous blunder. They shuffle more vigorously and Antonio says, 'I hope we haven't offended you. We all love this sequence. We think you look fantastic.'

'Perhaps you could explain exactly what it is you'll want from me?' I'm being grand and I have, of course, registered the enormity of being asked to appear on television but there are other issues here and that seems to me to be the least important. Apart from anything else, they've usurped my face.

'We want you to tell us – it'll be scripted, obviously – how it feels to be young inside, still hungry to do the things you haven't done, not wanting to be defeated by time. That sort of thing.'

'Why not ask somebody who's actually working? There are plenty of people you could use. I really don't understand why you're talking to me.'

'We'll be using a politician—'

'Who?'

'… and a presenter and a writer…' he looks at the sofa; the young men become thoughtful but say nothing. 'And a sports personality. Quite a few people, actually.'

'But why me?'

'You were famous. Loved. It'll be an honour to work with you.'

I really want to go home now. I want Leslie and several glasses of red wine. I get up. This startles them all and they get up awkwardly, uncertain about my mood. I smile. I must look deranged. 'I'll speak to my agent,' I say. 'And then we'll see, shall we?'

'Thank you so much for coming. We really appreciate it.' Antonio offers me his hand. I shake it and turn away from the clerks' chorus before I have to do the whole line again.

The journey home is appalling, standing the whole way. I want someone to offer me a seat and yet, of course, I don't. When I get in, I find two coats over the bannister. I know these coats very well. I need bonhomie to meet their owners and I am, at this moment, without bonhomie. I am also without courtesy, and enter the kitchen like a matron after lights out. Poppy and Rolf are at the table. Leslie's on his feet and turns to me. 'Darling, I'm so sorry. I heard the door but we were just having a little discussion about Rolf going to Manchester—'

'Bloody right,' says Poppy.

'Mim.' Rolf raises an empty glass to me. 'Welcome home.'

'Hi, Mim,' says Poppy without interest.

'How was it?' Leslie kisses me. His eyebrows are eloquent. I gather that all is not well with Rolf and Poppy.

To Leslie I say, 'Lots to tell you. Not now.' To Rolf and Poppy I say, 'I'm tired and hungry, actually. Would you mind if Leslie and I have dinner? We've only got two chops but there's cheese if you want.'

'We're going anyway,' says Rolf. 'Let you debrief. Get up, Poppy.' We follow them to the hall and help them into their coats.

As we open the front door – and it's not a particularly pleasant evening, with the wind blowing in – Poppy kisses me goodbye and says, 'I'm pleased he's got a job, for Christ's sake. I'm not saying he shouldn't work.' She turns on Rolf. 'I don't want you in digs with her. I won't have it.' Her face, so rarely agreeable these days, is distorted and she's clearly about to cry. I'm trapped in the draught by the door. Do I invite them back in? We'll spend the evening refereeing if I do. Or shall I be callous, push her out, and promise to phone in the morning? She's still talking and I'm trying to come to a decision when Leslie and Rolf solve the problem. They hug each other and say good night. Rolf goes down the steps.

I put my arm round her. 'Why don't we have coffee tomorrow?' I say. 'I'll come round at eleven.' To my relief, she agrees. We kiss again and she trails off to the car. Rolf opens his door first and she has to wait in the wind while he gets in, her neck bent low in defeat. I like Rolf. I like them both, even though they create turbulence. He's never behaved badly at home, only on tour, and Poppy's had a few liaisons of her own. Why is she so hysterical about this?

Leslie closes the door and holds out his arm to receive my hand. 'You all right, Missus?' It takes us twenty minutes to make chops, mash and salad, during which I tell him about the interview.

'Bloody cheek,' he says, 'turning you into an old woman.'

We're washing up when Leslie has an idea. 'Why don't you take the job and then get them to change it?'

'Change what?' I'm still not sure I understand Leslie's enthusiasm for this project. I can't remember the last time he tried to get me out of the house and working.

'Everything. Why didn't they show you the script?'

'I don't think I asked to see it.'

'That'll need work, you can bet your boots. Get them to change the lot. Agree to everything, be nice and then make a few suggestions. They're children, for God's sake. Who have they asked? What do they know? *You* know. *I* know. We could do it better. Tell them I'll do it. I'll write them something. They'll love it, I promise you.'

'Why are you so keen for me to do this?'

'It's a few hours' work. You'll be gone a day at most and then, who knows? This could open doors.' Leslie hasn't really grasped the full picture here. I think he still sees this job as a vehicle for his wife to make a comeback rather than an advert for some quack elixir. I know that if I agree to do it, I'll detest myself. I pour us both more wine. 'I could write you something anyway,' he says. 'A musical. Let's write a musical about getting old.'

'Sondheim's done it already.'

'Wouldn't be like ours.'

'You do it then. You write it.'

'Bloody will.'

'Bloody good. What's it called?'

'Gaga.'

We both think that's extremely funny.

When I ring Charlie, he tells me that he hasn't heard from them. 'I'll chase it up. How did it go?'

'Quite odd. They've made some film of me ageing—' I do my best Arthur Askey '... *and now, before your very eyes...*'

'Ridiculous.'

'Unsettling. Anyway, I don't want to do it.'

'You don't want to do it?'

'No. I'm not selling drugs. It's really not up my street.'

Leslie starts shouting. 'Of course she'll do it, Charlie. Let me talk to her. I'll sort her out.' I hand him the telephone and walk away. I can hear him saying that he'll talk to me, that he should meet the writer and make a few changes. I look out of the window and make a note to myself to plant something yellow next to the gate. Leslie rings off. 'Charlie'll get back to us,' he says to me. 'When he's got a bit more gen.'

'I'm not doing it, Leslie. Really, I'm not.'

'Wait and see.'

'Not doing it.'

'Wait and see.'

It's Friday and therefore very unlikely that anyone can be 'chased up', as Charlie puts it. As far as I'm concerned, there's nothing to chase. The morning brought its particular clarity: the whole affair is ludicrous.

*

Poppy and I are sitting in her kitchen. It's not a welcoming room. There's too much blue formica and nasty tiling: blue here, white there, garish fruit and veg border and all the wall space made grim with blue gloss. The chairs are hard, wooden and rickety, there are marbled blue tiles on the floor and the neon strip is absolutely ruthless. All in all, I can only endure this barrage by focusing on Poppy's puffy face and my mug of coffee. The mug is lime green and has the words *Dad Rules Here OK* painted on the side.

Poppy's crying. 'That was the longest time. The longest ever. I really thought he was going to leave. For that cow!'

'But that was *years* ago.'

'Nineteen eighty-three,' she says, offended, as if it was last week.

'Look, she's old now. They're both old now. You can't honestly think that Rolf's going to leave you for an old woman!'

What am I saying? Are we, Poppy and I, too old to provoke desire? One never actually says, *it's over now*. My façade may have started to come away from its mortar but in the dark, in bed with Leslie, I'm just me. There are no mirrors in the bed, nothing to remind us of what we've become, only reminders of what we know and love. As Poppy opens her mouth to argue, I add, 'And he needs the job. You can't stop him going just because he behaved like a prat with Doreen whatever-her-bloody-name-is.'

'It's six weeks.'

'You can visit. And he'll be home on Sundays.'

'That leaves six nights.'

'Five if he catches the last train on Saturday.'

'It's a long play, he'll miss it.'

'He can order a taxi.'

Poppy slumps down onto the table with her head on her arms.

Her voice is muffled. 'Christ, Mim. I never thought I'd have to go through this again. Don't you ever worry about Leslie?'

I say, 'No.' And the truth is, I mean it.

Charlie calls just after lunch. 'Dear girl. What did I tell you? I've just had a call from the client and they want to meet you again. I've suggested Tuesday at eleven. All right?'

Leslie's standing next to me with his ear bent to the phone. I take a step away and sit on the hall chair. 'Charlie… I don't want to be too bloody about this but I don't—' Leslie squats in front of me. I know this is hurting his knees and I stand again. 'I don't want to do this.'

'Why not? What's your problem?'

'I don't like these big drug companies. I don't want to be a part of it, that's all. It's not something I want to put my name to.' Even as I say this, I realize that it sounds utterly lame. If I'd been known for my scruples then I might have had some rationale for a late stand against the dark forces, but I was never uncompromising, never politically alert. I don't do crusades. It's an awkward moment. I say, 'Hold on,' and give Leslie the telephone. Charlie must be getting used to this by now, a word with me, then a handover to the man of the house.

'Charlie? Leslie here.' He puts his arm round my shoulders. 'Mim's had to answer the door… I'll talk to her, don't worry. It's great news… We're very pleased… As beautiful as ever… Of course she is. I'll tell her. Wait a minute, I'll get a pen. Off Portland Place, yes, I've got it… Tuesday… Of course I'll go with her. Bye, Charlie. Sure, bye.'

Without speaking, we go into the sitting room and Leslie sits close to me on the sofa. He says, 'So what's the matter?'

'I don't want to do it, that's all.'

'This drug rubbish. Since when are you against drugs? You're always taking a pill for something.' There's a long pause while he strokes my hand. Then he says, 'Do you want to know what I think?'

'I know what you think.'

'OK, smart-arse. What do you think I think?'

'I think you think I've lost my nerve.'

'You're right. That's exactly what I think. You haven't been in front of a camera for nearly forty years. Of course you're scared.' He turns my face to his and smiles. 'You'll be wonderful. They know that, that's why they want you.'

'Bollocks.'

'Why, then?'

'I don't know. I really don't. There are dozens of people better for this than me. I've been out of it for too long.'

'And whose fault's that?'

'You wanted me to stop.'

'It was the right thing to do, you were there for the children. I don't know what got into you later, turning your nose up at everything. Meet these blokes on Tuesday. See what they've got to say. Come on, Mim, darling. Don't let this go. You never know where—'

'I know, I know.'

'It's true. You don't. So?'

I'm thinking. Apart from the fact that I have absolutely no wish to work again, the horrible truth – am I really so vain? – is the unpleasant realisation that I don't want to be filmed. This is new. I never minded watching myself on screen. I never flinched at unflattering angles. I was interesting, and young.

Then Antonio showed me the maggots. 'I'm too old for this,' I say to Leslie. 'It's not nice, seeing yourself.'

'That's the point. You're getting on. We're both getting on. These people want you. Don't say no till you've talked to the others – see what they think.'

I don't care what they think. I know what I think. Leslie and I never take photographs. Apart from the occasional fuzzy party snap, my mirror face is the only one I see and it's not a true reflection. In the thirty-eight years since I retired I've been discreetly weathered by garden air; now I'd sooner swallow an endoscope than be examined by a television camera. Would anyone like a close-up of my stomach wall?

Two

We live in a small house, too small for three of us, which is why we bought a flat for our son, Max. It's nearby, a two-room, top-floor conversion with sloping ceilings and a good view of trees and sky, which suggests a dear little bed tucked under the eaves and a small square-paned window with sticky-out gingham curtains. Actually the bed's not dear at all, and the windows are permanently obscured with blinds that were once red and green with a design of coconuts and palm trees. They're faded now, bleached out by sunlight. The floors are covered with the original carpet, as thin as Ryvita, sea-green with dark stains. Leslie's old desk, the top piled with things that Max doesn't attend to, occupies the wall opposite the bed. His clothes hang on a metal rail, his shoes sit below. It smells, the room. It smells like a bar in the morning, before they wash the glasses. There's a kitchen, used to make coffee, a bathroom and a sitting room designed, you might say, by someone trying to capture student squalor. We offered him more furniture. We offered him money for paint, new carpets, new curtains, even a cleaner but, sad to say, he's made the place very much his own. He'll be forty-one next year.

I never visit socially. I go when I'm asked, to let in the plumber or collect the post if he's away but I don't pick up so much as an eyelash. And the extraordinary thing is this: the world never sees the Max that inhabits this room. On view, he's cashmere and Chanel cologne. I've come to understand that this is his inheritance. He puts on a good performance. To be frank, he does sober better than I ever did anything in my life.

We've eaten together every few Fridays since Leslie started doing retirement homes. These meals are always cooked by Leslie and me. Max attends. Tonight, as he reaches for bread, he knocks over his glass and it shatters on the floor. (Why should we deny ourselves wine? It makes no difference to Max whether he drinks from our bottle or brings down one of his own. If we put fruit juice on the table he'd only assume, rightly, that we were trying to set an example.) I clear up the mess while Leslie dishes up the pasta. Nobody speaks.

Max breaks the silence. 'We had this last week.'

Leslie's first in. 'I think we had omelettes last week, didn't we, Mim?'

'Smoked haddock,' I say. 'In milk.'

'Don't you want any, darling?' Leslie again, trying to appease.

'If that's all there is.'

I give Max a new glass and sit down. He's put the cashmere back in the cupboard and replaced it with a costume pieced together out of old horse-blankets. I hardly dress for dinner but I don't make a point of looking as if I've spent the night flat out on the Embankment. Max lifts his fork to his mouth and then puts it back on the plate.

'Charlie told me about the audition,' he says. 'That was a bit of a turn-up, wasn't it?' Max works for Charlie, or Charlie has the grace to say he does. I think he's doing us a favour. All the spaghetti's fallen off his fork and he busies himself with it, speaking into the plate while he twirls. 'Raise a toast and ring them bells.'

Leslie's about to speak but I interrupt with, 'Nothing's definite. Not yet.'

We eat for a few seconds more, then Max says, 'Well, I've got some news as well. Some definite news. I'm…' louder, 'going to get…' louder still, 'a dog!'

'A *dog*?' we cry, together.

'A four-legged friend, my friends. Good company, wouldn't you say?' Max is eager. A door opens briefly and we see a new – old? – expression on his face. 'Oh, yes! The wagging tail, the welcome, the slippers in the mouth. He's a good boy! A good boy!' He nearly laughs and pats the air beside him, and holds his glass out to be refilled.

Leslie is, as ever, generous. 'Lovely idea, darling. Marvellous company, a dog. And will you be taking him, her, it, to work?'

I can't bring myself to speak. The dog will a have a brief life with Max, a month at most. Then we'll be walking the dog, feeding the dog, training the dog, rushing the dog to the vet and eventually having the dog put down because it's too ill or too old to go on. Or we are.

Max says, 'No, no, no. I'm getting a dog-walker to come in. I've got a name, highly recommended, does masses of dogs round here. Lovely bloke, apparently. Makes it a family thing.'

Leslie touches my foot with his foot. This means I have to say something positive and soon. I can only think of one question. Size is all. 'What sort of dog?'

'Whatever appeals on the day.'

Leslie says, 'You're not buying from a breeder then?'

'Rescue centre.'

I say, 'I'm sure they've got rules. You'd have to be at home to look after it.' And there we are. I could have let him find that out for himself but I'm irritated and therefore blunt.

'Will you shut up!' Max shouts. 'Don't keep telling me what I can do!'

'It's a lovely idea,' Leslie soothes. 'We'll support you all the way, darling.'

'If I want a dog, then I'll have a fucking dog and that's the end of it. You won't have to see it. It'll be mine.'

He's defiant, head lowered and eyes up, glaring.

'Of course it will. But we'd love to see it, wouldn't we, Mim?'

I have a parallel world. Max lives there, in a house. Inside, there are items – books, loose covers, wardrobes, lavatory cleaner. Outside, a climbing frame, a tree or two, compost, a shed, a hoe. We visit, his family welcomes us. His wife is a delight. His children are a delight. *He's* a delight. A happy, sober Hercules. Once upon a time, in the real world, he was a nice boy. Our friends adored him. He was far more amenable than Constance, his sister, and went through school without a bad report until the day they found him under his bed, dead drunk. Bye-bye school, hello tutor. Ordinary education over by sixteen. Never found under the bed at home but drinking copiously when out and not pursuing a career of any sort. On his eighteenth birthday Leslie got him a job as general minion for an theatrical agent. And that's where he stayed until the place went bust and Charlie took him on.

Leslie's calmed him down. They're going to the rescue centre next week; somebody there can tell him that he's not a suitable candidate. My foot's being nudged again. 'Good idea,' I say, 'I can't wait.'

*

It's still dark when we get up. We've had a restless sleep, punctuated by trips to the lavatory and a police siren whooping down the road; now we're only too pleased to leave the rumpled sheets. Leslie goes down to make breakfast in his dressing-gown but the heating's only just come on and it's cold in the house. I need clothes. Instead of finding a jumper, I take a pair of knickers from the drawer and then sit on the bed in the dark, shivering and try to determine which way round they go by feeling for the bigger side, the back. I bend over and put a foot in each hole, then I pull the knickers past my knees and stand up. Wrong way round. I sit down and turn them, or so I believe, and then start to stand again. Still wrong. At this point, I ought to put the light on but I'm too stubborn. I sit down. I'm very cold. I take off the knickers. I inch them, slowly, slowly round and put them on again. If they're the wrong way round this time, then my body's back to front. I stand up just as Leslie calls to see if I've gone back to bed. Knickers on. Day begins.

Rolf and Poppy are coming to dinner tonight, with Aude, my oldest friend and her lodger, Alasdair. Aude introduced us to Rolf and Poppy in the summer of 1975. She'd been placed between them at a theatrical do and thought that we might all hit it off, which indeed we did, over a meal at Aude's flat. We reconvened a few weeks later, and during the evening we decided to make a regular thing of it every three or four weekends. Cooking protocol: a different house each time. We all take turns to bring food. Three couples, three courses and everyone has a go at making everything. The host table provides the wine and likes and dislikes aren't accounted for. If it's not up your alley then you eat more bread. My greatest flop still gets a mention – hairy turkey legs, almost black flesh, impossible to spear, overlapping the plate and smelling like a butcher's floor. I'd bought a cheap bag of them from a market, thinking they might stew up well in a bottle of red. Leslie thought I did well to get a laugh.

Aude and I met on a film set fifty years ago, two women at the scene of a car crash, one sobbing, Aude, and one heroically attempting first aid, me. Her husbands and lovers have been temporary attendees, passing through like cavalcades and leaving similar amounts of debris. None has lasted more than four years. Alasdair, in gardening terms, seems to be a doer; two years and counting. He's an actor too, a watchful, sprightly Scot in his early seventies, grey-blonde like me. As far as I know, and possibly because he's too decent, Aude has never shown the slightest interest in molesting him. Their friendship, therefore, blooms. To everyone's surprise, he turned out to have a second career doing psychic readings. None of us has ever asked him for a sitting, and he's only volunteered a few odd – and, it must be said, pertinent – observations in general conversation, none of which has been directed at me. It has crossed my mind to visit him for a consultation but the fear of finding out that he's a fake is too inhibiting. Either way, there's a danger of scuppering the friendship. What if he tells me that something ghastly's going to happen and then it does? I might blame him for bringing the ghastly thing about. If he's wrong and nothing happens, I'd blame him for frightening me anyway. Lose-lose.

During the eighties, some years into these dinners and in the early stages of an apparently successful marriage, Aude announced that she was going to retire. One might say, retire from *what*, exactly but that's entirely missing the point. Waiting for the call is integral to the job. One waits continually and, in the waiting, one is employed: waiting. Aude had done a few days' work that year – half a dozen lines in some police thing – and was 'up to pussy's bow with it'. We spent the rest of the evening debating the whole matter of acting and that's when Leslie came up with the idea of us reading a play out loud every now and again, 'Just for fun,' he said. 'No nonsense about getting it right.'

We adopted the cooking protocol, each of us choosing a play in turn. If there aren't enough parts we share the roles; if there are too many, we double and as there are always fewer parts for women, we play men as necessary. The food has become secondary, an entr'acte, although we still take turns with dinner: a plate of something you can eat with a fork. As with turkey legs, so with the drama. If you loathe Pinter or Ayckbourn or Christopher Fry and it's not your choice, then bad luck. This all sounds tremendously clever and one might think that we're as good, collectively, as anything you'll hear on radio. And we might be, if we actually read the evening's play from beginning to end and gave the thing some thought. What actually happens is that at some point, usually halfway through Act One, somebody remembers a good story – making your first entrance through the fireplace because the door's stuck, that sort of thing. Then we'll all chip in, then it's dinner, then Act Two and more of the same. Leslie says that getting our collective chins up comes first and the play comes second but there's an uncomfortably wild edge to us during all these backward-looking forays that makes me feel older than I need to. Like most people I've known, we make the past our safe house. Nothing much to anticipate? Reverse smartly into golden years.

Tonight, it's Poppy's turn to choose the play and our turn to do dinner. She's decided on *Under Milk Wood* and I'm sure it's because Rolf makes such a pudding of a Welsh accent. Poppy's accent is, of course, faultless. The rest of us are adequate, and who cares anyway as we won't get past Mrs Ogmore-Pritchard's front door without an interruption. By seven o'clock the four of us are gathered in the sitting room, waiting for Aude and Alasdair and discussing my interview. I'm still adamant that I don't want to do it. Rolf can't understand why.

'A *telly*,' he says. 'You'd actually turn down a job for *telly*!'

'It's not just telly, I keep trying to tell you. It's some awful pill and I don't want to be a part of it.'

I've decided to keep the ethics story going: it's the easiest lie.

Leslie says, 'You haven't seen the script yet, have you, my darling? But I've offered to help them with a rewrite.'

Rolf and Poppy laugh, reunited in contempt. She says, 'Leslie, you can't be that naive! You're dealing with an advertising agency here. You can't honestly think they're going to let you put your oar in?'

'I don't see why they wouldn't want some input from me. I've got a few things to show them. This'll be so wonderful for Mim –' he catches my eye '– *if* she decides to take it. Being the name behind a new wonder-drug, that's something, isn't it? We might all be on it by the end of the year.'

Rolf says, 'On what?'

'This brain pill,' Poppy shouts. 'Aren't you listening?' She turns to me. 'I understand absolutely,' she says. 'Of *course* you don't want to do it. I mean, it'd be wonderful to have your name everywhere, and interviews and God knows what by way of new work but you'd have to do it all as *you*. I mean, how horrible.

How absolutely horrible to be splattered everywhere, up on hoardings and everything. I understand, Mim. I do, really. Stop nagging her, Rolf. She's done the right thing.'

Marvellous reverse psychology, this. I immediately want to contradict Poppy and appear in public as an ageing crone. I stand up. 'Must see to the dinner.'

Rolf leans forward over his long, thin legs and takes my arm with his long, thin hand, drawing me back to the sofa. 'Listen,' he says. 'One, it's a telly and two, Poppy's talking out of her arse as usual and three, we'd all be very proud of you. I'm with Leslie. Take the job, change it if you have to. Use the opportunity.' He lets go. Poppy snorts. She starts to speak and so does Leslie, at which point Aude and Alasdair arrive and I escape to let them in. While I'm putting Aude's flowers in water and the pilaff in the oven, I can hear Rolf declaiming, which means he's probably standing up in his crotch-forward, shoulders-back position. I carry in the vase to find him doing exactly that, leaning on the mantelpiece. He stops when he sees me. 'Mim, you're just in time. I'm saying how television portrays us dear old folks.'

'Badly,' I say. 'Don't you think?'

'It's a scandal. We're being patronized and excluded.'

'Humiliated,' says Poppy.

'Sentimentalized,' says Aude.

'And ridiculed,' says Alasdair.

'Follow that,' says Leslie. 'Mind you, they're writing a lot more parts now than they were, don't you think?'

I propose that we start. We organize ourselves, finding specs and texts and filling glasses, then Poppy distributes the many, many parts. Rolf begins, he's First Voice. After a few lines Poppy rolls her eyes and says, 'Oh Christ, this a marathon. Let's go straight to First Drowned.'

We all know what she's doing but only Rolf responds. 'Why not,' he says, closing the book. 'Bad choice anyway. Too many characters.' He's a little bit drunk now, wanting corroboration of her shrewishness. He looks round, smiling very sweetly and taking time to bring us all into his Poppy's-crazy-so-you're-better-off-on-my-side club. We wait. There's no point interfering yet. Poppy might not rise to it.

They're not the only ones who do this. We've seen it so often, the public spat. Wife, usually drunk, says to husband but makes sure to include all present, *I can't bear it, the way you never…*

Husband, usually drunk, says to wife but makes sure to include, etc., *If you're so… then why don't you…*

Wife, now in floods, says to husband, *Because I love you, that's why…*

Husband abandons talking to wife and addresses company directly, *She won't tell me what she wants. For Christ's sake…*

With Rolf and Poppy, I usually go for the nursery approach and divert one of them. 'I'd sooner eat,' I say. 'Why don't we *not* go to First Drowned until after dinner? Will you help me carry in, Poppy?' She hesitates and looks at Rolf to see how vulnerable he is to further attack; he's started a conversation with Alasdair and they're smiling so she follows me out. I could ask her to behave until they get home but I might end up making things worse, so I hand her the pilaff and we deal with the food. It's a truce for now. I sit well away from Rolf while I'm eating and talk to Aude about nothing in particular – clothes, the garden, anything but television.

Afterwards, we try the play again, but it's no time at all

before we've got in a muddle over who's who, which is a general excuse to come back to the topic that's exercising everybody: me.

I'm betrayed by Aude. Extraordinary! She starts it all by saying, 'I can see why you don't want to do it, Mim sweetie, but even so, there's something rather appealing about being out there as yourself. I wonder if it wouldn't be liberating? Not for you, obviously, not if you don't want to do it…' She glances at me and trails off, then says, 'Sorry,' in a small voice.

Alasdair says, 'Perhaps this is a landmark, my dear.' We all look at him as if he's produced ectoplasm from a top hat.

'Oh, stop it.' Poppy bangs her play shut and slaps it onto her lap.

'I'm roused,' he says. 'Can't pass up the chance to spread a little sunshine.'

Aude tries to make amends. 'If Mim doesn't want to do it then she doesn't want to do it and we shouldn't bully her. If they're desperate for old actors, they can have me.'

'She's the only one of us who could carry it off,' Leslie says. This is the first thing he's said for some time, and it's the introduction to a ridiculously flattering speech about my talent and general attributes which has everyone except Poppy nodding and smiling. She's shaking her head and making faces at me which I interpret roughly as You poor cow having to put up with your soft, babbling husband even though I wish I had one because I feel so alone I want to kill myself. Leslie finishes with a flourish, raising his glass to me and making a toast to the future.

'I think it's marvellous, Mim,' Rolf says. 'You can't pass up the chance to be on TV. You strut your stuff! Show 'em what a real actor's made of!' Alasdair stares at Rolf. Poppy's still shaking her head. Aude covers her mouth with the play. Rolf holds his hands out to me, imploring. Leslie blows me a kiss. It's a mime class.

We're in the bathroom afterwards. I say, 'I'm letting you down, I know that.'

'You don't have to agree to anything now. Wait and see. Wait and see what happens. You might be surprised.' He folds his towel and hangs it on the rail, then turns to put toothpaste on his brush. I look at his old skin: the indentations, the long, curving lines of overhang, the white hair, the brown blemishes, the scar along his lower abdomen, his precious face, made monkey-like by the toothbrushing. He winks at me.

I say, 'Perhaps you're right. Perhaps I will be.'

He puts his head to one side. 'Mmph?'

'Surprised. Why don't I wait and see?'

He spits into the basin and rinses out his mouth. I put on face cream and brush my hair. We go to bed.

It's Sunday and I have to ring my father. He's ninety-four and lives on the other side of London, thank goodness, in a flat near Richmond Park. It's a supervised thing; he's got alarms round his neck and on the wall and anywhere else you can hang one up or screw one in. The warden checks up on him every morning. I ring him every Sunday and visit twice a year: his birthday in July and some time during Christmas week. Each visit is an interminable day, preceded by the gathering of gifts, none of which will be acknowledged. Over the years we've given him a television, an electric footbath, electric blankets, linen, a radio, a microwave, innumerable books and videos, various woolly clothes, slippers, house plants, photographs in frames and a great many bottles of single malt. When I married Leslie, he gave us handkerchiefs in a thin white box, bent at the corners and embroidered with his initial.

The journey's long, three-quarters of an hour at least, even though we leave early to avoid traffic. When we arrive we have a cup of tea and a biscuit. Lunch, supplied by me but ordered by him, is at noon sharp. Leslie washes up immediately while I dry and pack the containers. At two-thirty we have another cup of tea and at three we leave. So much for the catering. As to the passing of the day, the five long hours are filled, minute by minute, by my father, the monologist. I swear that we say nothing, except 'hello', 'goodbye', and 'do you want any more ham/tea/bread and butter?' If this terrible, vocal discharge was a colour it would be baby-shit green. It pours from him as we step through the door and persists until we step out again and for all I know he carries on talking when we've gone. It's mostly anecdotal; a loop of old stories told again at every visit to sustain his history and his significance, always to the detriment of the despicable other. Sometimes he's offended by a television programme, and then at intervals we have The Complaint, usually trivial but inflated to a feud in the telling. He rarely mentions my mother.

The Sunday telephone calls are monologues in miniature, some anecdote or complaint, some present concerns and very occasionally, a question: 'Is the car all right?' or 'Is it raining where you are?' Oddly enough, questions only occur on the phone. I think it must be safer for him to risk a little interchange when he can't actually see his opponent face to face. All in all, the five hours of the visit are determined by him. As his daughter and son-in-law, as life forms, we're of no consequence. We enter only as providers of food and carriers of auditory sacks, like colostomy bags, ready to take his baby-shit and process it, which we do by screaming as soon as we're in the car and playing music far too loudly as we drive away, happy, happy, happy to be out of the room and out of his life for another six months.

My lonely, bitter, malicious old father has a fork in each hand to drive away the world. He has no friends, none living in any case, and none that were close before. His children left home as soon as they could, his wife died of misery while her hair was still quite brown. He says his unhappiness stems from the day that he found her unconscious in the downstairs lavatory, but a happy man wouldn't have made a bonfire of his daughter's books because the daughter had neglected, at the age of five, to tidy them away in time for tea. Then there was the overnight-in-the-bathroom incident and the tied-to-the-desk incident and the drowned rabbit incident and the many, many more times when he was cruel, ill-tempered or indifferent to me, and yet, here I am, racing back to him on a regular basis as if I had some kind of obligation. Leslie says we must show compassion. Am I doing this to placate Leslie? He can't stand my father either but he says we'll expect Max and Constance to be there for us. To which I say neither of them would lift a finger if we were being eaten by rats, and furthermore I have no intention of ending my life without friends, even if I have to find some half my age because everybody else has died.

So I make my Sunday call. He always says how are you, but it's a reflex, a jerk after a whack on the knee. I answer, OK and how are you, but before the words are out, he's off, haring away with a rant about the woman in the room next door. Today it's all complaint. For ninety-four, I could say, that's a strong voice and a bright mind but to pay him a compliment would be to wrench my gut out through my mouth, so I never do. The call lasts fifteen minutes. That's how long it takes me to dust the house, one-handed. As I reach the last window-ledge I interrupt with 'must go now, lunch to cook', he hurls one last brick at someone and we part with nominal niceties, leaving me with my teeth bared.

As far as the visits go, I have to concede that Leslie has a point, one can't entirely abandon one's own father and twice a year could hardly be described as taxing, although, of course, it is. I wish he was dead but such wishes are not to be voiced. The phone calls, therefore, are a ridiculous penance, the hair shirts that I wear to make amends for my rage.

Although I don't want to go to this meeting on Tuesday, Leslie's persuaded me – 'On the proviso,' I say, 'that you won't make me do the ad.' On Monday morning we look through my wardrobe to find the perfect outfit. Leslie points at two possibilities: a blood-red suit or a white cashmere jumper teamed with black trousers. I've only worn the jumper once – last year at Aude's birthday dinner – and I spent the evening with my head lowered to my chest, checking for splashes. We might be taken to lunch. I opt for the suit. As we're going downstairs, the phone rings. Leslie's in front of me. He gets there first.

'Hello, Charlie! Good morning to *you!*' There's no need for me to wait. I go into the kitchen and start to make elevenses: milky coffee and a biscuit each, never more, never less. I can hear Leslie through the door. He says, 'You're joking.' I go out to the hall. He's shaking his head. When he sees me he beckons me over. 'Charlie, hold on. Charlie, I can't understand this, I really can't. Hang on, don't say any more. Mim's here, I've got to tell her. I'll call you back in a minute.'

'Tell me what?'

'I can't believe this, I really can't believe it. Your ad, Charlie says they're ditching it. What are they bloody playing at? Bunch of cowboys.'

His distress is on a par with my relief. Even so, I'm hurt. Why have they dropped me? I ring Charlie back. The conversation's difficult. He's reproaching himself at having, as he puts it, dragged me into a dud. There's no explanation from the client, just an apologetic withdrawal. We agree that the whole situation is bizarre and that their initial keenness was extremely misleading but hey-ho, as Charlie says, we've been here before and what changes? What changes, I could say, is that I'm seventy-one now. And yes, I went along with it to please Leslie but I could have said no and I didn't. So more fool me. Leslie's hopping about and signalling that he wants to talk to Charlie. I say goodbye and hand over the phone.

'Charlie? Leslie here. Listen, this is bad news. Mim deserves better – do they know who they're dealing with? Do me a favour, ring them again. Maybe there's a problem their end we can fix… I know… I know… God bless, Charlie. God bless.'

We have coffee and nearly half the tin of biscuits – a record. Leslie wants a re-enactment of the interview and I tell him what I can remember. Everything Antonio said has to be dissected for hidden intent and we spend quite a long time on the three clerk-clients and their malignant influence on the outcome. Were they taking notes? Not that I could see. Was there a tape recorder in the room? Not that I could see. I don't dwell on my grand manner, only mentioning it in passing as my response to their lack of information. Leslie brushes over the taking of the photographs – except to say that they should have booked a proper studio – but as I describe Antonio snapping away I suddenly understand why I've been dropped. It's funny and it's awful and I shall have to keep it to myself. This is what I think. I think I was asked to do the ad because of some old boy who runs the company. He'd loved me in his youth and had my film-face pinned over his bed. Was he hoping to meet me? To *touch* me? Now I invent a little more. Antonio shows him the new photograph. CEO looks at me with boy's eyes. His heart cracks. I've turned into his grandmother. Job's off.

I say none of this to Leslie. He's working on his own theory: the ignorance of the advertising class. 'I tell you what,' he says as we carry the cups to the sink. 'This has been good for both of us. You can't spend the rest of your life in that garden. We'll show them. I'm going to write you something. I want to build on this, Mim. I should have done this years ago.'

'Leslie—'

'Wait and see. I've got a few ideas already.'

We kiss, we part. He goes to the study. I need to do something physical to settle myself. There are tasks outside. The holboellia is winding itself round the guttering and herbs need to be gathered for the freezer. I collect the secateurs, put on my gardening apron and go outside. As I work, my face gradually disappears until I become no more than the parts needed for the job in hand; there are no witnesses to this. Stems and leaves are dropping round my feet. In the cool morning, I'm unobserved.

Three

I'm driving to Aude's flat through the dazzling autumn colour in Alexandra Park. Alasdair answers the door and beams when he sees me standing on the porch. 'Aude's still out,' he says, talking over his shoulder as he leads me down the passage to the kitchen. 'Isn't it your meeting tomorrow?'

'I didn't get the job.'

He turns round. 'Why not?'

'No explanation.'

The front door opens behind us. Alasdair shouts over my shoulder, 'She didn't get the job!'

I turn to see Aude, a carrier bag in each hand, standing open-mouthed. I go to help her with the shopping. 'No, no, it's all nicely balanced. I'll follow you, go through.' She shuts the door with her foot. 'My poor sweetie, after all that agonizing and not wanting to do it anyway, and then for them to pull the plug – you must be furious. Or are you?'

'Not really. A bit. Both and neither.' We arrive in line at the kitchen and start to put things away.

'Leslie must be spitting. He was so excited for you. Tell me what they said and what you said and what Charlie said—'

'I don't know what they said to Charlie. If they told him

anything then he's not letting on. Leslie's really upset. He's decided to write me the big comeback.'

'Has he? Is that what you want?' Aude's standing by the sink with a bottle of detergent. I watch as she bends. She can't reach deeply into the cupboard so the bottle goes at the front and then she lifts herself back up, crank, crank on the spinal pulley. I'm the same when I weed. Will we eventually have no access to the floor at all?

'No, it's not what I want. Not in the slightest.'

Alasdair asks, 'Tea? Coffee? Herb muck?' That's chamomile tea, Aude's new thing. We finish emptying the bags. She opens a box of caramel slices, Alasdair puts our mugs on the table and we all sit down. He's wearing the usual badly adjusted horizontal hold: checked shirt, striped waistcoat, paisley tie.

Aude says, 'I think those brain pills were a bit suspect. Anything strong enough to make a difference would have to be on prescription, wouldn't it? It's all very dodgy. Like the old monkey-gland thing. They've probably fallen foul of some regulation or other and it's all gone down the plug 'ole. Nothing to do with you at all.'

Alasdair leans towards me and rests his elbows on the table. 'But you didn't want to do it anyway.' There's an invitation in the way he says this, as if he's asking me to speak at length and from the heart about the whole event. Just as I'm thinking that I'd sooner talk to Aude alone, he says, 'I've got some lines to learn for tomorrow. Shall I leave you two to have a natter?' He picks up his mug and a caramel slice and waves it in farewell, then he's gone, slipped away.

'Alasdair's good like that,' Aude says. 'Never sticks around when he's unnecessary.' Sometimes when I look at her, I see the face I fell for, the doe eyes and the droll mouth. Today's one of those days. 'So,' she says, frowning. 'Leslie's writing this masterwork for you. And you don't want to tell him not to bother, but you don't want to have anything to do with it, and you're happy for him because he's happy working, and you're miserable because he'll be miserable when he finds out that he's been wasting his time. Is that it, roughly?'

'Roughly. Exactly.'

'What a bugger. I hope you didn't go to the interview dressed like the forget-me-not fairy.' She inspects my gardening jeans and old blue sweater.

'Don't be daft. I wore the black suit.'

'Good make-up?'

'Lots.'

'Hair?'

'Good. Anyway, this is all nonsense because I didn't want to do it, so good for them and let's talk about something else. Why's Alasdair learning lines?'

'He's got a few days on a corporate. I don't remember what, nothing worth mentioning. I don't want to pry, but are you having a mirror crisis?'

'Yes. I am.'

'Thought so. Listen, perhaps you ought to talk to Leslie.'

'Why?'

'Why not? If you really don't want him writing for you, you ought to tell him.'

'Are you, Mad Aude, counselling me on how to conduct my relationship?'

'Not really. Well, yes, I am. Or you could let him finish and see how you feel – it's not as if he'll get whatever it is produced.

34

And you could have fun, we could *all* have fun, reading it. Do you really not want to work again?'

'Not now.'

'You needn't have stopped. You could have gone on for ever, you know you could. You're still lovely.'

'Irresistible.'

'Well you are, you silly old woman. Perhaps Alasdair's right. Perhaps we all need a new experience, a landmark or whatever he said.'

We're both silent, contemplating this. What does Aude see? I see a tower on a bleak cliff. The sea's turbulent and the sky's dark, no moon, no stars. A small, square window at the top of the tower displays a guttering light. If this is meant to be a warning to sailors, I know they miss it. I know they believe the ship to be on course right until the moment when they ram into the rocks. I leave soon after, promising to talk to Leslie. Is this the kind of situation that makes people ask Alasdair for a sitting?

Of course I've had landmarks before, not grey towers, just universal rites of passage. Being born, for instance. I gather I made quite a mess of that. I was also a disobedient baby and a unpleasant child – my father's viewpoint, nobody else's. Puberty, earlier than most. My mother described my first period as an 'affliction'. I remember hiding my blood-soaked towels in the wardrobe for months on end. She must have come across them but I have no memory of the consequences. Marriage, an absolute change of life, nearly all for the better. Childbirth, camouflage, nausea. Being on a film set in my swelling body, longing for a soft, flat surface. When it came to labour, Max's passage was arduous. Constance was swift and supple and fled through me like a fish. Death of first parent. Terrible. I loved my mother. She was too thin-skinned, or so my father says. I think she did her best. All my memories of her are tender, except perhaps for those times when I wanted her to stand her ground. She never did, she never even raised her voice to him. A week after she died, I left home. Death of second parent. Soon, I hope.

Giving birth to Max didn't really change my life very much. I was filming again a month after he was born. There was the occasional phase when Leslie and I were home but most of the significant moments in his first two years took place in front of the nanny. Then I got pregnant again. I don't remember exactly how we arrived at the decision but in the event, I elected to clock off for five years. *The Curfew* was my last major film.

The significant moments of baby Constance were therefore all observed and applauded by me. The oddest thing – if never straying more than a quarter of a mile from the family bosom is any indicator of affection – is that Max is the more devoted child. I do sometimes think that if I'd left Constance to the nanny, we might all have been a great deal better off.

Two days before she started school, in the autumn of 1973, I rang Charlie. 'I'm back!' I said. 'The sailor home from the nursery!' He was delighted, he said, pleased as punch, but I'd have to be patient, things were rather quiet. The man who'd produced my last three films was in hospital and unlikely to get out… nobody was going to the cinema… kids were taking over. My name was respected, of *course* it was, but there were new people now, new blood in the system. As it turned out, the five years had done for me. 'Like digging up a body and expecting it to walk,' Charlie said, helpfully, after another of my wailing calls. The industry had adjusted rather too successfully to my absence and there was very little that an actress with my history could do – the odd 'featuring' perhaps, or the indignity of a fresh start in television, taking what was offered. Charlie wanted me to adapt but I retired again, properly, at the age of thirty-eight. I'm still not sure exactly why. Plenty of people did awfully well; a lot of our friends did more work on television than they'd ever done on film and were very happy doing it. It's too glib to say that I wanted to stop while my name meant something but there might have been a spoonful of that in the mix. Add a few cups of Leslie hoping I'd stay at home for the children, me not wanting to be any old actor on the set and a pinch of fuck you then, if you don't want me, that's your problem – and there I was, clocked off for good. I haven't been completely neglected. Over the years I've had some strange British requests, some stranger foreign ones, some old friends wanting me for cameos and a letter from a young American director wanting me to play – God forbid! – a tribal elder. I turned them all down. I wish I'd been as resolute last week.

Max rings on Wednesday afternoon and asks to speak to Leslie. He's writing in his study and is irritated at the interruption but he takes the phone from me and says, 'Hello, darling,' saving and closing down before I can look at the screen. 'What's cooking?' From this end, I gather that what's cooking is a dog. Max wants to go to the centre now. He says he'll pick Leslie up in ten minutes and he's there, tooting away outside, before Leslie's got his coat on. I wave them off, certain that nothing's going to come of the expedition.

When they've gone, I go upstairs to change into my garden

clothes. As I pull on my sweatshirt, a very bad idea begins to take shape and I find myself walking into Leslie's study. I say, 'I find myself' as if I'm sleepwalking. The truth is that I'm engaging in an ethical/unethical debate over what I'm about to do, while my criminal half is already busy getting to the crime scene. *You have no right*, the ethical voice says, *it's none of your business, this is despicable*. The other voice says, *He shouldn't keep things from me, if I'm going to be in it then I've got a right to see it, it's my life, my life*. By this time, I'm at the computer and turning it on. Unethical wins, hands down.

On first glance I can't see anything that's obviously the work in hand, then I realize that I have no idea what I'm searching for. Passing by everything familiar, I open the unusual. There are sketches, none of which could possibly be for me, song lyrics, brief ideas, lists of character names, even a synopsis for a children's film. There's so much here, and he hasn't told me about any of it. Is this what he does while I'm gardening? It's ridiculous, but I'm hurt. The phone rings and jolts me back to the room. Quivering with guilt, I answer. It's Poppy. She wants to know how I got on at the second interview. I tell her the job fell through and that I'm dyeing my hair and I can't talk because the dye's dripping onto the carpet. In her Poppy way, she carries on. While she's talking, I'm opening another document and there it is, the masterwork: *Near the Knuckle*. Poppy says, 'Hello? Hello?' I say I have to go and this time I'm brusque. We ring off.

Leslie. What is this? I know it's the big one because he's written *For Mim* under the title. There's a plot and character breakdown and a suggested cast list and then what looks like the first script. It's a series. A series about a brothel. The stories, 'some comic, some tragic' are narrated by and starring the madam –

me. I scroll on, scanning the pages, rushing to read as much as I can. He's halfway through the first story. It's well written but that's not the point. I read the first page again. He's cast our friends and several B-list television actors but there are no big names. He wants the big name to be me. The madam's described as an 'old whore, a bit hard-boiled but can lay on the charm if she needs to. Still flirts. Shrewd, looks after number one. Done everything, seen the lot. Brassy-looking, seen better days but still trading on them.'

I turn off the computer and go downstairs. It's cold today but I put on my jacket, make a mug of tea to warm my hands and then go out to the garden and sit on the bench. My heart's scraping against my chest and my arms and legs are stiff and numb. For the first time in our lives together, I don't want Leslie to come home. If he comes home, then I have to tell him that I know. And that I don't want anything to do with it. And that I can't believe he could be so stupid and crude. If he's slipping into senile erotomania or having one last stab at the big time, then let him do it for himself. I'm still sitting there, blue with cold, when Max and Leslie bang on the kitchen window and wave at me to come in.

I can't look at Leslie. Max is exuberant. 'I've got a dog!'

'What, here?'

'No, no, no. He's still at the kennel. They're going to visit me first and make sure the flat's OK. I can pick him up next week.'

'What about the walking?'

'I told you. I'm getting a dog-walker.'

'And that's good enough?'

'Sure, it's good enough. I might love this dog. I might just give this dog a fucking good home.'

Leslie says, 'Come on now, Mim. It's a lovely greyhound, an old racer. Give the boy a chance.'

'He's not a boy, Leslie, he's nearly forty-one. You two do what you want. I'm going to start the dinner.'

Leslie makes a leave-her-to-me face at Max and says, 'I'll come with you next week, darling, when you pick him up.' Max leaves. I hear the front door close. We're alone.

Leslie comes back into the kitchen saying, 'It's a brindle. Barney the brindle. Not bad, eh? Max thinks he'll keep it, the name. Reminds him of a cartoon or something.' I've walked off to gather what we need for dinner and Leslie's following me round, trying to stop me. 'Don't be like this, Mim. He really wants the dog. I'm sure he'll take care of it.'

'I'm sure he won't. Not for more than a few weeks, anyway.'

'Give him a chance, that's all.'

'So you'll stop writing and walk it round the park all day.'

'They don't need much exercise.'

'It's a bloody greyhound, of course they need exercise.'

'That's the amazing thing. They just want to sleep.'

'Who says?'

'The woman at the dog place. They're knackered, that's the point. You'll love it. It's a beautiful dog.'

I'm at the sink now, peeling. I can't spend the rest of my life with my mouth shut but the thought of having to explain and then be explained to and then excavate and dredge as we go into the issue and round and back again… I can't even remember what it is about Leslie that I like. I don't want any of this.

Then I tell him. 'I used your computer today, while you were out.'

'Oh, yes? Why?'

'Why not?'

'No reason. You can use it any time you like, you know that. It's just that you never bother.'

'Today, I bothered.'

'Right.'

There's a long silence while I put oven chips onto a baking tray and Leslie tops and tails the beans.

I take the eggs out of the fridge and bang the door shut. 'Omelettes, then.'

'Why not?'

'Did you think I wouldn't find it?'

'I wasn't hiding anything.'

'Why didn't you tell me?'

'I did. I did tell you. If I didn't tell you, why were you looking?'

'Why didn't you tell me what it *was*?'

'Do I have to tell you everything? You've had a rough few days, you've been feeling a bit blue. What's wrong with getting a nice surprise?' There's a bean hanging from his left hand and he's smiling at me with his mouth open and his eyebrows high on his forehead, urging me to be happy. I can't speak. He puts the bean down and scratches his ear. 'No good, eh?'

'I'm sure it's well written. That's not the point.'

A series of expressions passes across his face: he's pleased because he thinks I like the writing, he's uneasy because I'm upset, he's confused because that's contradictory and then he's relieved because he thinks he's worked it out. 'The narration's all voice-over so you won't have to learn it. Piece of cake, darling.' Leslie, Leslie. Who do you see when you look at me? Have I got the face to be running a whorehouse, an old whore cackling over her girls, fingering the money, leering at the men? Is that how I look to you?

'Mim? Say something.'

'No.'

I turn off the oven and leave the kitchen and, of course, he follows me. I walk round the hall and then up the stairs. I don't know where to go. One rainy night, after an argument with Rolf, Poppy jumped out of her bedroom window. He was watching football at the time and didn't see her whizz past or hear her land on the flower bed. To get in again she had to ring the bell, which he didn't respond to because he was busy with the football and because he thought she was somewhere in the house and would answer it herself. When he did finally open the door he couldn't grasp the situation at all – I think that's understandable – and there was apparently some delay before it dawned on him that the furious, sodden, mud-caked woman on the step was Poppy. Her story, that she was chasing a wasp out, seemed convincing enough and for all I know he believes it still.

'Mim? Come on, darling. Stop it, please.' We're on the stairs now. I'm near the top, he's halfway up. We can't tour all evening with me playing the injured wife. I turn round.

'Go back down then. Go in the sitting-room.'

'Not without you.'

'I mean *with* me. Please go and sit down.'

We usually share the sofa. Now I'm on one chair and he sits lightly on another. He's afraid of me, staring at my face and leaning forward with tears in his eyes, straining to understand. There's no precedent for this, we've never come to a point where one of us has become implacable. I can't bear his fear.

'I'm not doing it, Leslie. That's all.'

'OK, OK. I'll change it. You tell me what's wrong and we'll make it work. I don't want you to do anything you're not happy with. Tell me where you think I've gone wrong and I'll make it right. Anything you want, anything. There's nothing that can't be fixed – isn't that what we always say? Everything can be fixed. So what don't you like? Tell me. Go on. Tell me.'

'Everything.'

'Everything?'

'It's *crude*. It's horribly crude. Is that really how you see me? Like an old whore?'

'That's not how I see you, of course it isn't. But this is a great idea, Mim! It's perfect! It's got everything.' The fear retreats. The tears drain away. 'Think of the stories. You've got politicians, the clergy, big business, the ordinary bloke, the sick bloke. The girls have all got stories of their own. And then you're there, holding it together. It's not *crude*. It's drama with a twist, that's all. Nobody could do it like you, darling. Nobody's got the gravitas, the wit.'

'Or the face?'

'Or the face. Look at you. Definitely the face.'

There we are, game over. I stand up. 'So if I asked you to play an old flasher, I suppose you'd be thrilled to bits.'

'I might be. *Peep Show*. It's a good idea.'

'Shut up'

'All right. I've got the picture. You don't want to do it. That's fine. That's your prerogative, to say no. I still think it's a good idea but if you're dead set against it then I'll stop. Or maybe I'll go on but I won't write it for you. How about that? I'll write it for somebody else. How do you feel about that?'

'You carry on.'

'I will.' He gets himself out of the chair and comes to where I'm standing. 'You're stiff,' he says, holding me. 'Don't be stiff. I

43

wasn't keeping secrets. I was keeping surprises. All right? Are we all right now?'

I can't say anything. I grunt and he takes that as a yes. The honest answer is that we're far from all right. I don't want to know that I've got the face for this. She's an old trout of a madam; she's a lowlife, a misanthropic ruin. I think Leslie only really sees me when I'm wearing my happy hat. *Happy* to be in the audience, Leslie. Happy to applaud.

I was maid of honour at Aude's second wedding. Leslie was the late arrival. He says it was love at first sight, I say it was just the way he danced. We fed each other cake and sat out the dancing and then talked till dawn, sitting in his car on the Embankment. He let slip that he wanted a wife and children so I avoided him for months although the letters and calls kept coming, always funny, always encouraging, always telling me to amaze the director, stun the public, be gorgeous, be clever, *be loved* by him. I replied, once or twice. We met again. He made me laugh, so I said yes.

Five weeks before our wedding I got a job filming in Edinburgh. Leslie was working in London and couldn't come with me so I went on my own, clickety-clack up the railway track into my last stab at the single life. Everybody flirted on the set but this time, I went from a standing start to full infatuation in the first hour of rehearsal. The man was much younger than me and had almost nothing to say for himself but we met secretly for five days. He ended it by pretending not to be in his hotel room and when I asked for an explanation, he said I was deranged. An explanation! Where do you start? I couldn't stop crying, which was partly feeling spurned and partly feeling furious and rather more than partly, the thought of him telling everyone about it which, of course, being married himself, he didn't. (Much like the celebrated actor who gave me what I came to think of as the Famous Clap. I still wince when I see him on the telly.) I came home chastened and – until my recent metamorphosis into the very model of a modern madam – Leslie and I have continued to be more peaceful together than apart.

After we've eaten, Leslie goes up to his study to finish the scene he's working on. He asks me if I mind but what am I to say? In fact, I'm relieved to be alone. I still haven't opened my new book on dry gardening. I make us both coffee and then sit with a pad and make planting notes until he calls to tell me he's going to bed.

I lock the front door, fill a glass with water and turn out the lights. As I'm walking through the hall, without warning, I'm Max, alone in the dark, standing in front of a bulging bin bag. We're both dead, Leslie and I, and our lives have been piled high; bags for the charity shop, bags to sell, bags for the council dump. Constance, inflexible even in bereavement, has left Max to tidy us up. And then I imagine how I'll feel if Leslie goes first and I'm the one left standing in the dark, alone with the hammering silence. If he's here, even if he's locked away in his room, I can hear the wind-rattle and the boiler-thud. I can hear traffic, birds, children in neighbouring gardens. If he's out, I know he'll be back. If he was nowhere to be found, in or out, if he was dead, the house would be mute. I think I couldn't bear it, that silence. I think I might kill myself. That's what I think, even though I don't like him very much today.

Four

Rolf's going to Manchester tomorrow so we're having an extra-curricular meeting at their house. No play, just liver and bacon, mash and baked beans. 'A good old blow-out to see me through,' Rolf says when he rings to ask us over. He opens the door in his striped apron with a tea towel hanging over the pocket and a wooden spatula in his hand. Leslie follows him into the kitchen and Poppy takes me upstairs to see her new winter coat. It's a ploy. We examine it briefly and then sit on the bed staring at Rolf's suitcase which is open on the floor, ready for his tooth-brush and flannel. I know she wants to talk but I've been feeling estranged from Leslie all day and it's made me unresponsive. 'So he's off tomorrow,' I say. Better to be self-evident than to say nothing at all.

'I'm not going to his first night.'

'Why not?'

'Why the hell should I?'

'Because you always do. Because he'll want you there.'

'Tough.'

'Why don't you do something while he's away? Take some-thing up, you know. A course or something.'

'For Christ's sake, Mim. The only thing I want to do is stop him sharing a bed with that woman. I don't want to learn fuck-ing Italian.'

'Only a thought.'

We go downstairs. Aude and Alasdair have arrived and they're standing in the kitchen, talking to Leslie. The bacon's spitting as the lid on the potatoes bobs up, spilling scum onto the hob. Rolf tells us all to go away. We fill our glasses and sit on the wooden-framed sofas like battery hens waiting for seed. The only voice is Leslie's as he tells the story of the visit to the dog sanctuary and then delivers an address on the plight of retired greyhounds. Why's Aude so quiet? I haven't spoken to her since Tuesday but she was brighter then, full of plans for the garden and wanting my help. Despite her smile, she's guarded. Is this about me? When the greyhound address peters out, I ask her how she's doing and she perks up and tells us all a good story. The elderly woman who lives in the flat above her got on a bus, but was so preoccupied with getting her trolley up the steps that she didn't think to make sure where the bus was going. She asked the driver who said:

It's on the front.

I'm sorry, I didn't look. Could you tell me, do you think?

Like I said, it says it on the front.

I know, I'm sorry, but I forgot to look.

Get on anything red, would you? Jump on a fire engine if it happened to be passing?

And then the driver started the bus before she sat down and braked as often and as badly as he could for the rest of her jour-ney, making a particular effort to catch her out as she stood up to leave.

'They don't quite get it,' says Alasdair. 'They think they'll be forever young, these brass-neck boys.'

47

Rolf arrives with the food and tells us all to come to the table and eat. It's delicious, if swimming in grease, and nobody speaks for a while, except to compliment him. Then he and Leslie start a conversation about the new job and bad pay. Neither of them mention the cast at all, which is awkward as we normally talk about actors we know, particularly if one of us is working. The stifling of gossip brings the unmentionable Doreen to the table. By denying her we make her notable, the silently shrieking ghost. Poppy's getting drunk. She grabs Leslie and shouts, 'We'll all have a lot more to talk about soon, won't we? How Big Wolfie had a lovely time in Manchester with his little fwend in their inky-dinky little fwat.'

Rolf's sitting opposite her, behind a barricade of candles and dishes. He starts to get up but she mirrors him and he sits down again. They stare at each other, revving up for a scrap. The silence hollows out the table. Leslie prevails.

'My knees have been terrible this week,' he says, booming into the crater. 'How's your back, Alasdair?'

'It keeps my head off my arse. There's not much else I can say about it. Are you seeing anyone?'

'No point.'

Poppy fills her glass and sighs noisily. I turn to Aude. 'Have you decided what to put along that wall?'

'I'm not sure. A rambler, what do you think?'

I turn to the table at large and say, 'Aude's redesigning her garden so I'm giving her a few ideas.' Leslie winks at me, then gets up and starts to gather the plates.

Rolf, released, licks the potato spoon. 'Leave those, Leslie. No pud. But I've got some absolutely delicious little cakes we can have with coffee, home-made by the deli, or so they tell me.

Poppy's been talking about the garden, haven't you, my darling?' He waves us over to the sofas. 'Why don't you show Mim that photograph you found yesterday?'

'You all enjoy your little cakes,' she says, throwing her napkin on the table. 'I'm going to bed.'

Rolf smiles. 'Sleep tight. I'll save you one, shall I?'

Unusually, she lets that pass and says good night to the rest of us, kisses everyone, except Rolf, and leaves the room. I follow her, even though Leslie tries to stop me. She's walking very slowly up the stairs, holding the bannister and pulling herself along. Was she doing that earlier? Or is this dramatic emphasis for my benefit?

'Poppy? Why don't you come to dinner tomorrow? You won't want to be alone, not when Rolf's just gone.' She turns and sits down heavily on the step. This doesn't look like a performance. I go and sit on the step below her and the smell of perfume strengthens in the liver-and-bacon air. She puts her hand on my shoulder. I put mine over it. Her skin's soft, despite the creases, her nails are manicured balloon-red, the swollen knuckles bump under my caress, the rings scratch my palm. 'He's not going to leave you – you've been together since Moses. He wants the job, Poppy. He can't help it if she's there. He didn't cast the thing.'

'He should have turned it down. After last time.'

'That's history – you're punishing him for something he's got no intention of doing.'

'So?'

'So! What's he said about her? I bet he hasn't said anything.'

'He doesn't have to.' She takes her hand away and leans on the spindles.

I can't answer her. Perhaps she's right – perhaps Rolf has a few wild weeks with Doreen Whotsit then comes home, sated. Or she's wrong, and Rolf behaves like a monk. Either way, Poppy won't know and that's the worst thing, the imagining. She struggles to her feet and says, 'I'll come tomorrow, if the offer's still open.'

'Offer open, door open, you come when you want. Why don't you put something in his suitcase? A nice little gift.'

'Like what?'

'Trout.'

She sniggers. 'Wanker.'

The Rolf and Poppy show: we mock these two or get maddened or take sides. It's a lousy marriage where nobody listens and nobody really cares and neither one of them is willing to compromise or negotiate or even to be kind. And what about us – the Mim and Lesley show? We do our best, which is probably better than some, but now that a little worm has taken up residence in what I might whimsically describe as our love-plum, I'm not feeling quite so superior. I kiss Poppy. She goes upstairs, I go down and join the others.

As I open the door I hear Rolf saying, '… the simple approach. No fuss, don't need it.' He sees me and opens his eyes wide in enquiry. Is he asking if it's all blown over? I have no idea how to reply so I smile and head for the sofas. Leslie says, 'Hello, Missus, all sorted?' He's poured me coffee and put a cake on a plate. I sit next to him because Rolf's sprawling over two places and every other seat's been taken. Nobody mentions Poppy. As soon as we've finished the coffee we start to leave, wishing Rolf luck with the play and promising to get to Manchester before the end of the run. We know, and Rolf knows, that we won't even try but it's protocol and must be said.

Driving home, I tell Leslie that Poppy's coming to dinner tomorrow. He says, 'Poor old love. Poor old Poppy.'

'You don't think he's lusting after Doreen What's-her-name, do you?'

'I think he'd be only too delighted.'

'Meaning?'

'Meaning he's impotent.'

'*No.*'

Leslie nods.

'When did he tell you?'

'This afternoon. On the phone.'

'Why didn't you tell me?'

'I *am* telling you. You were in the garden, and then I forgot.'

'You forgot! How could you forget that?'

'I don't know. I forgot, I don't know why but I did. I'm sorry.'

I shake my head and look out of the window. It's raining and the rubber on one of our wipers is coming away, screeching across the glass. I speak without turning to Leslie. 'How long—?'

'A year or so.'

'A *year*! Why hasn't Poppy said anything to me?'

'Why would she? She probably thinks it's her fault.'

I'm sure she does. And I'm sure she sees Doreen Thing as a genuine threat. Will Rolf find new joy in his genitals? Will Poppy have to take the blame?

I'm about to ask Leslie if Rolf mentioned her when he says: 'There you are. Another good plot. The sad, celibate marriage saved by the helpful hooker.'

'That's awful. It's a cliché.'

'Depends how it's written.'

'It's a cliché, whatever you do with it.'

51

We're silent for the rest of the journey. I know Leslie's working on the storyline. I'm seeing Poppy and Rolf, back to back in bed.

It's Sunday morning and I ring my father, duster in hand. The conversation proceeds through the usual rat runs and then he says, 'I don't want that painting of Richmond Park any more. I've been given a photograph of Margaret Thatcher in a frame and there's nowhere to put it so I want to get rid of Richmond Park and put her there instead. The sun shines right on that spot. She'll look marvellous.'

I've always liked that painting. He takes a breath and I jump in and say, 'We'll have it if you're getting rid of it.'

He says, 'Well now, let me think. Your mother and I bought that painting on her birthday in 1951. I hadn't bought her a present, never had the time. You didn't realize that, did you? I had absolutely no time to myself. Anyway, as it happens, I took a day off because she wanted me to and of course I would have anyway, no matter how much I'd had to do because a birthday's a birthday and you have to have a sense of occasion, don't you? I didn't choose the painting, she chose it, but we said it was her present because it was her birthday. We paid fifty pounds. I think it must be worth at least ten times that now.' My father's rich. He has money in the bank, untouched. He has money under the bed and in bags in the wardrobe, untouched. He has bonds and stocks and shares and a firm to manage them. I know, because he's told me, that he's leaving most of this to be held in trust for any children that Max and Constance may have, and as neither of them are likely to produce progeny, the money will lie for ever without purpose, wrapped in bleeding skin, guarded by his spirit body in the

52

form of a diabolic beast with many hands and mouths and yellow eyes.

He wants to *sell* me the painting. I say, 'I'm sure you'll find a buyer.'

'Aren't you interested?'

'No, thank you.'

'I thought you liked it.'

'I do.'

He sniffs. 'Up to you.'

I'm nearly at the last window-ledge. 'Must go now, lunch to cook.'

'Say hello to Leslie.'

'I will. Goodbye.'

'Goodbye.'

At least the dusting's done. That only leaves the bathroom, the kitchen and the loos. I do some of it, badly, every Sunday morning. Leslie vacuums once a week and once a year we get someone in to clean the carpets but if you lie on the floor you're sure to find things you weren't expecting. When my father used to visit, the greater part of his entertainment was to snoop for evidence: the green crust behind the bin, the webs here and the stains there and the hairs and the corks and the fish bones; everything he found, he presented like a gift. Unbelievably, I thanked him. I should have put it all in his coat pocket.

I'm not as able as I was, less stretch, less bend, but the truth is that I've never had the least interest in keeping anything clean. When I stopped acting to give those years to Constance, Leslie was working. He was out. I was in. Was I going to spend my day on housework? Was I hell. When things got too squalid I'd put on the radio and scrub out, but it had to be done quickly, to loud music. You clean, you have a cup of tea, the house cavorts behind your back and makes itself filthy again. Is there any joy in that?

I still think of my mother, putting on a clean apron every morning before she toured the house with her box of cloths and scourers, talking to herself, lavishing attention on the taps so that they shone for her like little stars in the bathroom firmament, scurrying to our bedrooms, dusting here and arranging there, sweeping the floors, lining up the toys and making the beds so neatly that they looked two-dimensional, like cartoons. Then to the hall. Changing the flowers, dusting the table, dusting inside the phone, polishing the mirror, sweeping the floor and cleaning the doorstep, beating the mat first – never the other way round, silly! And then, in the sitting-room, taking all the ornaments off the mantelpiece and washing each one, then drying them carefully and dusting the mantelpiece before she put everything back. Dust and sweep, dust and sweep. Kitchen last. Scour and scrub. Every burner cleaned of its grease, every surface bleached, the sink burnished, the floor washed, the fridge emptied, wiped and restocked. And defrosted on the first of every month. And did I say that she always dusted the tops of the doors? That's how you define a real housewife: she doesn't only clean where you can see. She *seeks out* dirt and whisks it away. Bad dirt, dirty dirt.

I loved my mother very much, but I could see, even as a child, that she'd made housework holy because there was nothing else that she could do with her day. I'm not such a slut now. We're tidy, we leave no trail. Even so, my father, who holds that a badly folded hospital corner is grounds for a good slap, would be sure to find the dried broccoli floret wedged between the sofa cushions. Were he to visit that is, which, thank God, he will never do again.

Leslie and I have soup and bread for lunch while we read the Sunday papers, then he goes off to write and I get dressed for the garden. I'm still thinking about Aude's wary expression last night and get no further than the back door before I turn and take off my coat and boots. The phone's not on the table. Leslie must have it. I go upstairs. He's asleep, slumped in his chair, his hands resting on his stomach. Do I wake him up to spare him a stiff neck? I whisper, 'Leslie?' He says, 'Mmmm,' and makes sticky noises with his tongue but his eyes stay shut. I pick up the phone and leave him to it.

Aude answers straight away. We talk about last night's dinner for a minute and then I tell her about Rolf, knowing that she'll keep it to herself.

'Hell. Is it medical, do you think?'

'As opposed to?'

'I don't know – apathy.'

'Poppy must be thinking it's her fault or she wouldn't be making all this fuss about Doreen.'

'Of course it might be age. Does Leslie ever—?'

'Never.'

'Right.'

'Aude?'

'Yes?'

'I hope you won't think I'm fussing but last night you were watching me – I can't remember exactly when – and you had this odd expression…'

'Did I? I can't think why.'

She's quiet. I've become very anxious delivering this stiff little speech; I smell slightly of sweat. I'm glad we're doing this on the phone. 'I wondered if Alasdair might have said something about me or about Leslie or even about *you*, and you didn't quite know how to tell me. You know the sort of thing, we're going to die in a crash and if we stay in we'll die anyway because there's a tornado. Can't avoid your fate, that sort of thing. Something like that? Is that what it was?'

'Mim, sweetie, please stop. I'll tell you what he said. But you must promise not to tell him that I told you. Do you promise?'

'I promise.'

'Cross your heart?'

'Cross my heart.'

'Oh dear. I really shouldn't be saying this. I don't want to upset you.'

'Is it that bad?'

'No! No, of course it isn't. It's just that Alasdair thinks…'

'What? What does he think?'

'He thinks you're living in Leslie's shadow. Have been for years.'

'*What?*'

'That's what he said.'

'But I'm not in Leslie's shadow. That's ridiculous. You don't think that's true, do you? That I'm in Leslie's shadow?'

'I've known you both so long, I honestly don't think I think about you at all. Except nice thoughts, obviously.'

'Thanks.'

'I told him that as far as I knew you didn't want anything you hadn't got. And I'm sure he doesn't mean Leslie's doing it on purpose. I mean, he really likes you both enormously. I honestly don't think he meant anything by it.'

'But he said it.'

'Yes, he did. He did. Leslie's never stopped you doing anything, has he?'

'No! Is that all he said? Nothing else?'

'If there was more, I'd tell you. You're not upset, are you? I mean, it's ridiculous. I told him it was ridiculous.'

'And what did he say?'

'He said it again.'

'The same thing?'

'Same thing.'

'I don't know what to say.'

'I'm so sorry, sweet pea. I didn't want to upset you. I haven't, have I?'

'Good Lord, no.'

'Don't say I told you.'

'I won't. I promise. Thanks for telling me.'

'Anyway, Alasdair's got it wrong. You and Leslie are the happiest couple I know.'

Boots and coat on again and out to the garden. I didn't think to ask her why they were talking about me in the first place. Does Alasdair often make pronouncements to Aude? I'm beginning to feel aggrieved that he didn't ask my permission before he consulted his voices or whatever he calls them. As far as Leslie's concerned, it was my choice entirely to play the hermit. I was the star and I became the satellite; star to moon. I walked into the shade myself. Am I defending him? He couldn't have been more delighted when I got my degree, OU, years ago, but he never suggested that I should make use of it. Neither did I. I'm happy as I am. Which is to say I *was* happy as I am but am finding myself to be less and less so. I'm not blind to a neutral version of the truth here: husband wants best for wife, writes vehicle for comeback, wife horrified, demurs, husband wounded, retreats, idyll totters. Alasdair seems to be suggesting that wife needs to want best for herself. All well and good but how does that shore up the idyll?

Leslie comes outside, hugging himself in the cool air. 'Is it tea, Missus?'

'Give me five minutes to finish this and I'll be in.'

'Do you want a hand?'

'I'm fine. You put the kettle on.' And so it goes. No drama. Sunday afternoon in north London. Is this the moment to talk to Leslie about my life? I firm the earth around the viburnum I've just transplanted, pick up my kneeler and walk to the shed. The smell in here is so wonderfully *brown* that I close my eyes as always and drop away, a bit drunk in the nose.

'Mim?' Leslie creaks open the door. 'You all right, my darling? Tea's made. I wasn't sure what you wanted but I'm warming us up a couple of apple turnovers. OK?' He waits until the trowel's been wiped clean and hung on its nail; then we go back to the house, arm in arm.

Poppy comes by taxi; she's early. The chicken's only just gone in. It's too dark and cold for a tour round the garden so we put on Ella and Louis and sit by the fire, picking at the only nibble I can find, a bowl of nuts and raisins. We're used to spending the evening together whenever Rolf's away but this time it's more awkward: every topic we touch on seems to have some phallic implication. By the time we reach vigorous evergreen climbers, I'm feeling like Max Miller on the blue book.

The meal goes well until Poppy says, 'You two, you're like little duckies on the water. Smoothly, smoothly going on your way. Rolf and I are all paddle. Paddle, paddle, paddle, we never get anywhere and we make a lot of fuss. You two are simple. Simple love.' She looks at me with brimming eyes.

'Not always,' I say. 'The little duckies paddle furiously below the waterline.'

'Do we?' Leslie frowns. 'I don't. Speak for yourself, Missus.'

'Come on, Leslie. It's not *that* simple, is it?' I smile at him, trying to convey that we're doing Poppy a favour by describing our marriage as a little less than ideal. 'We've had bad times. Everybody has.'

'When?'

'Now and then.'

'When?'

Poppy isn't listening. She's helping herself to more vegetables, carefully arranging her plate and then waiting politely for us to do the same before she eats.

'No, you're right,' I say to Leslie. 'We're very simple. It's as simple as that.'

He lifts his glass. 'To ducks!'

Poppy and I lift our glasses. 'To ducks!'

Then we talk about her children and her grandchildren and Max and the dog, and marriage doesn't get another mention until we're back in the sitting-room having coffee. After a whispered request from me, Leslie absents himself, inventing an email he has to write. Poppy and I are close to each other on the sofa. She's tired now, full of food and a bit drunk and less able to hide her state of mind. I can see that Rolf and Doreen have settled in, her companions for the night. She stares into the fire. Her dyed hair's severe against her face and her clothes are badly chosen, a crude pattern of clashing colours.

'I was thinking,' she says, still staring at the fire, 'how I'd feel about going back to the house if he'd left for good.'

'And?'

'A part of me wouldn't mind at all. He can be a stinker, you know. A royal stinker.' She turns to me. 'In private.'

I nod, but qualify it by looking as if it's the last thing I expected her to say. I like him too much to be totally disloyal. 'And what about the part that would mind?'

'I don't like it, being alone. Going to bed. I usually sit in front of the telly until I fall asleep.'

'Is that all you'd miss, the company?'

'You know. You've seen us.'

'You're all right. Most of the time.'

'Most of the time, we're not all right. We haven't really been all right since the kids left – or maybe before. He doesn't like me. I can't say I like him. What's the bloody point?' She starts to cry. 'We haven't made love for more than a year. He can't. Or that's what he says. He can't, he won't. Either way I'm not allowed to say anything. And the heart pills he takes you can't mix with sex pills, which he says he wouldn't try anyway. He says he's too old, that's it. He says everybody has to stop some time.' She takes a tissue from her pocket and blows her nose.

I rub her ribby back with the flat of my hand. 'Poppy, love. I'm sorry. Perhaps he's embarrassed. Men hate doctors.'

She drains the cup. 'I'd better go.'

60

'Why don't you stay the night? I'll make you up a bed on the sofa.'

'I'd better not. Rolf might ring.'

I call a taxi and Leslie hears me and comes down to say good-bye. When the bell rings, she gives us each a hug and we promise to meet again within the week.

'It's all true,' I say, as I close the door. 'Rolf won't do anything about it though. So he might be lying.'

'She seemed calm enough. No tears?'

'A few.'

We lock up. On my way to the bathroom, I see Leslie at his desk – he's making a note about tonight, I'm sure of it. He's making a note about Poppy's behaviour for his damn script.

Five

It's Monday afternoon and Leslie's doing a show at one of his retirement homes. I'm starting the *Observer* crossword in our little conservatory. Next door's fence is being replaced so I've had to spend the morning undoing precious climbers; now I'm watching the men in case they get any funny ideas and start jumping about on the border. They're having a break, leaning on the fence posts and staring at the garden, mugs in hand. They must know I'm keeping guard but they seem quite equable about it, smiling if they catch my eye.

The conservatory's next to the kitchen so to make the best use of the time, I'm doing the washing while I wait. I get up to transfer the clothes to the drier and reload the machine, then I make more coffee and sit down again. That's when I hear the first buzz. I look up. A fly has trapped itself between the glass roof and the blind. I try to carry on with the crossword but the buzzing's frantic now, higher in pitch with long, sustained whining passages, the notes rising and falling as the fly attempts an escape and fails, beaten back by its own stupidity and the ever defeating blind. There's a gap big enough for a prawn to get through but the fly can't see it. I find the tool that unhooks the blind but there's no obvious place to clip it in, I'm not tall enough to see and Leslie isn't here to ask. There are dozens of dead insects on the ceiling, tiny silhouettes against the white fabric. I'll have to arrange to have the blinds taken down and the glass cleaned and the insects disposed of – I should have done this months ago. I use the tool to lift the edge further away from the glass but the fly continues to buzz, more fitfully now, and ignores the tunnel I've made. It's running out of oxygen – do flies breathe? I'm inhabiting the fly, it's a terrible death, choking and exhausted, trapped in what must appear to be open air, sky through the glass. If this were a whale or a dog, I could offer comfort and sit next to the thing, stroking its head until it passes over but I can't think of a way to offer comfort here. A stroking finger to a fly must be as consoling as a punch in the face. I transmit comfort instead, wishing the distress to be over quickly but there are limits to my compassion as I have no intention of ruining the blind by trying to tear it down. If this *were* a whale or a dog, which it obviously couldn't be but I'll pursue the analogy, then I'd destroy the blind. There are long silences now, punctuated by short, exhausted, single-note buzzing. Then a longer silence and a shorter, quieter *bzzzz* and it's over. The fly's dead. For some hours afterwards, in vigil below the corpse, I pity it.

Leslie comes home and we have a sandwich, then he goes upstairs. I've finished the washing and the crossword and read the papers. The men are still working on the fence and I might as well do the ironing as sit here staring out of the window. I go upstairs to fetch the hangers. As I reach the landing, Leslie starts to shout; it takes me a second to realize that he's trying out the script. I listen. I know it's possible that as the weeks pass, even though I don't want to be part of the thing now, I'll overlook how

upset I've been. A few weeks more and I might start to be helpful and that'll be the end of my futile little uprising.

Perhaps Alasdair's right. Perhaps I should have made more of
my life. Made more of *what* though? More tonnage in friends,
more yardage by the column inch? Does the garden count? Or
my degree? Am I wasting my allotted breath?

Scene: insolent youth at a garage, leaning on his bike with a
hissing air line in his hand. I face him out. 'If you're not doing
anything with that I'd like to check my tyres.'

'I've paid for this,' he says, 'so I'm using it up.' That's the ticket,
clever boy.

I call Aude on Tuesday morning. A strange man answers the
phone. Or I think he's strange until he identifies himself – it's
Gully, one of Aude's husbands, the worst. He's delighted to be
speaking to me, can't wait to hear my news, is in love with
London again after years in Italy. To see the Thames again! That
poker-faced old grey snake!

So she is, I say, spot on.

No reply.

So why is he back?

Long story, won't go into it now.

I ask to speak to Aude.

Oh, *Aude*. There's a delay. When she eventually comes to the
phone she says she's going out and can't stop to talk. Five
minutes later, she calls on her mobile.

'Gully's turned up.'

'I know, I've just spoken to him—'

'Out of the blue, no call, nowhere to live, no money.'

'You wouldn't—'

'Only tonight.'

'Aude, *don't*. Please. Please don't.'

She sighs like an old horse. 'I said he could have the sofa. For one night only. One night. And I'll give him dinner and he can use the bathroom and that's *it*. And breakfast tomorrow, and then he goes.'

'Why's he here, anyway?'

'He says there's a gallery that's interested in a show…'

'Oh, no. Do you want me to pop in and get violent?'

'No. No, no, no. I'll be firm. I promise. I know exactly how to get rid of him.'

'How, exactly?'

'I'll tell him the truth. There's no room. It's a tiny flat and anyway he's far too long for the sofa. I'd forgotten how tall he is.'

'Never mind the sofa. What about him poncing off you and owing you thousands?'

More sighing. 'You're right. I'll tell him. He can't stay.'

'Good.'

'I'll tell him that he's got till tomorrow morning. As soon as the moment presents itself. Really, I promise. I can't chuck him out now. Not when I said he could have the sofa.'

I'm silent.

'Stop it, Mim. I promise. You'll see, I'll do it. Must go, I'm shopping.'

A few seconds later she rings back. 'I forgot. Will you come for dinner on Saturday? It's Alasdair's birthday. Rolf's home for the weekend, so we can all meet up.'

'Of course we'll come. As long as Gully isn't there.'

'Banished. I promise.'

I know that it's not unusual for couples to con one another

and money can be the least of it but Aude has a very particular talent for indiscriminate intercourse. When it's over, she's no Piaf, she's all regret. And then, after the regret, she forgets. Here comes Gully, sneaking in. What does he find, a fist? A summons? No. Rose petals in the bath and filet mignon.

We didn't see Max on Friday, but he's coming tonight, with the dog. Before they arrive, I spend some time choosing an old bowl for water and put it near the back door. 'If the animal wants to eat,' I tell Leslie, 'He'll have to make do with what we leave from dinner. Unless Max has thought to bring a tin of food.'

Well, what do you know, he has. And two bowls. I empty mine and put it back in the cupboard. Leslie makes a huge fuss, showing me the dog as if it were a child. 'Look, Mim. Look! He's such a beautiful boy! He's a *good boy*, yes, he is!' It's docile enough, with extraordinarily thin legs. They're disturbing, too thin not to be injured or break. 'Its legs are very thin,' I say to Max.

'They're elegant,' he says. 'Barney's a very elegant lad, aren't you, Barney? A proper Fred Astaire. Yes, you are!'

Yes, he is and *yes, you are* and *who's a good boy, then.* Is the dog so depressed that it has to be consoled and encouraged with every sentence? I resolve to speak to it like an animal. It comes to me. I say, 'Hello, Barney.'

Leslie says, 'Pat him, then! He wants a proper hello. Go on, stroke his head.'

I stroke its head once to shut Leslie up. 'I don't want it roaming round the house, crapping everywhere, so we're going to keep the kitchen door shut. And I don't want it crapping in the garden either so you'll have to take it out to the street. All right?'

66

'For Christ's sake, Mum. He's as likely to crap on the floor as I am.'

'He's house-trained, Mim.'

'Maybe. But he's never been here before and he might not think it's a house. Let's eat.'

Fondling its ears, Leslie says, 'I think he's beautiful, Max. A lovely boy. Has he settled in?'

'No problem. Like he's always lived there.'

Leslie bends down to the dog and says, 'I hope you'll be very happy together. I wish you a long and happy life with my son.' The dog licks his face.

I turn away and get the casserole out of the oven. Max opens the tin, forks the meat into the dog's bowl and puts it down for him with more patting and baby talk. He and Leslie watch as the dog eats. Then we eat. During the meal, Max is positively garrulous. 'The dog-walker's fantastic – he's got six on his books and he takes them all round the park at once – can you believe it! Amazing, six dogs! Barney's going to have a great time. And I've got him a basket and a rug and some toys so he doesn't get bored during the day. And then I take him for another walk when I get home. I leave the radio on for him as well, to keep him company. He likes music.' Max helps himself to more stew. 'This is nice.'

What? And he hasn't had a drink or said fuck since he walked in. Even if this turns out to be a very short run, it's thumbs up for Barney. Max tells us what's going on at the agency and we talk about what we've seen on television and all the time the dog's asleep, curled up by his feet. It stays there until the meal's over, then it untangles its legs and stands patiently while Max collects the bowls and attaches its lead.

'See, Mum? This is how it is. No crap. Nothing. He's a good boy.' The dog looks up. 'He *is*.'

Leslie's excessive in his goodbyes. As we watch them go round the corner, he puts his arm round me. 'I reckon Barney's going to be the making of him. Man and dog. It's lovely, don't you think?'

'If it lasts.'

He pulls away and goes inside. 'Can't you ever be positive? It's no wonder the boy's got problems.'

I close the door and follow him into the kitchen. He's clearing the table. 'Are you saying it's my fault?'

'I'm saying you could be happy for him, that's all. You're always ready to criticize. Always ready to give him a bad time.' He turns on the taps and squeezes washing-up liquid into the sink. 'I think he's going to find his feet now, with old Barney. It's what he's needed all along. Shall I wash or dry?'

'You wash. Is that what you really think?'

'What?'

'That it's my fault. That Max is like he is because of me?'

'Just give him a break. Let him enjoy the dog.'

'You don't know what kind of time I gave him because most of the time you weren't there to see it. And tell me one time when you raised your voice to him. One time. You can't because you didn't. You were always so bloody busy being *nice*.'

'I love him. Why should I shout?'

'Because he could be a little bastard. Because he was a child. Because I had to do it. Because I still have to do it. *Because you never shout!*'

'I'm shouting now!'

'It's too late!'

'For what? What's it too late for?'

I take a plate and throw it on the floor. It bounces. 'It's too late because it's too late. Too *late*.' I pick up the plate and throw it harder. It bounces again.

'You've got the beginnings of an act there.'

I don't want to but I laugh. It's jerked out of me. I've made him angry and he can't stand it. Turned out nice again, Missus. Turned out well for the funny man.

I'm waiting to see the doctor. The reception desk is behind me so I don't know who's speaking, but I hear the outermost reaches of a voice, high-pitched and quivering. I think it's a man but I can't hear what he's saying and neither, apparently, can the receptionist because she asks him to speak up. 'I haven't been to the toilet for four days,' he says, loud enough now for us all to hear. He's told to sit down and wait. I sneak a look: he's tiny. An elf. Shuffling to the nearest chair – which happens to be the chair next to mine – he sits, leaning heavily on his stick, and puts a shaky hand on my arm. I say, 'I think the doctor's late in this morning.'

'Bloody marvellous,' he says in his elf voice. 'That woman's deaf, you know.' The other people in reception are intent on their magazines or on the floor. They shuffle in their chairs. 'You have to keep your pecker up.' He leans in. 'You look after yourself, love.'

I'm being called, I'm next. I wish him luck and gather my coat – why did I take it off? – and the paper and my glasses and my handbag and, clutching it all to my chest, I blunder my way to the consulting room, bent double like a panto witch. Another bad entrance, so many in my life. The doctor sighs as I come in.

I don't think it's directed at me. The phone rings and he lifts his hand in apology. I lift mine in return. Patient means patient, I say quietly but he misses it and the moment's gone. I sit down and organize the muddle in my lap, then I glance out of the window at the dead shrub in the centre of the courtyard. The poor thing was going downhill last time I was here, parched in its tub, and now it's a pile of twigs. Can I be the only person in the building who thinks this is a depressing view – twig as metaphor? The doctor's still on the phone; he turns to me and mouths *sorry*. I shake my head and mouth *no problem*. I've exhausted the view. I look at the clutter on the desk and the posters on the wall and the couch where I've had such grand times exposing myself. He rings off. He's very sorry he's kept me waiting. I remind him about my blood pressure and tell him I'm not happy with the side-effects of the drug I'm on. He peers at the screen, does the thing with the armband and writes me up something else. I leave, trying not to fumble – another bad exit. As I walk through reception I see the old man. He's asleep, or pretending to be. Not for the first time, I pray for a future without public humiliation.

The older we get, the more our friends and acquaintances seem to die in threes and fours – we get the hats out for one funeral and they stay out. And then I spend days thinking about my own funeral and planning the perfect do – making sure it's got me in a nutshell so they all know who I really was, even if they didn't when I was here. I've decided on this: for the filing in and sitting down, the theme from *The Curfew* – big string section, solo violin, nicely distressing – then Aude reading 'The Mower' by Larkin, everybody singing the twenty-third psalm, Rolf reading 'That Is The End Of The News' by Noël Coward so that they can all have a laugh, everybody singing 'Somewhere Over The Rainbow' so that they can all have a cry, Leslie saying whatever he pleases, unless he's already dead in which case it's whoever wants the job, and then the theme from *The Dam Busters* as they winch me through the curtains. I update this from time to time but I've written the current version out in case. We all seem well enough now but if one of us goes – not that I want to wave the shroud – it's probably ta-ta to a couple more. Surgery visits make me morbid.

After lunch I drive down to Crouch End to see if I can find a gift for Alasdair, despite his analysis of my marriage. His birthday usually passes without a celebration, and I can't remember any helpful details about his likes and dislikes except that he wears contrary patterns and admires J. B. Priestley. I assume he has the collected works of same, and I don't think I can contribute to the warring wardrobe – far too intimate. There's music, but I've never heard him express a preference so that's off. Food, possible. Wine, predictable. After a useless tour, I finally see a rack of sale ties in a shop window and give in about buying him clothes. There's a red forties job at the front, with a swimsuit blonde stretching up to the knot. Ten pounds, and if he thinks it's ghastly at least he'll know I've tried. Then I go into the stationery shop for a card. As I pass the display table my eye's caught by a notebook with an exceptionally red cover and a deeper red stripe down one side. I have to touch it so I pick it up, feel its weight and open it. The paper's heavy. It's exciting, like a new exercise book. I want to write something at the top of the first page and underline it perfectly with a clean ruler then fill in the space with neat black words. I close the book and go to put it back – what could I do with such a thing? I already have a notebook for the garden and I'm only halfway through it so there's no excuse for buying a spare. Nonetheless, I choose a card for Alasdair and take it, with the book, to the till. I leave the shop still not knowing why I'm spending money on something I have no use for. When I get home, I put the book in my chest of drawers. It's a secret.

Aude rings as we're watching the early news. 'Gully says he's got nowhere to stay while he finds a flat…'

'Really?'

'… And there's no-one else in London he can ask. I mean, I can hardly put him out, not in this weather. And he's given me thirty pounds towards the food. And he's being so good, folding his blankets every morning. What do you think? It won't take him long to find a flat. I think he's learned his lesson, I really do.'

'Why can't he stay in a B and B?'

'Don't be silly, they're too expensive. And it's not as if he's costing me anything. That thirty quid, that's more than enough…'

'For what?'

'… And he's keeping a strict list of all his calls… so what do you think? Do you really think he ought to go?'

'Isn't Alasdair getting pissed off?'

She hesitates, trying to frame Alasdair's pissed-offness in a good light. 'They get on very well, actually. Mim? Tell me honestly, do you think I'm being a fool?'

'Yes.'

'Because?'

'Oh, *Aude*, for Christ's sake. Because by tomorrow he'll probably be in your bed, and by the day after he'll have borrowed back the thirty quid and the day after that he'll have unlimited access to your bank account and he'll have given you crabs. And then you'll be angry because I didn't try to stop you.'

Leslie, who's been trying to listen to the news, says – loudly enough for Aude to hear – 'Tell her to tell him to shove it.'

'Was that Leslie?'

'Who else?'

'God…'

'Tell Gully to go. Please.'

'Even if it means he's homeless?'

'Even if.'

'Are you cross with me?'

'Yes.'

'I know I'm being annoying. He's such a nice man, really. He can be such a sweetie-puss when he wants – making us all a Chinese meal and offering to wash up. He's very good in the kitchen. Shall I tell him to go, then?'

'Yes.'

'Is that your unconditional, unqualified answer?'

'It is.'

'I don't know if I can do it.'

'You can.'

'I don't think he's got crabs.'

'Be brave, Aude. Tell him now.'

'I'm in the car.'

'Tell him when you get home. And then tell me you've told him.'

'All right.' Almost inaudible. She can't bear to do this – she'd sooner have a squatting Gully than be thought of as a vindictive old shrew. 'Bye.'

Six

I don't want to wake up but Leslie's calling my name. There's a nice smell. I do my best, squinting against the light.

'Good morning, my darling! Happy Anniversary!' He's barely visible behind an enormous bouquet of greenery and jumbled flowers – where's he been keeping that? He sticks his head round the foliage. 'Forty-one years, Missus. Forty-one!' He waits, eyes a little red with potential tears, mouth in the first creases of a smile.

I make room for him next to me on the bed. He sits with the bouquet on his lap. 'They're beautiful,' I say. 'Where did you hide them?'

'Next door. She wishes you many more years of happiness.' He says this in a Liverpool accent, our neighbour being Liverpudlian. It pleases him and he carries on. 'All you need is love, eh? Isn't that the truth, my pet?' He puts the flowers on the carpet and kisses my face. 'I want us to have a special day. What do you think?'

I think I can't believe that I've forgotten. 'Happy anniversary, darling.' I cup his ear and he leans into my hand. 'What sort of special day?'

'I've booked a table.'

'Sounds good.'

He gets up. 'We can have a bit of breakfast and see what we feel like doing. D'you fancy a film this afternoon?'

'Why not.'

He kisses me. 'I'll put these in a bucket and get breakfast going.'

'I'll be down soon.'

Later, pretending that I need mascara, I walk up to the bookshop. There's a new biography I know he wants and I buy a sheet of wrapping paper, a card, a jar of stem ginger and two Danish pastries. When I get home I wrap the book, make coffee and put everything out on the table. He's writing, of course, but comes as soon as I call him. He loves the presents. After lunch, we go to the pictures – some comedy thing – then home for a cup of tea before dinner.

The restaurant is one we've been to before. It's very charming, very French and we're very early. There are no other diners. We order. The first course arrives.

Leslie lifts his glass. 'To another lovely year.' We clink. 'And to you.' We clink.

'And to you,' I say. We clink again.

He lifts my hand and kisses my ring finger. 'We're doing all right, you and me.' He polishes the ring with his thumb. 'When you think of poor old Rolf.'

'And Poppy.'

'And Poppy. We're lucky. We're still here, we're happy, we've got great lives. We're *very* lucky. Let's eat.'

'Not that we haven't had our problems.'

'Have we? Like what?'

'Like the script. You know, all that stuff about me playing the madam.'

'I thought we'd sorted that out. Me writing it for someone else. Isn't that what you wanted?'

'Absolutely.'

'So, no problem then.'

'No, no problem.'

He pours me more wine and fills his own glass. 'You had me worried there.' He smiles. 'How's your artichoke?'

'Delicious. How's your terrine?'

'Perfect. I really like this place.'

'So how's it going? The script?'

Now I'm being perverse. Not only do I not want to know, but the very act of discussing this is like exploring a cut with a hot fork. Fifty years ago it would have been 'so tell me about your old girlfriends'. Leslie says the writing's going well. The madam's been needing a foil so he's brought in a brother. I ask if this brother bears any resemblance to mine, but Leslie laughs and says he's laconic and dangerous, 'like Clint Eastwood'. Bernard's more like the man who bored the pants off the King of Spain – that's a joke but I only remember the punchline. He's not laconic, he's prosaic and only dangerous if he's talking when you're trying to stay awake, i.e., at the wheel. At least Leslie isn't grubbing through my family to populate the plots. We eat the second course in silence for a while and then he tells me more about the next few storylines – 'you'll never know it's Poppy and Rolf but they've been useful, very useful'. I manage not to say anything and then the waiter takes away our plates and we sit quietly, holding hands and watching passers-by through the bay trees in front of the window. Leslie's been attentive all day but the more he pursues me, the less love I feel. I'm as remote from his affection as if I was on celluloid. I'm two-dimensional.

Flat-hearted. And all he's done is to see me quite differently from how I see myself.

And how do you see yourself, Mrs Lyons? I see a woman, M'lud. Adequately fit and able. Quite clean. Not maggoty-old or cackling-old-whore old. *But you were an actress, Mrs Lyons, and able therefore to assume manifold identities.* How in the swim you are, M'lud. Yes, I was indeed an actor, as the current idiom would have it. But Leslie – Mr Lyons – is also my husband. Being driven to write for me, as he undoubtedly was, I would have appreciated a part more in keeping with who I am. *Which is what?* There you have me. I don't find it easy to put my finger on what I might presumptuously call my Self. What I am sure of, and of this you can be quite certain, is that I don't see my Self as Leslie appears to see it. *Which is how?* What is this – Colombo? He sees me one way, I see me another. That's it. Curtain. *And do you see him as he would wish you to?* I have no idea. *Plaintiff has no grounds for complaint. Case dismissed.* Plaintiff thinks you're probably right, and she's beginning to realize that the basis for her malaise is more serious than botched casting. She is abstract, with no distinctive markings. All she has to show for herself is a small shelf of film and two strange children. And a garden.

Leslie's saying something, '... Lemon tart, fig and port sorbet, a plate of tropical fruit or go mad and have the chocolate mousse. Go on, go mad. Have the mousse. I am.' We have the mousse. He ends the meal with another present, pulled from his breast pocket with a flourish. A voucher for the garden centre. He wants me to choose a tree, a marker for our forty-first year.

My tears surprise us both. Why am I crying? He's gone to

such trouble to prepare for today. I ought to, I should, I can't respond in kind. When we get home we go straight upstairs. I know Leslie wants to make love but as soon as I've washed I get into bed and start to read, hoping he'll change his mind. He doesn't. I put the book down and turn out the light. We make love. Two perimeter walls tight up against each other – I see you, you see me, one eye each, up against the spyhole. If he doesn't know that he doesn't know who I am, and if I don't know who he is, how have we survived forty-one years of marriage?

Leslie's gone to the garage. It's cold and overcast but I sit at the garden table warming my hands on a mug of coffee and reflecting in a disorderly way on last night, and Max's dog and Aude's tribulations, and whether I can find a way of talking to Alasdair without letting on that I know he thinks I'm a thwarted wife. This morning, at the mirror, I made hideous faces at myself, distorting all my features until I got frightened and had to stop. A director once described me as the captivating fusion of Vanessa Redgrave and Diana Dors. If he could see me now, I think he'd be more likely to opt for Walter Matthau and a baked apple.

I've brought down the red book and it's open in front of me. The paper's white. The pen, capped, is black. What shall I do with it, this bare page? I uncap the pen and immediately remember a story about Winston Churchill thanking Lady Astor for nudging his arm as he stood paralysed with a loaded brush in front of a blank canvas. Imagining Lady Astor to be behind me, I fling my hand towards the page, making a line with a slight curve towards the right-hand corner. Churchill was right. The

79

white space is less daunting with ink on it. No other line suggests itself and I stare at the page, reluctant to spoil the design. Then I eat the biscuit and drink some coffee, looking out at the garden. Perhaps I'll try to draw the birdbath. Picking up the pen – should have used a pencil, bound to make mistakes – I use the curved line I've already made as a starting point and work at it for some time, looking intensely at the structure. I think I've finished. I hold the drawing at arm's length. It stinks. It spoils the book. Very carefully, I tear out the page, fold it and put it under the coffee mug, ready for the compost heap.

The book still looks new. The second page has got top billing now. I write Miriam Shaw. Her Book. London. England. Her Book? I must have bought this with some intention. The more I look at it, the more I'm back at school. I write:

> *This book belongs to Miriam Shaw*
> *Sure she was, but sure no more*
> *To some a crone or else a whore*
> *Poor deluded Miriam Shaw*

That's good. I quite like the page having writing on it. I'll try something else. Stay with school… what about the story exercises they used to give us? 'The Picture That Came to Life', 'A Night in the Waxworks', 'It Was All a Dream', 'Three Wishes'… that was a good one. I wished for people to do to unto me as I wished to do unto them, a good marriage (and long) and a boat for my mother and me to sail round the world in as soon as the war was over. Without my father. I probably didn't say that at the time. And what would my Three Wishes be now?

My first wish would be that Leslie and I should die together, in our bed, without dementia or any agonizing illness. My second wish would be

I can't write any more. I can't think of any other wishes. I close the book and get on with the garden. Leslie should be home from the garage soon and we'll have lunch.

Seven

Max rang this afternoon to say that he'd be coming as usual. Why not, it's Friday. He's still happy with the dog. He's even put on a half-decent shirt and proper trousers. He talks to Leslie while I dish up. Leslie tells him about our anniversary, which provokes an apology for having forgotten to send a card and congratulations 'for sticking it out'. We eat. We talk, as always, about what we're watching on TV, and we hear more about the exploitation of greyhounds. Then he tells us that he's going down to Putney on Sunday, to introduce the dog to Constance. Leslie says, 'Tell her hello. Give her our love.'

'Any message from you, Mum?'

'The same.'

At the mention of her name, each of us withdraws into an internal drama, the most brightly coloured red-letter day, the most colourless loss. In the first days, these were my dreams: that she would love me as I'd never loved my father. That I'd never make use of my father's weapons: inconsistency, cruelty, neglect, the endless bloody melodrama. That I would salute my girl's achievements, no matter how different from us she turned out to be. That my love would always outweigh her flaws. That I would keep my mouth shut. In the first days, I may have found it possible. And how did she do, despite me? She thrived at school, was industrious and po-faced, took no notice of me one way or the other, behaved impeccably and was as remote as a duck, arse-up in a pond.

Twenty years ago, a few months after her eighteenth birthday, she left home. She also left most of her belongings, some of which are still in a box in our attic, and set up house with a school friend in Wandsworth. We had no idea what she actually intended to do but gave our permission – unsought – and then helped her to the taxi. Her income, a small allowance from us, could be beefed up with a part-time job. Why not let her play at being grown-up? The joke was on us. She'd joined the police. I found out when the friend's mother called and said how relieved we must be that Constance had chosen a stable career. I could hardly admit that we hadn't been told. I must have found some devious way of getting this woman to spill the beans. We wrote to Constance that afternoon saying how proud we were, asking for a photograph of her in uniform and reassuring her that we were terribly pleased and so on but it was weeks before she replied, no photograph, only a letter thanking us for our 'good wishes'.

Over the years her visits grew less and less frequent and then, after my sixtieth birthday party, they stopped altogether. Leslie had arranged a show, a sort of *This is Your Life* affair with friends getting up to tell stories, a few clips from my films and some old home movies. The first reel: scenes from our tenth anniversary. Constance was seven at the time, a very self-contained, rather prim seven, handing round cigarettes – we all smoked then – and bowls of cheese footballs. We'd asked the children to sing a number with Leslie, him playing the piano, them doing a bit of soft-shoe. They tried to get out of it it but we persuaded them, Max more easily than Constance. In the end, they performed the song with sullen little faces, resenting every second, which somehow made it all the funnier for the guests. I apologized the next day, which she endured with her usual deadpan resignation, and that was the last time she came to a party, until my sixtieth that is.

As soon as she saw herself on the screen, she left the room. Max followed her and I went after them both. By the time I reached the door, she was pulling on her coat and shouting. It's a loud voice, probably highly effective with criminals. I said that she was a baby then, that no-one would think any the less of her. She said rather more in return. Since then we've kept the cell door open, as Leslie says, by sending cards on her birthday and at Christmas. Max meets her occasionally, always in her house or at her choice of restaurant, and although he isn't keen to gossip – loyalty's one of Max's good qualities – he does give us some news. We know that she's married to a man called Neil, another policeman, that she has no children and that she's risen quite successfully through the ranks. Her hair's still blonde, she hasn't put on any weight, she's well and she asks how we are from time to time. She visits my father, but he refuses to discuss her. Would she like to see one of us? Both of us? No, she wouldn't. She seems happy. She seems well. We have a theory and it's this: Constance believes us to be disappointed in her; we're not. If she can't bear to see us, then that's the end of it. There are no explanations and certainly no apologies due, on either side…

… Leslie and Max are talking about Charlie and the problems he's having with the business. I offer them both more food and then Max says, 'Will you be in on Monday?'

I know exactly what's coming next but Leslie bounces into the trap like a baby bear. 'I'm sure we will. Won't we, Mim?'

There's no point trying to fudge an excuse. Leslie won't pick up on it and we'll end up with a senseless conversation about something in the diary I can't verify. 'As far as I know,' I say with the least possible enthusiasm, 'yes, we're in.'

Max is delighted. 'Fantastic. Look, this is how it is. The dog-walker's got some hospital thing and Charlie's in Birmingham so I can't take the day off.'

'Can't you take it in with you?'

'No! With Charlie's cat?'

'What cat?'

'*The* cat.'

'I didn't know he had a cat.'

'He's got a cat.'

'So who looks after it?'

'Charlie. Who do you think?'

'And what happens when he's away?'

'*I* look after it.'

'What, it lives in the office?'

'Mum, for fuck's sake, it lives in his flat.' Max shifts into his withering voice. 'I feed the cat in the flat.' Then he lifts his shoulders, raises his hands and look at Leslie. 'What's the big deal?'

Just as I'm about to say *so why can't the damn dog go with you if the cat's upstairs in Charlie's flat?* Leslie says, 'Forget the cat, will you, Mim.' He turns to Max. 'So we're having Barney for the day.'

'Is that all right?'

'A pleasure. A real pleasure.' He pats the dog. 'We'll have a lovely time, won't we, Barney boy? Yes we *will*.'

I've spoken to Poppy several times during the week and she rings again on Saturday morning. Rolf's home today and they'll both be at Aude's tonight. She's had a manicure and streaks and a Shirley MacLaine haircut and she's found a yellow shirt that goes so well with the skirt she bought last year that you'd think they'd been made from the same bale of cloth… And she hasn't got cancer. Cancer? Diarrhoea, she tells me, and something awful stirring in the bowels. The doctor says she's anxious and eating badly. Last time it was a bruised ankle, the time before that a mouth ulcer, before that, a cough. All certain to be the first trumpet blast.

I ring Aude. Dinner's still on. And Gully? He's out. 'Out or *out*?'

'Out. As in not here. He's gone to the chemist's – there's a boil or something on his neck, and don't worry about tonight, he's going to be out. Actually, I wanted to tell you something.'

'What?'

'He's asked me if I'll marry him again.'

'*What?*'

'He says our divorce was the worst ordeal of his life, that he's never recovered, that I swung him round the court by the balls. That I left him a broken man.'

'Good, yes. So why does he want to do it again?'

'I've got no idea.'

'You won't, will you? Please tell me you won't.'

'I don't think so. But it's nice to know I can still have sex. Of a sort.'

The idea of that crook getting into Aude's bed is more than I can bear. I tell her. She tells me that I have no idea how lonely she's been. I tell her that she'd do better if she picked a bloke up on Muswell Hill Broadway. She tells me she's tried. I beg her to end it. She tells me to mind my own business. I tell her not to ask me for help when it gets nasty. She tells me it won't get nasty. I tell her I loathed Gully the moment I clapped eyes on him. She tells me to bugger off. I do.

After lunch, while I'm in the garden sweeping up leaves, I think about my three wishes. Am I stuck at one because I don't want to waste the other two? If I had dozens of wishes, would I wish for many things? We're luckier than most, we're not broke – Leslie was very careful when he was earning and I saved more than I spent – but how would it be to have more? I immediately think of the garden, more choice, more rarities. But there's no point. I can afford anything I want and I love what I've got. Clothes? The house? Holidays? We have everything, we don't want to go anywhere. What if I could change my past or guarantee my future? Should I wish for a different marriage, different children, a longer career, a different career, a different father? And what about Leslie? Should I wish him blessings? What do I wish Max? Or Constance? How do people in fairy stories ever wish for anything? It's onerous, this list. I can't possibly narrow it down to three.

When I come in I find Leslie asleep on the sofa with the paper falling out of his hands. I make tea, get the red book and go to the conservatory. The first page is a bit of a mess with the rhyme and the abandoned single wish, but I can't keep tearing things out so I leave it as it is. The effect is enigmatic, a bit Mary Celeste. And here I am on a clean page, the same problem all over again. I've gone off the idea of a school essay, and I'm certainly not going to attempt a play. A fairy story might be fun.

Once upon a time there was… what was there?… a… plate, a huge plate that belonged to a giant and his wife. The plate was big enough to hold a whole roast cow or a pie made with two sheep or an orchard of apples, stewed with a sack of sugar. Every morning, the giant's wife would put the plate on the kitchen table – a table big enough to stand an army on – and she would say this to her husband:

'Mr G, O Mr G, what are we to have for tea?'

And the giant would shoulder his enormous gun, a gun big enough to do for the largest of animals, and he would go in search of provender.

Not bad. I've got no idea what happens next and I can't say I care terribly, but I quite like the plate. I've got a better idea.

Once upon a time, there was a shadow. The shadow had no show of its own but tailed the person it was fastened to, changing as the light changed. Sometimes it was a flat thing. On staircases it was bent. In the wrong light it could be alarming – the monster on the stairs. Sometimes it disappeared altogether, into the place where shadows wait until they're wanted. One day, out on the road, the shadow hovered over a puddle. The puddle, which was in a hollow and rarely dried out except in the warmest weather, had had time to think about life. 'I envy you,' it said, 'being on the move. Even so,' the puddle went on, 'I can't say I envy you your conditions of employment.' As the shadow began to slip away, the puddle shouted after it. 'Haven't you ever thought of cutting adrift? Be like fog… be free…'

The meeting with the puddle upset the shadow's normal composure. Day after day, pulled this way and that, it began to accumulate resentment. Then one afternoon, as the shadow was being moved from a bright lawn to the place where it was made to disappear, it snatched away a tiny wisp of itself that it left on the grass, alone in the sunshine.

Alasdair might have a point. I couldn't have thought up this little allegory without some internal provocation. Am I tailing Leslie? Trailing Leslie? No shadow exists without its begetter. It's nonsense to think that the wisp could survive alone. There's a gust of wind and I look outside to see next door's cat, hurtling – flying – like a black and white leaf towards the shelter of the border. The cat should be grateful that I won't let the dog go out there on Monday. There'll be no caticide, no trampled beds. I close the book and go inside to wake Leslie.

We're the first to arrive at Aude's and we're too early. She's still in the bath. Alasdair makes us drinks and we sit round the fire, then we give him his tie which he loves and puts on immediately, even though he's wearing a polo-neck jumper and a waistcoat. I ask him, quietly, about Aude and he tells us that Gully's got a huge boil on his neck, the louse, and is obviously angling to be allowed to stay. 'He wants *me* out,' Alasdair says. 'Out of my room. Tries it on every which way, never lets up.'

I haven't told Leslie about the marriage proposal, and I don't know if Aude's told Alasdair so I just say that Gully's a vile shit.

'You never saw any of Gully's exhibitions,' Leslie whispers to Alasdair.

'Mercifully, no.'

'*The Many Faces of Cod*, that was a cracker. Cod in love, Cod waiting for a bus. He had baskets of raw fish all round the gallery. And fish and chips wrapped in paper and some hairy berk doing fishing songs on a guitar. Horrible, the whole thing. Very smelly.'

Then Alasdair tells us about the man at the BBC who bet him ten quid he could say arseholes three times at the Savoy Grill and get away with it. The man gets the menu, looks up at the waiter and says, 'Ah, soles I see. These are soles, aren't they? Our soles are bigger than these.'

As Leslie tries to top it, I go out to the loo to look for Aude. The bathroom's empty – she must be in her bedroom. She is. Lying on the bed, dressed and made-up, her legs curled round and her hands folded against her throat.

'I'll be out in a minute. I was feeling wobbly.'

'What do you mean, wobbly?'

'Shaky. A bit shaky.'

'Push over.' I sit inside the half-moon of her body and put my hand on her hip. 'I'm worried about you. You're in a mess, girlie.'

'Don't start, Mim.'

'Why not?'

'There's no point. I think I'm going to have to marry him. He's lonely. He's old and lonely.'

'How appealing.'

'And I'm old and lonely. And I hate being in this bed by myself. Let me get up, will you?' I move out of the way and watch her walk to the mirror.

'Would you not wait, just for a while? You might change your mind.'

'Nothing changes,' she says to my reflection. 'It only gets worse.'

I'm about to point out that getting worse is the sort of change that Gully excels at when Leslie knocks to say that Gully's on the phone.

She's out of the door before I've got up. It turns out that Gully doesn't like any of the films at the local cinema and he doesn't know what to do with himself. And his boil's hurting. Aude heads him off by suggesting that he spends the evening having a meal and a nice read in the pub. Of course, if she marries him again, we'll all have to be friends. Hell. She's asking him if he's got a paper… he could probably still buy one if he tries a few late shops… and take some aspirin? Aude's happy again, playing nurse to a wounded outcast. She always swears she's learned her lesson, that whoever it is can whistle if they think she's easy, that she's merciless now, as impenetrable as a mermaid. The call's effected a cure. She's not wobbly any more, but opening the door to Rolf and Poppy with a radiant face.

Poppy's had the full works – spiky hair and the bright yellow shirt and skirt. Straight from an American musical, primary and brash, refusing to give Doreen What's-her-name the upper hand. Rolf's exhausted but says he's happy with rehearsals and during dinner we all chat away, jolly as monks over the fish pie. So far, so pleasant. Then there's a small delay while Alasdair fills our glasses and that's when Leslie says, 'I've been writing this thing, you know, about a brothel.' He looks at me as he's speaking. 'Mim thinks it's rubbish,' he adds, as a pacifier. 'She's probably right.'

'I never said it was rubbish. It's a perfectly good piece of work. I don't want to be in it, that's all.' I smile at Leslie. 'Do I?'

Nobody speaks and then everybody speaks at once. The

loudest wins – Rolf, of course. 'Why don't we make it our next play-reading?'

'Not if Mim doesn't want to be in it. That wouldn't be fair.' Thank you, Aude.

Rolf isn't listening. 'She doesn't mean she doesn't want to be in it with *us*, do you, my darling? Nothing to be precious about. You can't mind if it's just us.'

'But I do mind.' I might as well split open at the breastbone and expel an alien onto the tablecloth. 'I don't want to be in it. I don't want any part of it. If you want to do it, then you carry on and do it. I'll make other arrangements.'

Leslie's staring at me. His face is flushed. As the silence reaches its climax he says, 'All right, my darling. We'll shelve it. It's not ready, in any case. Not nearly ready. Why don't we do an Ayckbourn? You love an Ayckbourn. That'll be fun.'

'Good idea,' they all say, desperate to shut me up. I'm unrepentant but looking for a way out when I remember that we're here because of Alasdair. As a diversion, I start to sing 'Happy Birthday'. Aude gets the cue, dashes out to the kitchen and comes back with a cake circled in a tartan bow. There's one candle, off-centre. As Alasdair blows out the flame, Aude says, 'Make a wish then.'

He closes his eyes and I think, lucky man, he knows what he wants.

Leslie says nothing on the drive home. Neither do I. When we're in the house we wash, get into bed, pick up our books and still we're silent. Unheard of, this. We read for a while, then I put out my light and lie on my side away from him, unable to find the phrase that might allow us to speak. I can't sleep. The bed shakes a little. I look round, over my shoulder.

He's bolt upright. Tears are sliding down his cheeks and his nose is running but he's trapped, immobile, staring at some awful thing that I know I've helped to make.

'Leslie?'

He can't hear me. I call him again. He looks down, sightlessly. I sit up and put my arm round him and then we subside slowly back onto the bed together. He cries for a long time, very quietly. When he's still, he says, 'I'll never amount to much.' That's all. That's all he says before he turns away and falls asleep. His nose is so blocked that I can hardly make out the words, but that's what he says, I'll never amount to much. Do I believe he's made the best of it? Maybe not...

In the morning, still red-eyed, he kisses me and we get up and make breakfast as if nothing out of the ordinary's happened. As I'm buttering the toast, I say, 'I was a cow last night. I'm sorry.'

'My fault. I should never have said anything. Bloody stupid, not asking you first.'

'I think we should do it.'

'Do what?'

'Your play. I think Rolf was right, I'm being too precious for words.'

He finds the yogurt and closes the fridge door. 'Rolf's a prat. It's not finished anyway, not nearly. Do you want some of this?'

'No thanks. If you change your mind...'

'...unlikely...'

'...but if you do.'

'I'll tell you.'

'OK.' And that's it. He will never mention last night again and neither, of course, will I.

We spend an hour with the Sunday papers, interrupting each

other as always. Then I get dressed, gather the duster and tele-phone my father. He's started to make his Christmas list for my brother and me. Bernard, who lives in Spain, gets his copy through the post. I take dictation. This year, my father wants a new bed with a pressure-foam mattress. We can club together if we want, he won't mind. And some new clothes, the listing of which precipitates:

'I've always taken pride in my appearance, Miriam, unlike you. I must say you've settled for being a bit of a landgirl since you stopped acting. I can't abide women in slacks. Your legs aren't that bad. Why don't you wear skirts? Anyway, I'm chang-ing my wardrobe. I'm tired of it all. Now, listen. The man in the next flat says…' And so begins The Complaint. Today it's histor-ical: the distance Bernard and I have put between us and him. Other people's children and grandchildren come nearly every Sunday. Even from far away. He has to make excuses. He has to say that Bernard's too ill to get on a plane now and that he's retired to a warm country because of his health. And his daugh-ter – 'That's you,' he says, as if I might have got myself confused with some other poor bastard – his daughter gets sick when she travels in a car. 'I tell them I couldn't put you through it. I tell them you have to take pills when you come and the pills upset you and then you have to get over the pills as well as being in the car in the first place. It rankles, Miriam. I don't like to lie but I can hardly tell them that you don't come to see me because you can't be bothered. I gave up my life so that you two could be properly dressed and educated, and what have you done with yourselves? Bernard's a nobody and you're married to an enter-tainer.'

'Doesn't Constance visit you?'

'That's irrelevant.'

I've finished the dusting. 'I've got to go now. Time to get the lunch on.'

'Don't forget the bed.'

'I couldn't possibly.'

Monologuists. We do our best to avoid the ones we know but you can't avoid other people's friends or the person you thought was normal until you asked them to lunch. There's a pole, that's how Leslie and I describe it: at one end you'll find an ear and at the other, a mouth. Most of us live in the middle, having ordinary conversations, my turn, your turn. At the mouth end it's like that play by Beckett, disembodied lips jabbering. The ear end just drifts off. Why listen? Partners often share the pole: one talking, one twitching, glassy-eyed. Bernard's the windbag type, piddling on and on and on, dull, dull, coma. My father, although he's adept at The Complaint, is really an ear-mugger, hectoring and lecturing, loud enough to reach the gallery. Got an opinion? Got facts? Don't bother. You're wrong.

The top of our top ten ghastly encounters – we list them sometimes, to torture ourselves – was with a drama teacher at Max's primary school. His wife asked us to dinner. We arrived at seven. We left at eleven. If we spoke at all, it was only to ask for salt. They told us about their children and their recent holiday in France, with photographs, their expertise in theatre and film, their years at university, the work they'd done on the house, with photographs, and then, with brochures, the possibility of their emigration to Canada. Not a day too soon. At the door, the wife wrapped her arms round me and said, 'Dear Mim, it's been so nice to get to know you better.' Like all monologuists, my father

Eight

It's Monday and Max has left us the bowls, the basket and the dog. Leslie's taken complete control but even so, I couldn't be more aware of its presence if it was sitting on my lap and chewing my hair. After lunch, we take it for a walk on the Heath. There appears to be no-one about, but as we turn a corner, we see two people in the middle distance. One is standing, the man. He has white hair and an ex-army posture, shoulders back, head high. He gives no indication of having seen us, although he's facing this way. The woman, the two cheeks of her bare arse pointing towards us at his side, is clearly pissing on the grass, her trousers around one ankle and her hand on his arm. There's no shelter here, it's cold and she's been taken short. She can't squat because her back and her legs are ramrod-stiff, she's wishing she'd worn a skirt, she's wishing she hadn't agreed to go out so soon after lunch. I pull on Leslie's arm and we wheel round, walking back the way we came. I can't bear it that the man should have to stand by his almost naked wife in an open space, that his wife has to urinate in public because she can't wait and she's too fastidious to soak her trousers, that their marriage, whatever it's like, has to include this act. How do they administer the embarrassment? Perhaps they never refer to it, or else they laugh it off, or he'll snipe at her for some other, less involuntary act. Or they're so fond of each other, so tender, that he kisses her and helps her dress without having to say a word. 'If that happens to me,' I say to Leslie, 'please make me wear a nappy.' Leslie says if that happens to me, he'll phone the *Sun*.

Who expects to be pitiable? Who expects to end up in a circle of chairs, unreliably fed, head lolling, anonymous? You don't need shoes. You wear slippers for that lurch between your bed and the depot where you sit, waiting for death to pick at your sleeve. You don't remember the last time you went through a front door or put on a coat or used a telephone. If anybody's dutiful enough to visit, you certainly don't play the hostess. Do choose a chair, won't you? Don't go, take me with you, let me smell the street...

And what if you're home, on your own, determined that you won't leave for good unless it's in a box? What then? If you're helpless, it's Alcatraz, without the company. Who thinks they'll come to this? *And when does it start?*

Consider that woman in the park: if she'd had the chance to see her future on film when she was twenty, say, or even forty, would it have changed the way she lived her life – to know that she was going to piss herself in public? Is there something I should know about what's in store for me? Might it change what I'm doing now?

While we're walking, we start to talk about my father and the new bed. Leslie thinks it might be an investment to get a good one. 'We could always use it when he's gone,' he says. 'Max might like it.'

'Even if it's been slept in?'

'I don't see why not. Unless your dad's incontinent.'

'Oh, Leslie, *please*.' We walk on. The dog's walking with us. To my amazement, it doesn't pull on the lead or stop at every tree. I'm not warming to it, but I'm thankful.

'Not that your dad's ever going to die,' Leslie says. 'He's shrivelling, that's the best he can do. Poor old soul.'

'Shrivel, Drivel—'

'... and Snivel. Solicitors.' I want to settle the last ghosts of Leslie's tears, to assure him that I'm on his side, that I'm not the enemy. On the way back to the car, he stops to kiss my cheek and presses his nose into my face. 'You smell very nice. Like a nice wife should.' He kisses me again and we walk on, hand in hand. It's not that I'm capitulating about the madam business but I don't feel exercised about it, not today. When we get to the car, the dog climbs onto the back seat and curls up on an old towel. As Leslie drives off, I turn to make sure it's behaving itself. Without moving its head, it raises its eyes to me. I'm not ready for it, the feeling in those eyes. As any B-movie hack would have it, I respond. He's too far away to touch but I extend my arm towards him. He straightens out and lays his head on my outstretched palm, as if he's giving me a gift, an unexpected prize. We look at each other.

'What are you two doing back there?'

'Nothing.' I turn round and open the glove compartment to find the sweet packet. 'Only making sure he wasn't getting mud on the upholstery.'

'Oh, yes? And was he?'

'No.'

'That's good then. Only I thought I saw you being nice to him.'

'We're getting along.'

Leslie glances into the mirror. 'Who's a good boy, then? *Who's a good boy?'*

When Max comes to collect the dog, he doesn't leave straight away but makes himself a coffee and sits at the table, work-smart in apricot cashmere. 'I've got a problem,' he says, crossing his legs and looking at Leslie. He doesn't have to say a word because I know exactly what the problem is and of course I'm right, in every particular. Charlie's stuck in Birmingham because there's some shenanigans with the play and he can't leave until his actor's happy, and the dog-walker's visit to hospital uncovered some ghastly illness and the poor man's got to stay in for a few more days. Ergo: hello Barney for the duration. Yesterday, I would have been seriously annoyed but an unforeseen rapprochement has been pulled off in the back of the car and while we're not quite chums, we're certainly straying into good-will, Barney and I.

'That's marvellous, isn't it, old son?' Leslie says to the dog. 'We're really enjoying having him here, aren't we, Mim?'

'We had a good walk. He behaved very well.'

'Mum, for God's sake. What did you expect?'

'He might have got himself into mischief...'

'... savaged all the old biddies, bitten their ankles...'

'... with children, other dogs, whatever. The point is, he was OK and we're all getting on fine. So if you've got to leave him for another day or two, it's perfectly all right.'

Leslie says, 'So is he staying the night? Only you're welcome, if it's easier.'

'No. I'll bring him back in the morning.'

I say, 'We might as well buy him two bowls to use while he's here.' They both look at me as if I've turned into a singing sardine. 'Well, why not? You're bound to leave him again. It makes much more sense to have two sets.'

'Good idea, my darling. We'll get them tomorrow.' Leslie gets up and puts his hand on Max's head. 'I'm going to start dinner. Are you eating with us?'

'No thanks. I've got a friend coming over.' A friend? He gathers his things and puts the dog on a lead. Bye-bye, Barney. Bye-bye.

We cook and talk about Max. I'm interested in the idea of a visiting friend. It's novel enough to be remarkable. We never hear about visits to or from anyone – which isn't to say that he doesn't have friends, or even lovers, but if he does they're kept secret from us. Of course Max can have my father's single bed. He's never had a double. We don't refer to his apparent celibacy, not even to justify it. The whitewash stays in the bucket, partly because Leslie can't bear to talk about anything which might challenge his world view and partly because I don't want to pry. Max comes to us, he works, he presumably makes conversation with people and for all we know, he runs a non-denominational prayer group every Wednesday night with tea and biscuits after. But tonight, openly, he's being visited.

'So who do you think this *friend* is?' I say. 'He hasn't mentioned anyone to you, has he? I suppose it's easier with the dog. You can chat to people round trees.'

'He wouldn't tell us, would he? What boy tells his parents what he's up to? He wants to keep his private life private. That's why it's called a private life. It's private…' Leslie ends the line on a fade, as if he's given up with it. 'If he's got a friend coming round, that's marvellous. You never know where it'll lead. Good luck to him.'

Good luck indeed. I'd like to think that Max could be happy, in or out of marriage. From what we can see he hasn't quite got the hang of making conversation but then it's possible that the kind of conversation he makes is an absolute hit, standing-room only, with the fortunate few who've been given an audience.

I haven't spoken to Aude or Poppy since Saturday. When we've eaten I ring Aude. Alasdair answers and says, 'They're out, thank the Lord.'

'That bad, eh?'

'I tell you, Mim. If he was good for nothing it'd be an improvement. I've never seen Aude like this.'

'I have. It'll stop eventually but we've all got to be patient.'

'I suppose you've tried telling her what you think?'

'It's pointless. She won't chuck him out, not yet. Not till he pulls off some unspeakable stunt. So what are you going to do?'

'I can't stay here. I'm going to have to find myself somewhere else to live. If you know anyone with a room…'

I ask him why he doesn't call on his spooks for counsel, but he says it doesn't work like that. 'It'd be like trying to take out my own appendix.' He says they don't even give him advice of the 'Think twice before passing water' kind. I want to ask him why, and what's the point of being psychic if you can't use it to get one up on fate, but he's saying something about trying to find the good in Gully…

'… I wish I could. Never mind enlightenment. As far as our man's concerned I only want to stick his head down the toilet.'

'I wish you every opportunity.'

I report this conversation to Leslie and he suggests that Alasdair could move into one of our spare rooms. 'We get on all right, don't we?' he says, looking up from the paper. 'I wouldn't mind having him round the place till Aude pulls herself together.' Leslie thinks I'm asking him to approve the idea but the truth is I don't want anyone else in the house. That's why I didn't offer. Even though I like Alasdair, I don't want to have to meet him over breakfast. I'd inevitably end up doing my hair and putting on make-up the moment I got out of bed. And what about lying on the sofa when I want to snooze? And sharing a fridge?

I ring Poppy, and immediately wish I hadn't. She's very drunk and incoherent and the only words I can hear clearly are all connected to her having terminal cancer and not wanting to die alone. 'Have you seen a doctor?' I shout, not because I expect an answer but because this is what we do, Poppy and I, when she's having a bad night. Now she tells me that the cat's got cancer as well and she's going to have her put down, first thing in the morning. Tibbie is Rolf's special friend. She lies across his shoulders when he's reading the paper and sits in the basin when he's in the bath and as far as I know, she's in perfect health. The cat's a weapon, the cancers come and go according to Poppy's state of mind. Rolf knows she's lying, but there's always the possibility that she's cried sick cat once too often, and he sometimes rings me from wherever he's working to see if I know the truth of it. Act Two coming up: the suicide threat. Apart from the futile jump out of the window, Poppy's never actually tried to kill herself but I've been known to race round in the car, just in case. Tonight, I nurse her away from the pill bottle and back to feline cancer. She's almost asleep now, cursing Rolf and threatening to sell the house – a new ploy! – if he doesn't start to… love… never said… waste…

She's quiet. I say, 'Put the phone down, Poppy, darling. Put it back on the receiver,' until I hear the click. Rolf's only been away for a week. We're in for a long run.

While we're getting ready for bed, Leslie says, 'I still think about that audition of yours, you know.'

'Do you?'

'Don't you?'

'Occasionally. More as a breach of the peace.'

'I think it's as well you didn't get it.'

'Really?'

'It's been for the best. I mean, you didn't want to do it anyway.'

'Not really.'

'So it worked out well.'

'It certainly did.'

'I'm glad.' He puts toothpaste on my brush and hands it to me. Then he asks me if I've ever thought of presenting a gardening programme. I ask him if he's joking. He says he is. I'm not so sure. He goes to sleep very quickly, book in hand, while I lie awake, thinking about Antonio. Castings were always a horrible business. That mile between the door and the director's table is as exposing as any dream of waltzing naked in Piccadilly. I remember an audition in the early days. I was shown into a room, not introduced to anyone and left to think good thoughts while the director – I'll call him Cocky Snook – carried on talking to his pals. I was patient for a while, said nothing. More waiting. As I was on the verge of shouting *I'm laying an egg on the lino*, he looked at me, shook his head and said, 'I told your agent to send me someone attractive. Go, please.' I never forgot him. You don't. More tales came my way, none of them in his defence. When I was successful, I longed for him to cast me in something so that I could look him in the eye and say, 'I only work with good directors. Fuck you.' Of course, things being how they are, I never got the chance. I console myself with this thought: when he reaches the celestial Odeon, his wretched little life will be balanced against the pain he inflicted and he'll be judged and made to wait by a silent phone for all eternity. I'm wide awake now. Why was Leslie so cheerful about the audition? Perhaps he's secretly pleased that I didn't get the job – that's what inspired him to start his brothel play. This is a bad thought before going to sleep. I want us to be friends. I want Leslie to feel that he *has* amounted to something. I take the book from his hand, which wakes him up enough to allow him to turn off his light and snuggle down.

'G'night, my darling,' he says. 'Who's a good girl, then?'

I'm still not in the slightest bit sleepy. Poppy's misery is a stimulant. I turn over and start to list my plants, in Latin, going clockwise round the garden from the pots by the back door. This usually sends me off long before I get to the bottom fence but tonight I can't concentrate. I reach a clump of alchemilla mollis and forget what's next. Do I have to go downstairs and find out? I try to go anticlockwise instead but lose track and revert to Poppy. The worst sort of phone call, just before bedtime. And then there's Aude. Oh, dear… Breathe slowly, counting. A taxi stops in the street, the engine idles, there's knocking on a door, shouting, swearing, more knocking. I peer at the clock in case I have to call the police. It's twenty to one. The taxi drives away, everything's quiet again. I get up and go to the loo, drink some water, scuttle back to the warm, puff up the pillow. Leslie's lying on his side away from me, snoring. Something thumps and cracks deep in the house…

… And the red book drops into my mind, as does Leslie's idea of me as a presenter. It's a good story. I can see the main character. She's a morning-TV person who's made to front a gardening show. She's loathed gardening all her life because her father grows exhibition begonias and prefers them to his children. Are begonias funny? Or dahlias? Sweet peas, sprouts… Sprouts are funny. It's sprouts. The producers suggest that her father should be brought in as a special guest. He's a huge hit and she's sacked. How does she avenge herself? A midnight visit to the studio garden, secateurs at the ready… a stroll through her father's sprout beds with a large box of Cabbage White caterpillars.

Max delivers Barney at nine o'clock and goes off to work, promising to be back by six. There's no mention of last night's visiting friend and, true to form, we say nothing. The dog greets us both as if we'd been abroad, drinks furiously from his bowl and then retires to his favourite spot – the floor by the boiler – where he curls up on a blanket I've found for him and goes to sleep. We're sitting down with the post and the paper when the doorbell rings. Leslie answers it. I hear him say, 'Bloody hell!' and go out to the hall to find Alasdair, standing between two large tartan suitcases. Leslie's helping him off with his coat.

'I'm so sorry, I should have rung. There's been a bit of a crisis.'

Leslie says, 'How's Aude…?' while I'm saying, '… Is Aude all right?'

'Aye, she's… she's fine.' He sees me glance at the suitcases.

'Don't panic. I'm on my way to a hotel.' His hair's sticking out like Struwwelpeter and he's in a T-shirt and jeans. Obviously a quick getaway.

'You can stay here till you know what you're doing,' Leslie says. 'Can't he, Mim?'

'Of course.'

'No, no. Not staying. That's not why I came. I'm not sure why I'm here, really. I think I needed a bit of oil on my troubled waters.' He'll never leave. This is our lodger, our boarder, the gentleman in the third-floor back. I'm Kathleen Harrison in a floral pinny. One bath a week, no cooking in the rooms, no musical instruments, no guests, no flushing of the toilet after nine p.m.

We go into the kitchen. Leslie makes us all tea. 'Toast?' he says, waving a plate at Alasdair.

'Please.' He runs his fingers through his hair – 'I must look like a bog brush' – and then sits at the table with his face between his hands, pushing his mouth in like a little beak. I sit opposite him and wait. He says, 'We've had a bit of a set-to.'

'You and Gully?'

'Aye. Me and him.' He sees the dog. 'And who's this lovely fellow?'

I explain. Leslie's getting impatient, hitting a mug with a teaspoon. 'So what happened, Alasdair?'

'He's got me out, that's what. I'd explained about what I do, you know, enough for him to keep quiet when I've got a reading. Then this morning, he walked into my room. No knock, nothing. Said I was evil. Said he couldn't sleep in his bed, waiting for some devil to creep in and gobble up his soul. Can you believe it? Can you *believe* it? He's insane.'

'He should be locked up.' Leslie puts a mug of tea on the table. 'What do you want on your toast?'

'Honey, anything. Thanks.'

'What about Aude? Was she there?'

'Yes. At the end. When Gully said' – Alasdair bends low over the table and drops his voice demoniacally – 'There are unearthly things loitering outside your room.'

'Christ Almighty.'

'That's horrible.'

Alasdair gulps at his tea. 'You know, I reckon that skunk was making it up. He wants me out and that's as good a way as any. Very overwrought. No need for all that devil stuff.'

Leslie says, 'Why didn't Aude tell him to pack it in?'

'Come on. There's only two solutions to this. Either I go or he does. It has to be me. She's deluded, he's crazy. It's as well it's over. I'm fine with it. Really.' He takes a bite of toast. 'She's not in any real danger. This'll pass, don't you think?'

So there we have it. It's done. When Alasdair was in the flat, Aude had a friend, a human bookmark to remind her where she was before Gully turned up. All I can do now is to phone her regularly and repeat, '*Do not give him money. Do not give him money,*' until she does and he disappears again.

Leslie persuades Alasdair to stay for a while. We make up the bed and give him towels, then I pick some flowers for his room while Leslie shows him how to work the cooker and the TV. He's flying to Scotland tomorrow for a children's telly but he'll be back here for the weekend and he says he'll look for a new flat straightaway. I hope that's true. When I've taken up the flowers, I put on some warm clothes and go outside to sweep up.

The leaves are luscious, an inch thick on the beds and paths and I settle into the job, happily mindless, until Leslie brings me out the phone. 'It's Aude,' he whispers. 'I haven't said anything.' We make faces at each other then I shoo him away and lean on the broom.

'Aude?'

'Mim! Alasdair's gone.'

'I know, he's here.'

'*Is he?*'

'He is.'

'I suppose he's told you then?'

'Of course he has.'

'Oh. Are you cross with me?'

'I'm appalled. What were you thinking?'

'Gully was genuinely scared – he's very religious. Did you know that? From his point of view—'

'Gully's point of view doesn't interest me. The man's an oaf. You've lived with Alasdair for years. Did you ever think he was wicked?'

'Of course I didn't. I know it's nonsense but—'

'It is. It's absolute nonsense. Gully's a bully and he wants the place to himself. Stop this, Aude. Tell him to go. Tell him to go today.'

'I'm sure if Alasdair stopped doing the readings, Gully wouldn't mind a—'

'Baloney.'

'Don't, Mim. I want to talk to—'

'Why?'

'To apologize.'

'There's no point. Not if nothing changes.'

'Let me talk to him. Please. Please, Mim.'

There's nothing to be done, not while she's in this frame of mind. I call Alasdair and we meet at the conservatory door. 'It's Aude.'

He mimes, *Well, well*, takes the phone from me and says, 'Hi, Aude. How are things?' I leave him to it.

It's a still day. The leaves haven't moved. I pick up the broom and travel the garden, sweeping. After a while, Leslie comes out to help me and we work quietly together, picking up the leaves and heaping them in their chicken-wire coop. When we've finished, I put my arms round him and hug him as best I can through our thick clothes. He kisses my woolly hat and holds me to him. 'How was Aude?'

'She's nuts, and Gully thinks he's the Pope.'

'Why don't we take Barney for a walk?'

'Good idea.'

By the time we get home, Alasdair's rung his agent, washed his hair and put on his odd, ill-matching clothes. I think he's in recovery.

We have a sandwich lunch and go off to our various holes. I've got the red book out. What about finishing the garden presenter's story? Success, disenchantment and dead sprouts, a night-time tale. I'm bored with it already. If I want to write anything at all, it's a morality play about the folly of reaching the last quarter of one's life without having learned the first thing about the other three-quarters. Are we all guilty of it? Alasdair had the nerve to pass judgement on me but we've never been told if there's an Alasdair junior tucked away, or an ex-Mrs A. or even a Loved and Lost in a glen somewhere. As for his work,

I don't believe I've ever heard him brag about anything spectacular. He's a reticent man. Does that mean he's defeated? Or at peace? I open the book and the first thing I see is my wish for us to die peacefully in our bed. I turn two pages, not wanting to read the shadow story again, and as my fingers release the clean paper, Leslie's mother makes an appearance, fully formed, flat on her back in a pink brushed-nylon nightie. I start to write.

There were three nighties, a pink, a yellow and a blue, and I washed them in rotation for eleven weeks, along with three crocheted bedjackets, all pink, and a flood of white knickers. Two plastic bags a day – out with the dirty and in with the clean. I hated the nylon, the nail-scraping static of it, so I bought her some cotton nighties, pretty ones with lace and ribbons. She said thank you but they came back in the bag, unworn.

If you were casting Joan, she'd be in a film about a World War. Ration-starved, thin lips, button eyes and always expecting the butcher to run out of scrag-end just as she reaches the head of the queue. When Leslie took me to meet her for the first time, she actually sniffed me out. I could hear her as she took my coat, smelling it. She made a great show of not knowing who I was or what I did, even though Leslie insisted that he'd told her several times. The whole thing was show, of course – belittling her boy and his tart of an actress. It was enough for Leslie to be an entertainer, a fact that she excused by saying that he'd inherited inability from his father and couldn't help himself.

After a few years, we began a more civil friendship and I understood that her disappointment was universal; nothing had ever pleased her, no-one had ever relieved her of her philosophy: Things are against me, I'm alone. It was true, she was, but only because she'd pushed everyone away to prove her point. Why has she turned up today? If it's because I'm thinking about dying peacefully in bed, she's a fine example of the opposite – horrified, staring at us whenever she was awake, like a monkey being tortured in a lab. Near the end, as she was falling into a coma, Leslie took a chance and stroked her hand, not expecting her to register his touch but needing it for himself, the closeness. Then he began to cry. She groaned like a harmonium revving up, lifted her head off the pillow and shouted, 'Stop that!' So that was what she'd learned, about life, about Leslie, about her loneliness. Sod all. And it killed her long before she was dead.

I read what I've written and close the book. Joan would have been appalled. She couldn't stomach any sort of reflection or, as she would have called it, 'me-me twaddle'. I'm not sure that I'm terribly keen on twaddle either, but here I am doing it. We're all under scrutiny. Especially me-me.

Nine

It's Friday night and we're on our way to a party, a golden wedding at the Hendersons'. I'm wearing a frock. It's black and unremarkable and will, I hope, invite no comment. At their last party, for no other reason than to cause distress, the Hendersons told us all to come as 'something from Sainsbury's'. Leslie and I went as Grey Suits and Clipboards and were accused of not playing the game by the others who'd spent far too much time trying to look like tomatoes and tins of sockeye salmon. Leslie had worked with John and Lena in the mid-sixties, the three of them uniting against the director in some lame production that folded after a week. I didn't mind John but I took against her immediately – she affects a rather oily charm when you know she'd like nothing better than to kick you in the teeth. We've met over the years but I'd never describe them as friends, so when they rang a few months ago and asked us to this do, I was very surprised. Of course Leslie didn't turn them down, primarily because he was so touched to have been included.

The function room is typical of its kind, decorated with yellow flowers and clusters of gold balloons hanging from the ceiling. There are younger people here, presumably John and Lena's children and grandchildren, some of whom are running wildly round the dance floor, screaming and drowning out the band that's already playing on the small stage. Some couples are braving the kindergarten and doing a foxtrot while the singer glares at the children with open malice, and the keyboard player and the drummer up the volume to such a degree that we're all shouting to make ourselves heard. After an hour or so of this there are speeches and toasts and the balloons are dropped and we all stand to sing 'For They're A Jolly Good Fellow', and that's when Lena does the dreadful thing. 'Ladies and gentlemen!' she says, pushing the singer out of the way and bawling into the microphone. 'I reckon you're fed up with dancing. It's time you got to know each other better!' She turns to the drummer. 'Give us a roll, maestro!' He does a listless rattle, gazing at the floor. 'Right,' says Lena. 'Let's get saucy!'

Even Leslie can't stand this. He looks at me with his 'shall we go?' face and I mouth, *now*, but before we can leave we're being pushed into a line. Lena's been saying something and we've missed the beginning '... and you'll all know each other very well!' Everybody laughs, except us.

'What did she say?' I ask the child at my right.

'You have to pass a orange behind,' she cheeps, 'from under your chin to under their chin and if you drop it you're out and you die.'

'Die?'

'Fall over.'

If half the people in this room fall over they'll never get up. What does Lena think she's doing? 'Let's go,' I say to Leslie. We link arms and march to the door. A man I haven't noticed before – a tall, thickset eyesore – is standing in front of it, arms folded. We assume he'll move and let us out, but he doesn't.

'Yes?'

'We're leaving,' Leslie says with a smile. 'It's late. Past our bedtime.'

'Sorry. My orders are to keep everyone in.'

'*Excuse me?*'

'That's what I've been told to do. Sorry, mate.'

'Who by?'

'Mr and Mrs Henderson. Who do you think?'

We look at each other. This has to be a joke. We both laugh. 'Gag's over,' Leslie says. 'We're leaving.'

'Sorry, mate. You're staying.'

Panic. My chest's tight. I say, 'I'm extremely ill and if you don't open this door immediately and let me out, I'll hold you personally responsible. *I want to go home.*' My voice is weak, almost a whimper.

Leslie picks it up. He's whimpering too. 'Let us out, come on. My wife's not well.'

The man laughs. 'I hope you enjoyed your evening,' he says, standing aside to let us pass. As soon as the door's shut we run through the corridors and down the stairs to the car, desperate to get away before Lena or John or one of their brutes comes after us and drags us back to the orange game. It's some time before we can speak and when we do, it's only to swear.

At home we change silently into our dressing-gowns and sit, dazed, over a cup of tea. The post-mortem: Leslie's angry that he wasn't heroic, couldn't face up to the effing gorilla, didn't punch him or push him aside. And why didn't he confront Lena and John? He rewrites it, dragging them over to explain themselves. I'm angry because I feigned illness. Neither of us can under-stand why they chose to bar the door. Then again, the gorilla might have engineered it. Leslie puts on his dolt voice. 'Let's have a laugh,' he says. 'Let's lock 'em in. Ha, ha.'

Talking about it doesn't help to calm us down, in fact it riles us further and we sleep badly, reliving the scene. By morning, we're baggy-eyed and fractious.

'Are you going to ring them?' I say when we're making breakfast.

'What's the point? It's over.'

'Last night you…'

'That was last night. If we see them again, I might mention it. It's over. Let's have a nice day, shall we?' He turns me away from the sink. 'Come on. It's over. We can do what we like.' A noisy kiss on the forehead. 'What do you fancy? Apart from me?' Leslie won't discuss the party again, not seriously. By the time Alasdair comes downstairs, the whole incident will have been turned into a story in which our helplessness becomes a tremendous part of the joke.

I really did want to kill that man. Even now, up to my wrists in good brown earth, I'm thinking about his stupid face and his stupid arms folded across his stupid chest, and I'm thinking how satisfying it would have been to knock him to the floor. What did he see when he looked at us? Were we such would-be buffoons? What's he to me that I can't laugh it off? And then, trowel in hand, I see the line, the long line of obstructions and Leslie's tactics, my tactics, to skirt round, lie or walk away. I try to think of a time when either of us might have tackled a blockade. I can't, not one. I cover the last tulip bulb with soil, put my tools away and go indoors to get ready.

After lunch, Alasdair has appointments to visit three flats and as the addresses are all local, I say I'll walk there with him. We've left Leslie and set off down the road when I realize that my offer might be mistaken for eagerness to get him out of the house. I say, 'Don't take any old dump. You're welcome to stay with us until you find something you like.'

'I think I'll find something today. But thank you.'

'Is that a divine scoop?'

'A fizzy feeling. That's the way I'd describe it, a fizzy feeling in the fingers.'

The first flat is far, far from fizzy. The young man who greets us says 'uh' and slouches off, expecting us to follow. It's grim – a storage container – with a hardboard partition separating the bathroom from the bedroom. Years of scale have gathered on the bath like shit spread on sandpaper, glued to the enamel. There are knickers soaking in the basin and towels on the floor. As we leave the young man says 'uh' again and then, 'see ya'.

'I don't think so,' Alasdair says. 'But "uh" to you anyway.' The next one's much better, a garden flat with a decent kitchen, and the third doesn't answer to his knock. We go back to the second one and Alasdair asks if we can view it again. The woman who lives there welcomes us, the garden could be delightful, the windows are lovely and everything's clean. We agree that it'll be perfect. Her lease doesn't expire for another seven weeks but I tell Alasdair – because I must – that he can stay with us in the meantime. He thinks for a second or two, staring at the carpet, then says yes, he'll go straight to the estate agent and put down the deposit.

I leave him and walk home, thinking of the place that Leslie and I rented when we were first married – a three-bed, fourth-floor flat in an austere brown block somewhere near Tottenham Court Road tube. We were both new to real sharing but it was easy. Two people, one inclination: general aesthetic disorder. Not one cross word about who did what. The kitchen had no windows and the ceiling was miles up, with a hideous neon strip that we never turned on. Leslie brought in a table lamp with a silk shade – grease-spattered within a week – and we cooked together, in twilight. There can't have been a general shortage of windows but I seem to remember that the whole place was a sort of soupy grey. Our bedroom was the darkest, overlooking a central well, littered at the bottom with giant dustbins and threaded with fire escapes. If we were at home, we kept the curtains in there drawn all day. Why did we live in such a ghastly place? It was meant to be ritzy. We wanted to live together, we were both busy, we didn't have much time to look for anything else. I don't think I've ever been as happy since.

We left the flat when Max was born and bought this house. It cost a few thousand, certainly no more than ten. It's worth eight hundred and fifty now, apparently, silly money, not that we'll ever sell. The back garden was barren except for a coal bunker, a shed with a corrugated-iron roof and ferocious roses on every boundary. At the front, a great lump of a rhododendron – a plant I hated long before I could give it a name – spilled over into the road. As neither of us had the first clue about gardening, Leslie got someone in and I came home after two weeks of filming to find a lone conifer in the front and an immaculate rectangle of lawn at the back with a dismal central bed. For two more years, we paid the gardener to hack away at everything. Then Constance was born, I announced my first retirement and we were asked to a lunch. I have no idea who asked us, where or why but I *do* remember the garden we ate in. Epiphany! An abundant, joyful shambles. The next day I bought some tools and all the useful books I could find and told the gardener that we wouldn't need him any more. Leslie's thought of moving once or twice but I can't leave this place, not after everything I've given it.

Alasdair's definitely staying until he moves into the new flat. There's no need to entertain him as if he were a visitor because he has a particular, rather self-effacing way of getting on with his own life. He's not that different to the man we've been meeting at dinner over the years, but watching him close up I've noticed things that I've never been aware of before. His hands, for instance; the fingers never quite close. Folding the paper, making phone calls, buttering bread, talking – they're always waving, like a sea anemone moving in water. He's fastidious. His clothes may be random in pattern, although I'm beginning to doubt that anything he does is random, but he takes extraordinary care in ironing a shirt. When we're alone, I ask him if he finds us too disorganized.

'Not a bit,' he says. 'I only look a foot or so in front of me.'

'How does that work when you're doing readings? Don't you have to branch out a bit?'

'It's perilous,' he says. 'But I force myself.'

Is this true? Having him here makes me even more curious about his psychic life. He's very deliberately not asked us if he can see clients in his room and I think he's right. I say, 'Is it going to be difficult for you, not being able to work?' I don't explain that Leslie would feel particularly awkward because I know I don't need to.

He says that if anyone really wants to see him, they'll wait. We talk about Aude. Should I ring her? Should he? We decide to leave it for a few more days. Then he says, 'This ad affair. Why didn't you want to do it?'

For a second, I don't know what he means. 'The ad? Oh, that. Why didn't they want *me*, you mean?'

'You said no before they did.'

'Like I said, I disagreed with the principle of the thing.'

'It's changed you.'

'Has it?'

'You're on the prowl. I'm not sure why, but you're nothing like you were a few months ago. I don't mean to pry. It's only an observation.'

A part of me's curious. Does he have something to say? I'm flattered that he's noticed a change – how have I changed? – and suspicious that he's trying to make himself important. I decide to change the subject. 'I don't mean to pry either, but what are you thinking of doing about the flat? I mean, do you think you'll go back to Aude when Gully's gone?'

'Maybe. Buying something, that's crossed my mind. Maybe moving out of London a bit. What do you think?'

'What do *I* think? I've got no idea. Could you afford to buy something?'

'I could.'

'So why live with Aude? I mean, I can't see why you'd want to share if you don't have to.'

'You do it. You share.'

That makes me laugh. 'I'm married!'

'But you like him, don't you?'

'Of course I do.'

'I like Aude. I like her company. I was married, you know. For twenty-five years.'

'*Were* you? Aude never said.'

'I didn't tell her.'

At this point, I don't know what to follow up first: the marriage, not telling Aude, telling me, whether he's divorced or widowed. Children? I leave too long a gap. He answers anyway. 'Divorced. 1985. A slight difference of opinion about the man she was having an affair with. There were no children, thank the Lord.'

'You never talk about it.'

'There's nothing to say. Not now. It's not something you chuck into the conversation – oh, and *by the way*, I was married to pally old Greta and she left me for a drummer in a pit band.'

It's obvious, really. A man in his early seventies is unlikely to have spent a life without at least a trial 'marriage'. I see Alasdair by himself and I cast him as a bachelor. He sees me with Leslie and casts me as a wife. I once had a life alone; he's had a life with pally Greta. All our conversations over the years must have been very inconsequential – what else has he done that I don't know about?

He says, 'You've diverted rather successfuly there. I was asking you about your ad.'

'There's nothing to say. It's history.'

'What's history?' Leslie's at the door. I'm immediately disconcerted, as if I've been caught holding Alasdair's hand. It's not that I'm feeling in the slightest bit amorous but there's an intimacy between us that's only become apparent in the breaking of it.

'The ad,' I say, too loudly. 'Alasdair's just asked me about the ad.'

Leslie comes in and sits next to me on the sofa. 'She's right. The past's the past. You can't live your life wishing things had turned out differently. That's my philosophy, Horatio.' Do I mention Alasdair's marriage? The phone rings and I leap up, happy to be out of the situation. My father's had a fall. He's in hospital.

By the time we arrive, he's dead. We're told about the stroke that followed the fall and then we're ushered into the side-ward where they've put his body. Leslie takes my hand and we stand to attention, watched by the nurse. I ask her if my father said anything in his last minutes. 'I'm afraid not.' She turns to him and then back to us, as if to verify that he isn't about to speak. 'I'll leave you now. You'll want to be alone for a while.'

I nearly say, *Oh no, we won't*, but of course I do what's expected and say 'thank you' with that tight little smile you adopt when you're trying to hold your feelings in check. Which I suppose I am, except that the feeling is liberation. I look down at his face and the only change I can find is a slackening around the jaw. He gave nothing, he gives nothing.

'You all right?' Leslie's arm goes round my shoulder. 'Do you want to sit down?'

'I want to deal with this as quickly as possible and get the hell out.'

'Not much different, is he?'

'Better. He looks better.'

'Mim…'

'What do you want me to say? Let's go home before he changes his mind.'

We do what we have to do and get in the car. If my mother's waiting for my father, I hope she's brought a sizeable posse of magistrates. The man needs to be properly judged. As for me, I'm an orphan now, a seventy-one- year-old orphan. Nobody's daughter, one role gone. Unfortunately, I'm still a sister. I ring my brother in Spain as soon as we get back from the hospital.

'I don't know what you want to wake me up for,' he says. 'Couldn't it have waited till morning?' He's making a face. It's transmitting itself over the continental mass. 'I suppose I'll have to fly over.'

'Up to you. The funeral's paid for, apparently. We'll go to the flat tomorrow and find the paperwork.'

'And the will?'

'No idea. Stuffed in a drawer somewhere. This might be nonsense but he did mention that he'd be leaving most of it to Max and Constance. Well not actually to *them*, more to any children they might produce.'

'And have they?'

'No. Not yet.'

'It'd be absolutely bloody typical.' Bernard, or Barnyard as Leslie calls him, begins to drone. The will, contesting it, the flat, photographs, mementos, the executor, inheritance tax, his wife's feet, his heart, air pressure, inner-city violence, Spanish weather… and as he talks I become more and more enfeebled until in the end I'm lying on the sofa with my eyes shut and the phone resting against my hand on the cushion. He ends, '… I suppose I'll have to let you deal with it.'

'Yes, Bernard.'

'Regards to Leslie.'

'And to Linda.' I ring off and close my eyes again. Bernard Shaw the bore. I tried Bernie for a bit once but it never caught on, probably because he's such a pompous pig. Not comfortable with the diminutive, our Bernard, more of a 'be assured of my best intentions' man. Thank God he's staying put.

'Mim?' Leslie's standing by the sofa. I open my eyes. 'It's two o'clock, my darling. Shall we go to bed?'

It's Sunday and I would have been ringing my father now. I take the red book out of the drawer and sit on the bed. This is going to be a letter. I start, *Dear Dad* – that's rubbish. I can't use the word 'dear'. *Dad*. No, that's no good either. Forget epithets.

'I'm so pleased you're dead. I'm so pleased I don't have to ring you today, or ever again on any Sunday for the rest of my life. No more visits. No more shifting about on that bloody chair trying not to SCREAM while you roll on like a Sherman tank, patrolling against the Thing, the terrible Thing, keeping it banked up outside the door. I bet it always got you when the lights went out. If I'd arrived at the hospital in time, if you'd taken my hand and said, 'I'm so sorry, Miriam. I'm so sorry, my darling girl. I was bad. I was cruel. I was selfish and unkind and I never appreciated you or your mother or your brother. I've lived an awful, empty life. Forgive me,' would I have said, 'Don't be silly, you dear old, silly old dad. Die happy. Of course I forgive you.' Big kiss, tears. You die in my arms. Cut!

Or would I have said, 'A bit late in the day there, chum. Live with it.' Or die with it. Which of course you have. I wish I'd told you how I felt before, I wish I'd had the gall. Not that you'd have heard me.
  'Dad?'
  'What.'
  'You're dying.'

'*So what. Who cares.*'
Nobody, Dad. Nobody cares.

Somebody walks past the bedroom door. I close the book, remembering an article I once read about children losing their parents. There was a photograph of an essay by a recently bereaved boy. 'My father is a strong man,' he'd written. 'He was tall.' And the teacher had scrawled, 'Stop mixing your tenses,' across the bottom in red ink. The boy was right, of course. His father inhabited every tense, as does mine. But I would have written, 'My father is a weak man. He learned nothing.'

Leslie's rung Max and left a message, written a note to Constance, put black bags and cleaning materials in a box and made us a picnic to take to the flat. He gives me the note to sign.

'Loins girded?' Alasdair comes into the kitchen. 'I'll get a chicken or something. Ring me when you're leaving and I'll put it in the oven.'

'There's no need.'

'There's every need.'

The mothering touches me and I do a bit of diverting business, accepting with a deep bow to hide my tears. I had no idea I was so shaky; what have I got to cry about? Except that we've got to drive all the way to Kingston and spend the day combing through a dead man's drawers. We're there by noon. I know the combination to open the front door but I'd feel like a trespasser now, just walking in, so I ring for the warden, Mrs Wilmott, a robust northerner who greets us with a perfectly proper amount of concern. We follow her into the flat and stand shoulder to shoulder, looking at the sitting-room. The paintings have gone, as have all the good pieces of furniture.

'You know I was very fond of Mr Shaw,' she says. 'He had a good innings, a very good innings but even so, it's always sad when we lose the people we hold dear. If there's anything I can do to help, please ring on my bell. I'll be here all day.' She nods and turns to leave.

I'm speechless. Leslie says, 'Where are his things?'

The warden stops. 'What things?'

'All his stuff. Where is it?'

'Didn't he tell you?'

No, good, kind warden. The old bastard didn't say a word.

'He decided to get rid of it all. All the things he didn't need, the paintings and suchlike. You'll find all the receipts in the bedroom. In the cardboard A-to-Z thingy at the bottom of the wardrobe. I put them all away for him. I'm so sorry, I really am.' Her open face knits together, she seems to be genuinely upset by the situation. 'That must have been a bit of a shock, coming in like that and finding everything gone.' My father's surpassed himself. After finding the A-to-Z thingy and reminding us that she's there if we need anything, Mrs Wilmott leaves us to it. I take off my coat and spread it over my father's chair to cordon him off.

Leslie says, 'He never mentioned it then?'

'Not a dicky bird.'

'Do you think he knew he was going?'

I can't explain how he anticipated his death but the rest's easy. Everything's been sold in order that we shouldn't profit from any item that could be carried to the car. The proceeds are in the bank, and therefore part of the assets and therefore in the half-world of the never-to-be inherited inheritance. If we want any of what's been left here, we're welcome to it. It'll all be tat. We can't pitch into the flat without a bolstering cup of tea, so we go off to the kitchen with the picnic bag. While Leslie puts on the kettle, I explore the cupboards; they've been stripped of the silver and the good china that he didn't have room to display. We can choose between three supermarket mugs, three plates and three sets of ropey old cutlery. Did he keep them in case of one more visit from us? And what would he have said if I'd questioned him about the bare walls and empty spaces? *Stop complaining, Miriam. Always making dramas.*

We sit on the hard chairs and drink our tea. Then Leslie says, 'One good thing about him selling everything – it'll save us the bother.'

'Do you have to?'

'What?'

'You're always looking for the *one good thing*. It drives me up the wall.'

'There's enough bad things. Why not?'

'Because sometimes the bad's just bad.'

'You didn't want that money, did you?'

'It's nothing to do with the money.'

'I know.'

'He's unbelievable.'

'Saved us the bother, though. You have to give him that.'

We finish just after four. There are no photographs anywhere, no letters, no cards, no memories at all. He's thrown everything away. We put clothes and linen aside for charity and gather bits and pieces from the kitchen and bathroom to take home. We leave the curtains hanging, clean the surfaces as best we can and make several journeys to the front door with the file, the television, the radio and the remaining single malt. If he'd timed the fall better, he could have sold the telly after he'd watched *EastEnders* and made a few extra quid. On our way out, we offer Mrs Wilmott the house plants and ask her if she can arrange for a charity to collect the bed and the other furniture; she's eager to help and wants to go to the funeral, if we'd be kind enough to let her know the arrangements. I honestly believe she liked him. We finish loading the car and ring Alasdair to say we're on our way. I look back once. It's the last time I'll see that door!

Ten

What Leslie doesn't tell me until we've eaten and settled ourselves at the kitchen table in front of the cardboard file, is that he's already seen the will.

'When? Just now?'

'At the flat.'

'You didn't say anything. Why didn't you say?'

'I thought you'd sooner do it here. In private. I was trying to make it easier for you, my darling. That's all. That's why.'

I'm fishing around in W. It's empty. 'So where is it?'

'It's in A.'

'You hid it in A?'

'In case you tried to find it before we got home.'

'Why? What for?'

Leslie's expression says, *Brace yourself.* 'It's not good news, Missus. You look. You'll see.'

I look. My father's left half his estate to Constance and the other half to the warden. Great – half to a woman we don't know and half to a daughter we don't see. I'm not angry. I'm not even shocked.

'That's why I hid it in A,' says Leslie.

'What's why you hid it in A?'

'In case you went charging off, accusing her. That's why I hid it. If you're going to contest the will…'

'Why would I contest the will?'

'Because your dad hasn't left you anything!'

'But I never thought he would!'

'I know. But I didn't know what you might do.'

'What, duff up Mrs Wilmott? Honestly, Leslie. I don't care.' I write down the solicitor's details and put the will away, in W this time. We start to go throught the rest of the file.

'Very nice for Constance,' Leslie says. 'I've got his BT bill here. Do we deal with this?'

'I don't think so.'

'She'll be over the moon.'

'I expect so.'

'We should tell her about the will.'

'We should.'

'She'll ring soon, when she gets my note. Her and your dad, funny compadres. They must have got on bloody well for him to leave her all that money…'

'If she rings, we'll tell her.'

'… something in him we never…'

'… or something in her…'

I pull out some papers from C. There's an envelope, addressed to my father. I know who it's from. I hand it to Leslie. 'Here. It's a letter from Constance.' He takes it from me with a *swipe me* face, opens it with the kind of care he might give a letter bomb and scans the single sheet of paper in seconds before handing it back. I read out loud:

Dear Grandad
Neil and I are so grateful to you for helping us to buy this
house. You've made such a difference to our lives, and no
amount of thanks could possibly express the gratitude and love
we feel. Your gift was extraordinarily generous, matched in every
way by the support and love you've shown me through the years.
With my love, always.

I read it again, to myself this time. There's a knock at the door.
It's Alasdair, wanting to know if he can watch television. Leslie
says yes, of course, and then gets up and stands behind me, his
hands on my shoulders. I can't think of anything to say and it
seems that he can't either, so I rock backwards and forwards
against his chest, holding the letter. A silly thought comes, that I
want to bandage my eyes for a while, not to have to look at
anything else my father's hidden here. They're the same, him
and Constance, two marble peas. Of course they loved each
other, stone meets stone and thinks it's found a friend. I take
Leslie's hands off my shoulders and put them on my head. He
says, 'A gift like that, from him, it's extraordinary.' He ruffles my
hair then strokes it flat again and goes back to his chair. 'Nice for
Constance, that's the thing. Lovely for her. Amazing, really.
Who knows why people get on. Great shame for Max, but it's
very nice for Constance, it really is.' I still can't think of anything
to say. We carry on with the file for a minute, then Leslie looks
up. 'Hadn't you better ring Bernard? I'll bet he says your dad was
nobbled.'

I ring him. That's what he says, more or less.

'He's been coerced! I've been making enquiries.' Bernard's
spirited, a little piggy in his shit. 'It's perfectly possible that he

was made to sign this will under undue influence, that's the phrase, under undue influence. What's she like, this woman? It's obvious, isn't it? She's wormed her way in.'

'No, Bernard, there was no worming. She's very nice. I think they really liked each other.'

'Rubbish.'

'I know. It's hard to believe but if you met her—'

'I don't have to meet her. It's the oldest story in the book...' And so on. He wants the solicitor's number, which I give him, adding that I'll be ringing them to disassociate myself from the proceedings. He tries to pretend he's pleased for Constance but he won't be coming over, he doesn't even know if he wants to send a wreath and he's only glad our mother isn't alive to see the day.

I can't face the A-to-Z thingy again tonight. Leslie finds the funeral directors' details, then we say goodnight to Alasdair and go up to bed. We've got two more journeys to Kingston, registering the death and then the cremation. I should have claimed for petrol while I had the chance.

I'm trying to remember how they were when she was small, Constance and my father. Scene: she's two or three and he's reading to her from the newspaper. She's engrossed, staring at his face. Another scene: she's at the piano, a little older now, learning to play a simple piece and he's beating time with his hand on the piano lid. She falters her way to the end and he nods. She nods too, and then plays it again until she gets it right. It irritates me, the repetition, and I make a point of walking out. Nice mummy.

The terrible stone-face, the one I'd dreaded all my childhood, that was kept for Max. Scene: he's still in nappies. My father's trying to teach him to build a brick tower. He demonstrates and sits back, waiting for Max to copy. Max laughs, knocks it down. My father growls and builds it again. Max laughs and knocks it down again. My father whams all the bricks back in the brick bag. Max cries. I say, 'He's a baby, he doesn't understand.' My father picks up the paper. I take Max away.

We're on our way to register the death, crawling through traffic. Leslie's listening to the radio but I'm thinking back to…

… My mother, dying. And what did my father do afterwards, when he was alone? He found solace in Constance. He made her the centrepiece. The good granddaughter, the solemn and meticulous girl. She was nothing like me. Nothing in me ever offered solace. Everything I did made him mad because everything I did was wrong. He took one look in the cradle and decided I was odd, a lost cause, impossible to train. Bernard did better. He was humdrum and got immediate praise for it and the more praise he got, the less he was able to forfeit. And the more my father found fault with me, the more I believed I was to blame. Until… Guy Fawkes Night, 1950. I'm fifteen, standing next to the bonfire in my friend Martin's garden. My father's just dropped Bernard and me at the party and said something unpleasant and unnecessary to me as we go in. I can't remember what – why would I? Martin's mother slips her hand into mine. She doesn't look at me, we're both facing the fire, but she says I'll always be welcome in her house. I thank her. She squeezes my hand and goes indoors for the sausages. And I do go there, often.

Scene: Constance is fifteen – a tall, fair, rather beautiful fifteen. We're taking her to the theatre and dinner for her birthday, not her choice but we're keen, so we compromise and book for *Romeo and Juliet*, the play she's doing for her O-levels. She comes downstairs in her uniform. I say something like, 'Aren't you going to change?' She says she thinks she's clean and tidy. I say we're going to a proper theatre, not the bloody school play and why doesn't she put on something smart, there's enough in the wardrobe. Leslie says she looks lovely. I offer her some lipstick. She says no. I say she looks as if she's been dead for a week. Doesn't she want to make the most of herself? Does she really want people to think she's dowdy? Does she want to *embarrass* us? Leslie's trying to intercept me. Max has gone to his room and slammed the door...

It's too painful, this memory. Regret barges into my body, somewhere in between my heart and my stomach. I press my hands to the ache. Leslie says, 'You all right, Missus?'

'I'm fine.'

He rubs my knee. 'This'll all be over soon.'

I don't think so, Leslie. I think it's just beginning.

Eleven

It's a long day. When we get home, we find that Alasdair's let Max in and then gone out for the evening. Leslie's delighted. They greet each other, we say hello to Barney, then Max tries to give me a hug but chooses the moment when I've got one arm out of my coat. I do what I can to respond but it's awkward and he moves away.

'I thought I'd nip round. See if there's anything I can do, see how you're doing.'

Leslie embraces him. 'Thanks for coming, darling. Your mum's a bit tired. Give us a minute to get out of these clothes and we'll be with you.' Upstairs, he says, 'That's nice, isn't it? Coming round to see if you're all right.'

'Very nice.'

'What about the will? I'll do it if you want.'

'We can't tell him yet.'

'Why not?'

'Because Constance doesn't know.'

'But we can't sit there knowing and not say. Anyway, he'll tell her, won't he? As soon as he gets home, you can bet your boots. We could ask him to. We could say, you tell her, you give her the good news. Poor boy. Your dad could have left him something, a few quid, something.' He puts on a jumper, poses in front of the mirror, takes it off again and goes back to the wardrobe. 'He'll get money from us. And you never know, Constance might come up trumps and give him a share of your dad's.' He's in his underpants now, choosing tracksuit bottoms. 'I'll tell him if you like. As long as one of us does it, that's the thing. I don't want him thinking we were playing him along. All right, Missus?' Leslie's right. I say so. We finish dressing. As I go to open the door, he puts his arms round me. 'They're good kids, they'll sort it out. Why don't we ask him to stay and eat?'

I think, let's tell him to go home. I say, 'Sure.'

He kisses me on the forehead. 'I'm so glad my lot died broke.'

We go downstairs and gather in the kitchen where Leslie makes another big fuss of the dog. Max gives me a floral card from Charlie – *I know how you felt about your father but I send fond wishes and commiserations nonetheless, still a difficult time whatever the sitch. xxx* – then Leslie tells Max the funeral's going to be on Friday and sketches in the last few days while we cook. We don't mention the denuded flat, the warden or Constance. As far as I know, Max never visited my father but in case I'm wrong, I ask. I'm right.

'No point me going round there. He didn't like me.'

'Don't say that!' Leslie twists round, the potato peeler in his hand. 'He's your grandfather, of course he liked you.'

Max shrugs. 'He liked Constance. He *loved* Constance.'

That's my cue. 'Max?'

'Yeah?'

'We haven't been able to tell her yet, not till she phones, but the thing is, Max, we had a look at the will last night—'

'Oooooh, boy. You must be gutted.'

'What?'

'Him not leaving you anything. You must be really pissed off.'

Leslie abandons the potatoes and joins us at the cooker. 'How do you know?'

'Constance told me, yonks ago. When she helped him draft it.'

'So she knows?'

'Yeah! Course she knows. That's what I'm saying.'

'And you don't mind?' Leslie puts a wet hand on his arm. 'You're not upset?'

'I'm not upset. She tried to change his mind but he didn't like me. He didn't leave me anything. Period.'

'Is Constance going to share some of it with you?'

'She says she is. We'll see.'

Relieved, Leslie pats him on the shoulder and goes back to the sink. 'That's good. That's very philosophical, darling. I'm proud of you both. You'll be getting your share from us, and you know it. That's a promise.'

So everything's turned out well. Leslie only read the will first to save me from humiliating myself. Max isn't upset about it because he's known for years and he'll probably get something anyway. Constance wrote the fucking thing so we don't have to tell her either. I'm the last to know anything. Thank you all. I put the lemon back on its plate and head for the door. 'You can make the bloody dinner yourselves.'

'Mim?'

'Mum?'

'Go to hell.'

I hear Leslie calling out and then he's behind me. 'Mim?'

'I'll be all right. Give me a minute.'

'Are you sure?'

'I'm sure. 'I'll be down in a minute.'

'Or I'll be up to get you.'

I go to the bedroom. If I was young, I'd probably throw myself on the bed now, weep and then sleep till morning. As it is, I walk about, too conscious of what I'm doing to find any relief in it. I can hear the director: No need to make faces. Let the walking tell us. Stop. Turn round. Sniff. Sit on the bed. I do. I sit on the bed and blow my nose. What did I expect?

Hello, Mum.

Hello, Constance.

I've just helped Grandad write his will. You're not in it.

If my father had died with nothing to give, it wouldn't have made any difference. He'd have made trouble with shredded newspaper. So is it the money? The truth is, I don't think I'm crying because of the will at all. And Max is no more like me than a monkey's like a cuckoo, so how are we the same? Or did my father find something specific in each of us that he disliked enough to turn his back on? Then there's Bernard. It's a surprise how badly that's turned out, given that he was Father's little footprint. He was always the measure, the basis for my father's 'If you had ten per cent of Bernard's…' and, 'Because Bernard deserves it and you don't…' and once, but unforgettably, 'When will you realize that, unlike Bernard, you're incidental to me?' He rarely refused Bernard anything, but Bernard rarely asked because he'd learned that People Who Ask, Don't Get. And until Bernard decided to retire to Spain, they got on. Not *got on*, as in matey or demonstrative, more like fogbound ships hooting at each other in the murk. But that really did for the money, abandoning my father and going to Spain. Good boys don't rat on their obligations, not unless they want to become incidental.

I don't believe that we necessarily have to share characteristics with our children. Apart from the fact that we're all blonde down the female line – grandmother, mother, Constance and me – all brown-eyed, ditto tall and slim, there's nothing else to link us that I can see. Apart from the colouring, I'm nothing like my mother, the lion in her so sadly deposed by the lamb. As for my father, I used to pretend that my mother had found me in the Odeon foyer and taken me home, wrapped in her mohair scarf. I was no part of it, the family Shaw, only a small blonde impostor.

I'm still sitting on the bed, sniffing. I don't want to sleep. I don't want to read. I get up and take the red book from the drawer but as soon as I have it in my hands I'm self-conscious again, the wretched adolescent, confiding in her diary. The director's back. He says: Hold it there. What are you doing? You look nervous. Is this a journal? It's me-me twaddle, mate, that's all. It's a new diversion, raking up old stories and finding lack everywhere I go. It's quite self-indulgent, wouldn't you say, this cosy misery of being misunderstood. The food smells good. I'm hungry. I open the book and write…

My last will and testament. The final word. Whatever you fancy, take it. It's yours. If Leslie survives me, it's his. The garden will look after itself for a year or two, then you'd better get someone in. If Leslie's gone, the house, the money, these things can be divided. Please do it politely. Please cut nothing in half.

✳

Leslie's coming upstairs. I put the book away. He opens the door and peeps in. 'All right, Missus?' There's nothing but kindness in his face. 'Dinner's on the table if you want to come down.'

I nod. 'I'm coming.'

'You'll feel better with some hot food inside you.'

'Is Max still here?'

'He is.' Leslie comes to the bed and pulls me up by the hands. I submit and lean into him.

'I don't feel like talking.'

'So shut up.' He kisses my cheek and we go down to the kitchen, hand in hand, with me trailing after him on the stairs.

I can't look up from my plate but Leslie tells stories and Max responds, and eventually the meal passes. Then Leslie asks Max to tell Constance the funeral details. Max says, 'No problem. Actually, I'm going too, with a friend.'

I'm forced to speak. 'A *friend*?'

He tilts his head. It's a coquettish gesture and suggests that the 'friend' is certainly close, if not intimate. 'I bet you're curious.'

Before I can answer, Leslie says, 'Only tell us as much as you want to tell us, darling. Or keep it to yourself.'

Those big black eyebrows go up and down, a comedy on their own. I'd say he might just be handsome enough, just young enough, a bit plump maybe but plenty of hair. The lips are a touch flabby, the skin and eyes a little spoiled by drink but he's not entirely unalluring.

'So who is it?' I ask. 'Anyone we know?'

'No.'

'So who is it?'

'She plays the viola.'

'The *viola*!' we both parrot.

'Well, she *did* play the viola. She wants to teach now.'

'Does she?'

'So you're learning?'

'As if!'

'That's not how you met, then,' Leslie says. It's accurate, if self-evident. I know he's got dozens of questions but we're both reluctant to pry.

'What's her name?'

'Jackie.'

'Jackie!' We do it again, both parroting.

Max laughs. 'This is all a bit sitcom, isn't it?'

'Is it?' Leslie laughs with him. 'Number one son introduces girl to family. Family too nosy. I'm glad you're coming. It'd be simpler if we all went in one car. Do you want to bring her round on Friday morning?'

'We'll go on our own. It's simpler for us.'

'Why are you going at all?' I ask. 'It's not as if you really knew him or anything.'

'It's a family thing. Why shouldn't I go?'

So he wants to show her off.

Leslie says, 'We'll meet at the funeral then, unless you want to bring her round before. I'm really looking forward to it. Aren't you, Mim?'

An introduction to Jackie, a possible reunion with Constance and farewell to my father. Shake hands with first, take cue from second, wave off third. For a small do, there'll be no shortage of golden moments.

Twelve

I'm going plant shopping. Alasdair offers to keep me company –
'If you'd like a boy to do the carrying.' Why not?

Poppy rings as I'm picking up the keys. 'Hello, Mim, my
darling. How are you?'

'I'm fine. My father's just died, but I'm fine.'

'I'm so sorry.'

'Thanks.'

Alasdair picks up the paper and sits on the stairs. Poppy's
talking.

'… And here's *my* news. I'm going to Manchester.'

'Really?'

'Today. Any minute now.'

'That's nice. Well done! You're going to the first night. Rolf's
going to be so pleased.'

'*Noooo*. That's not for a week yet. I'm going to *catch them
at it!*'

'Oh, Poppy, no! Poppy darling, please don't. You can't
honestly think this is a good idea?'

'It's the best idea I've ever had.' She's drunk – last night's
residue or a fresh start with breakfast. 'Can't stay here. Anyway,
the whole point is that if I surprise them, they won't have a

chance to tip each other off. I'll get there this afternoon, early. I'll just walk in. Then I can catch them at it.

'At what, exactly?' I've got my coat on, I'm very hot. 'They'll be in a rehearsal room. What could they possibly be doing?'

'Whispering. Kissing in corners. I don't know. Giving the game away, that's what.'

'Why don't you wait till the weekend and talk to Rolf? Tell him you're unhappy. Tell him you're scared that he's going to leave you. If you tell him face to face, he'll be able to settle things. See what he says. Won't you do that?'

'Can't.'

'Why not?'

'Because he couldn't give a fuck.'

'So why go up there and make a fool of yourself?'

'Because it's better than sitting here. I'm going nuts in this house. Don't tell me that woman won't… it'll be like it was before… she's been waiting for this… years… can't say no… he never could say no…'

I interrupt. 'Right, then. Manchester it is.'

'You don't think it's a good idea, do you?'

'It's a bad idea. You know it is. As soon as you get there, you'll wish you'd stayed at home. Poppy, look, I'm sorry but I've got to go. Why don't you ring me when you get back?'

'Wish me luck.'

'I do. I really do.'

That's Poppy and Aude, then, both losing on points and me with my head up my arse. Are we all in this, grinding to a stop? She'll find Rolf on his own and assume Doreen's hiding behind the arras, laughing herself sick. Then she'll accuse him, make a scene in the pub, sleep it off and start again until he's forced to send her home. She'll say she's been thrown out. For Poppy, that's victory. Aude won't be calling me for a while, not till she's been milked and dumped. And as for me, the view up my arse is a family portrait, obscured by the proverbial glass darkly.

I tell Alasdair what Poppy's doing as we walk to the car. He says, 'Shall we warn Rolf?'

'I'm not sure. Would it help?'

'Maybe. Maybe not. A punch-up might do them good. There's no use in things steaming on the way they are.' He puts on his seat belt and then pulls his jacket out so that it lies over the buckle. 'What's being bought today?'

'A rose or two. Anything appealing.'

We're quiet as I drive up to Green Lanes, then Alasdair says, 'So the funeral's soon.'

'Friday.'

'Big do?'

'Tiny do. Just family and the warden of the place where he lived.'

'No friends?'

'He was ninety-five. If he had any, they're all dead.'

'You sound a bit sour there.'

'As a lemon. At least I haven't had to organize anything. He's paid for it all in advance. Even chose the readings and the hymns.'

'Anything interesting?'

'No. The usual. "When I was a child I thought as a child". "Abide With Me", blah, blah, blah. The only thing we have to do is turn up.'

'And the wake?'

'God, no. No wake. Enough's enough. Are your parents still alive?'

'Died years ago. Mum first.'

'Were you fond of them?'

'They were always there. But we didn't show our feelings much. No poignant moments over a fish supper. You got on with it. Did what you had to do. They were kind enough, and decent, and as far as I can see, that's rare.'

'You sound fond.'

'Do I? Perhaps I am. So what did he think of you being an actress, your dad?'

'What do you think he thought?'

'He hated it, right?'

In my father's harsh voice, I say, 'Actors are the scum of the earth.'

'Scummier than musicians? That's scum indeed. So what did he want you to do?'

'Vanish.'

If the car behind me gets any closer we'll be holding hands. There's a young woman at the wheel. When she sees me looking at her in my mirror she makes a face and then gestures at me to move over. I pull in enough to allow her to overtake, preferring submission to a dent. As she passes, she leans over her passenger and shouts, 'You shouldn't be on the road, stupid old cow.' She's only gone a few yards when the lights turn red. We cheer and wave.

'Max is a nice chap,' Alasdair says when we're moving again. 'So's that dog of his. I've never met your daughter. She's in the police, isn't she?'

'She is.'

'You don't see her much, then?'

'How do you know?'

'I don't. I'm guessing. She's never turned up when I've been there.'

'I don't see her because she doesn't want to see me. Us.'

'Is that right?' He asks why. I say enough to explain. Then, even though I had no intention of it, I tell him about the will. He says, 'right' and 'mmm' and 'bugger me', and then nothing for at least a minute. I'm relieved when he speaks. 'Life's full of little alleyways, my dear. I'd say you're right up one.'

'Up one? Why?'

'All of it. Everything that's going on.'

'Isn't that a bit dramatic?'

'Aye. Sorry. I'm speaking out of turn.' He reaches down to the radio. 'May I?'

'Sure.'

If Alasdair means that my father's just died, the will's a slap in the puss, I never see my daughter, and that I'm apparently labouring in Leslie's shadow then he's right. It's dramatic. I pull into the Clockhouse Nursery and park. As I switch off the engine, Alasdair undoes his seat belt and speaks without looking at me. 'Can I say that I don't think the alley's a cul-de-sac. It's more of a cut-through.'

'To what?'

'I've got no idea.'

'That's not very helpful.'

'You're right.'

'Is that it? No more advice? I thought you might have a few pithy ideas about how I'm supposed to cope with this funeral farce.'

'Well... you could always not go.'

'*Not go?*'

'Aye.'

'But I have to!'

'Who says?'

I raise my shoulders. 'Anybody… you can't not… not your own father's… I mean… *everybody*…' It's lame but I'm coming unstuck. The possibility of retreat is as exhilarating as spotting the first daff of the year. But then I wouldn't see Constance. And what about Leslie? Leslie!

'I can't, Alasdair. I can't do it. I just can't.'

'It's up to you. I shouldn't have said anything. I'm sorry.' He pats my arm, gets out of the car and walks over to the trolleys while I pull on my hat. 'I take it we want one?' he shouts across the car park, the red and blue check of his trousers horribly at odds with his green jacket. I give him a thumbs-up and we meet at the entrance.

'I didn't mean to be rude,' I say. 'Thanks for trying to help.'

'My big mouth.'

'Shall we shop?'

'I'm your boy.'

I love this place, it revives me. We walk round for an hour or more, buying roses and a fatsia with a big pot for Alasdair's new garden. By tacit agreement, we spend the drive home listening to the radio. As I reach the house and start to park, Alasdair says, 'I think Poppy's going to ring.'

'Why?'

'Because of Rolf.'

'How do you know?' Silly question.

Leslie calls me from the back door, the phone in his hand. 'It's Poppy. Rolf's just had a heart attack.'

I didn't count my father's death as the first of a run of three. That might have been an error. Poppy's on a train to Manchester, shouting at me over the noise.

'He's in intensive care. Come up, darling. Come and hold my hand.'

'What happened?' I'm shouting too. Leslie and Alasdair are either side of me, listening. I put the phone on speaker and hold it in the air between us.

'He got up and fell over. Didn't say he felt ill or anything. He's in hospital. It's his heart.'

'Was he with anyone?'

'Everyone. It was the middle of a run-through. He got up and fell over. Didn't say he felt ill, just fell over clutching his chest.'

'And how is he now?'

'They won't tell me anything over the phone. Stable. That's all they'll say.'

'That's good.'

'But you can't believe them, can you? Stable could mean anything. It's so unfair! He was walking *such* a lot. And having that yogurt thing, you know, and that woman's probably there already, pretending she's next of kin.'

'You go and find out what's happening, Poppy. You're his wife. He'll want you there.'

'She'll be by the bed.' The whole carriage must be leaning forward on their seats, desperate not to miss a word.

'Then you'll ask her to leave.'

'Come up. Please come up. I need you.'

'I can't, Poppy. My father's just died.'

'Has he?'

'I told you. The funeral's on Friday. I can't leave now.' I make a face at Leslie and mouth, 'Shall I go?' He shakes his head. 'I'm so sorry, Poppy, I really can't come. But we're here if you want to ring. Please give Rolf our love. If you give us the address when you get there, we'll send flowers.'

She starts to cry. 'He's going to die and I've been so horrible to him. Suppose he never wakes up? Suppose the last thing I said was the last thing he remembers?'

We all grimace. Leslie shouts, 'Leslie here. You listen, Poppy. He'll still be able to hear you, even if he's unconscious. It's the last thing to go. You tell him you love him. You make sure he hears that. All right?'

'Yes.' A tiny yes, almost inaudible.

'Call us soon?' I yell.

'Love to you,' shouts Leslie. 'And from me,' shouts Alasdair.

'I'll call you soon,' she says. 'Bye.'

We all chorus, 'Bye.'

I turn off the phone. Leslie says, 'Poor old Rolf. Thank heavens he wasn't on his own.'

'Are you sure I shouldn't have gone?'

'Nothing you could do, Missus. He's in safe hands.'

'I should tell Aude.'

Alasdair says, 'I'll do it if you like. I need to speak to her anyway.'

Leslie makes coffee while I carry the roses out to the garden. Of course, Aude wants to speak to me too. She's dreadfully sorry about my father, 'even though I know you hated the old sod', asks me about the funeral, says she can't bear to think of Poppy being on her own and that she'll go up to Manchester tomorrow. Hearing her voice, I realize how much I miss her. We reach the moment where there's nothing more to say if I don't ask about

Gully. I can't do it. She doesn't mention him either. The good-byes are reasonably affectionate.

Then we gather solemnly round the table to consider Rolf. The shock isn't so much that he's had a heart attack – he's been wretchedly careless of his health. The shock is that he's in hospital, inaccessible to us, possibly on his way out. Leslie says there's nothing we can do now. I glance at Alasdair to see if his expression suggests recovery but he's inscrutable, nibbling on a biscuit, so I don't mention the clairvoyant episode until I'm in the garden with him, potting up his fatsia. 'How did you know Poppy was going to call? Is it a voice, or what?'

'It's a feeling. You must have had it, when the phone rings, knowing who it is.'

'The phone hadn't rung.'

'I must have thought I heard it, then.'

'Is Rolf going to be all right?'

'I honestly don't know. Is that enough soil, do you think?'

'An inch more.' When it's done, he goes inside. I stay in the garden to plant the roses. The three roses. Alasdair might be able to pre-empt a telephone call but I've gone one better. I've bought the memorials before we've got the full tally.

At half-past one, not unusual, the post arrives. There's a letter from Constance. She thanks Leslie for writing and says she's thinking of us at what she's sure is a very sad juncture in our lives. She ends, 'and I expect I shall see you at the funeral. With best wishes to you both.' Leslie reads it to me and then hands it over. I read it to myself. Her handwriting's the same: smooth, swooping, the characters so neatly formed that they could be machine-made. Her style's no different, either. She's administrative, a Chief Constable in embryo.

'Good. That's good.' Leslie holds out his hand for me to return the letter. He puts it back in the envelope. 'We'll meet her husband, won't we? She's bound to bring him.'

'I don't see why.'

'Why not?'

He takes the letter out and reads it again, then puts it away and holds the envelope between his two palms. 'You don't know where to start, do you? I mean, there's so much you *could* say, all the catching-up and whatnot, but there probably won't be a chance. I could write back and suggest that we all go and have some lunch somewhere. What do you think? That'd be the best thing, go somewhere where we can sit down and have a proper old talk. Find out what she's been up to. I'll get it in the post this afternoon. Good idea?'

'Good idea.' Is it? If we were going to have a proper old talk, we'd need weeks, not hours. And we'd need a private place to do it and something clever in a hypodermic to pull Constance off her high horse. A lunch! Imagine it! Sit. Open menu. Choose meal. Open napkin. Pick up breadstick. Discuss general topic such as value of imprisonment versus rehabilitation. Lean back as plates arrive. Discuss merits of individual choices. Eat. Discuss general topic such as accuracy of police dramas. Lean back as plates are taken away. Go to loo for breather. Open menu. Decide against pudding. Too late for coffee. Call for bill. Say goodbye. Agree to keep in touch. She won't want to do it either.

Thirteen

It's Guy Fawkes day. After breakfast I try to ring Poppy and Aude but both their mobiles are switched off, and as we don't know where Rolf is I can't even send flowers. Leslie says he doesn't think you're allowed to have them any more. As a Frenchman once said to me, a piss without a fart is a parade without a trumpet. What's a hospital stay with no chrysanths in fake cut glass? Unless Rolf comes home to recuperate, we decide that we'll take the train up on Sunday.

'Could be that this brings them back together,' Leslie says. 'You can never tell, the way things work out.'

I'm at the back of the garden now, building a bonfire, nothing monumental but big enough to keep us warm if we want to watch the sky. We've been annoyed by fireworks for weeks, especially the bombs let off by the mad bastard who lives somewhere nearby and thinks it's clever to wait till after midnight before he gets his matches out. We can't identify the street but we think he's sixty, works in soft furnishings and lives with his cantankerous mother. He wants to kill her but he never will, they couldn't manage without each other, so he stores fireworks under his bed in a big brown suitcase and then every October, he starts to take them out…

Max calls me from the back door. 'Hi, Mum!' Leslie's behind him. They walk down the garden, the dog close to Max's heel. I meet them halfway, sticks in my hand.

'Big favour.' He's in his raincoat with a dark brown trilby pulled low over his forehead. 'Dad says you'll have Barney.'

Leslie chips in. 'He's scared of the bangs, aren't you, boy?'

'Just for the day. I'll pick him up after work.'

Barney comes to me, lifting his head forward for attention. I offer him a stick and he takes it, then stands waiting for me to do something else.

Leslie says, 'See? I told you it'd be all right. He's pleased to see his granny.'

'Great,' Max says. 'I'll see you later, then.'

I call, 'What time?' as he's halfway up the path.

'Seven?'

Leslie's catching him up. 'No problem. Whenever. I like the hat. New, is it?'

I've got the dog, apparently my grandson. He settles down on the grass, chewing at the stick. I finish laying the bonfire and stand back. It's a good piece of work, a small funeral pyre. We could cremate my father here. Build up the fire and lie him on top, get a choir in, entertain the neighbours. Send Bernard the ashes and keep the teeth for Mrs Wilmott. She can string them together and dangle them over her bed. The funeral… going to the funeral, not going to the funeral. I don't want to go, of course I don't, but that's not the same as actually staying away. You do some things because you must, even if you're hating every minute of it. This isn't a must. This is an ought. And that's Alasdair's trick: dropping the consequential statement, lightly said but in such a way as to hack open the forbidden thought. So here are the pros: it's the last visit, the finale. I see Constance for half an hour and possibly meet her husband. I do my duty in the eyes of God and Leslie. The cons: I don't want to visit him again, whatever his state. I don't want to see Constance for half an hour or possibly meet her husband. I don't want to fake respect or say hollow prayers or—

Something's wrong. If pros are *for* and cons are *against* then pro should be *for me*. And if it's for me, then the pro is this: I don't want to go. And the con? How I'm going to tell Leslie. And my father.

Miriam?

Yes?

This isn't about choice, girl. What about self-respect?

I'm trying to be honest with you. It's never too late.

This isn't honesty, it's defiance. You're selfish. You're incorrigibly insolent. My last day on earth, my last day!

So what?

Without me, you'd have been nothing.

Without you, I'd have been happy.

Happiness isn't important. Without me, who would you have been? I drove you. How else did you do it?

I was lucky. I had enough talent, enough luck.

Who taught you how to work? Who taught you to persist? You were a defiant, unruly girl. I gave you values. You've reverted, but that's inevitable. Leslie's weak.

You gave me nothing. It weighs heavy. I want to give it back.

You should be ashamed.

I'm not going. That's it, my announcement.

You sicken me.

It's mutual.

Barney and I go indoors. There's no-one downstairs so we go up, the dog loping a few steps ahead. He's more beautiful than I thought, more elegantly curved and coloured. At the top, he waits. I can hear Leslie singing with Louis Armstrong, 'What A Wonderful World'. Indeed. I put my head round the study door. 'Busy?'

'Not really.' He turns off the cassette. 'Request from some old boy. Thought I'd brush it up. You all right?' I go in. The dog follows. 'Hello, there! Who's this?' Leslie looks up at me, his hands on Barney. 'Finished the bonfire?'

'Yup.' Now I'm here, I'm not sure I can say it. Perhaps I should wait and ask Alasdair if he's got any ideas. I ask Leslie about the shows he's doing at the retirement homes. He tells me about a few of the people he particularly likes, people who join in, people who make sure they sit at the front so that they can be included in the patter.

'Leslie?'

'Yes, Missus.'

'I've been thinking. I don't want to go to the funeral.'

'Of course you don't.' He gets up and puts his arms round me. 'I knew I shouldn't have left you alone down there. You've been brooding.'

'I mean I *really* don't want to go to the funeral. As in, I'm really not going.'

He pulls away. 'Not going?'

'Not going. At all. Staying at home.'

'You can't!'

This is turning out as expected. Now he's going to say —

'But it's your father!'

'That's why. The thing is—'

'Mim, listen. I know. I know exactly what you're thinking but there's a time and a place and this isn't it.'

'I don't think you do know what I'm thinking.'

'I do.'

'You don't.'

'You're thinking that now you've got your chance it's two fingers and goodnight. Right?' He demonstrates a big fuck-off with both hands.

'Maybe.'

'But he's your father! You can't let him go on his own.'

'He won't be on his own! He'll have you and Constance and Mrs Wilmott. He'll have the bloody Dagenham Girl Pipers. But he won't have me. That's it.' As I turn to leave the room, Barney gets up and waits, uncertain which of us to be with.

'Mim?'

'What?'

I turn back. He says, 'What about me? Won't you do it for me?'

'It's nothing to do with you. I can't do it for you because I'm doing it for me!'

He shakes his head. 'And what do I tell everyone?'

'Tell them I'm ill. Tell them whatever you like.'

'And what about Constance? She'll think you're not going because you don't want to see her. Please come, please. Not for your dad then, for Constance. Let's all be there together, the whole family. It's been years. We don't even know what she looks like any more.'

'She's had ten years to send us a photograph. If I'm not there, she'll be relieved. Why don't you go without me? If it matters that much, then go on your own. Stop telling me what to do!' We're shouting now, ugly-faced shouting. The dog starts to whine.

Leslie lowers his voice. 'Because that's what we do. We pay our respects. It doesn't matter to me that you're there. What matters to me is that it doesn't matter to you. It's not nice. It makes you cheap.'

I hit him. I hit him hard on the upper arm, with the full force of my open right hand. He doesn't speak. He just looks at me, red-eyed. I clasp my hands together, not because I think I'm going to hit him again, but because I want to reassure us both that I'm harmless.

'I'm trying to be honest, Leslie, that's all.' *Whisper it, Mim. Stop behaving like a thug.* 'My father's dead. He won't know if I'm there or not. It's not two fingers. I'm not cheap. I've got to stop pretending, that's all. I'm sorry I hit you. I'm sorry, Leslie, really.'

'You have to do what's right for you. Understood.' He rubs his arm. 'You pack a good punch.'

'I'm sorry.'

'I'll tell them you're not well.'

'Whatever you like. You say whatever you want.'

'Suppose Max sees you up and about?'

'It was sudden. A bug.'

And there we are, standing in front of each other, lost for words. 'Are you all right?' I point at the arm.

'Nothing a good surgeon can't fix.'

'I'm sorry.'

He shakes his head.

'Do you fancy some lunch?'

Fourteen

We've forgotten – or chosen to forget – to ring Bernard. Leslie
says he'll do it and comes down to report that we'll see the wreath
but not the man. He's 'initiating legal proceedings'. Why send
the wreath then? I was thinking he might like to pay for a line of
floral letters, something along the lines of *YOU OLD SOD*.

Leslie's gone back up to his study and I'm starting to water
the indoor plants when Aude rings. Rolf's recovering, she says,
and Poppy's been at the bedside for hours. 'It's very sweet, to
see them.'

'Are they keeping him in?'

'A few more days I think. He's very weak, poor love, you'd
hardly know him. His little white face on the pillow, and wires
all over the shop.'

'Poor man.'

'I'm staying another night. Just for Poppy, really. The rest of
the cast have been wonderful but she hasn't got any mates here,
not that she can talk to.'

'Is she behaving?'

'She is. And she's sober. Thank God it happened in front of
everyone, or Doreen would have copped it.'

'What if he'd been with her?'

'That's the first thing I thought, Doreen trying to get out from under. Actually, nobody I've spoken to thinks there's anything going on. Too old, sweetie, that's the consensus. How about you? When's the funeral?'

'Friday. I'm not going.'

'You're *what?*'

'I don't want to talk about it now. Give me a ring when you get home.'

'Are you ill?'

'No, no. I've decided not to go, that's all.'

'*That's all!* Mim! What does Leslie think?'

'Ring me when you're home.'

'Of course I will.'

'Love to all of you and a hug for Rolf.'

'And you, sweetie-puss. What a bad girl! Love to you.'

I tell Leslie the good news and we make a definite decision to go to Manchester on Sunday. I'm so buoyed up by having a proper talk with Aude that I water the rest of the plants badly, overdoing several and then having to empty saucers and mop up drips with tea towels. Telling her that I'm not going to the funeral seals it. This is proper news, confirmed by a reliable source. Me. No more obligations!

As I water the last pots, the balloon of my exuberance begins to lose height. I might have faced out my father but letting Leslie go without me – isn't that selfish? Or is it a case of facing out Leslie's appetite for keeping people happy, even the dead? If he's said more than two words to a corpse while it was alive, he'll turn up at the funeral. He says it's a tribal thing, that we should all gather together and cheer the departed to the new world. Then again, the possibility of seeing Constance, of meeting her husband, of reconciliation, that might be the real draw. Can I really say that I'd sooner cold-shoulder my dead father than see my living daughter? Then again, my living daughter has no interest in seeing me and will bring a cold shoulder of her own. Back to the first premise: not going is good. If Leslie feels he must, that's his look-out. But in thinking that, I flinch, replaying the moment when my hand crashed into his arm. Why didn't he retaliate? I've never hit him before, he's never hit me. His blood-red eyes bearing it, that stays.

Alasdair's to blame. Conjure him up, drag him to me. He's small, he puts up no resistance. When he's so close that I can see the hair in his nostrils, I tell him he's an agitator, a mixer, a man on a mission to make trouble. He smiles. I tell him to keep his opinions to himself in future, not to presume that we're all agog waiting for his insights. What's he got to say to that?

'There's water dripping on the floor.'

That's no answer. I shake my head and at the furthest extremity of the turn, I see Alasdair, walking towards me, his hand outstretched. He takes the already wet cloth from me and catches the flow. A pool gathers on the table top. I run out for more towels and we swab and wipe and I find a dry mat that's big enough to cover the stain.

'Leslie tells me Rolf's on the mend,' Alasdair says as we head back to the kitchen. 'Good news, eh?'

'Very.'

OK, this is it. I'm going to ask him, firmly, why he launched his little missile into my life. Is it Leslie's shadow I'm in, Alasdair? Or was it my father's? Or both? And what's to be gained by disrupting my marriage? Corroborative evidence, Alasdair, nothing less.

Leslie shouts from the hall. He's taking Barney for a walk before the fireworks start in earnest. Twenty minutes and then tea? Yes, I shout back. Tea in twenty minutes. When the front door's shut, I say that I want to make a quick tour of the garden and ask Alasdair if he'd like to come with me. We put on our coats and start at the front. There are already a couple of dead fireworks lying on the beds where they've fallen or been thrown. The metaphor isn't lost on me, the symbol of rockets and squibby things: a short sizzle of noise and a flash of colour and before you know it, you've got muddy cardboard. Alasdair's keeping quiet, following behind as I check that all's well. We go in again and then out to the back garden, still hardly speaking except to marvel at the colour of a vine or the lustre on a stem. A dozen times I think I'm going to challenge him, and a dozen times I hesitate. We're nearly back at the house before I get to the point.

'It wasn't really all that helpful,' I begin, 'you saying what you did. Why are you poking your nose into my life?'

'What did I say?' We turn to face each other, except that I'm taller and he has to look up, not a good position for a serious interchange. He walks away, backwards, until he can look at me without tilting his head. 'Well?'

'You said I needn't go to the funeral. In fact, you said a lot of things.'

'Are you not going, then?'

I don't answer. I glare.

'So I wasn't helpful?'

'No. In fact, it upset Leslie. It upset us both.'

'Are you saying that's my fault?'

If the neighbours are in their gardens they'll be hearing all

162

this. I lower my voice. Now I sound threatening. 'It was your idea. I never would have said anything if you hadn't told me to.'

'Whoa, *whoa*. It was a suggestion. Not an order.'

'Please don't shout.'

'I'm not shouting. You're whispering.'

On cue, there's a deafening burst of noise from a nearby garden. From a directorial point of view, the setting's formulaic: argument, bangers. I can't talk out here between the eavesdropping neighbours and the bombardment.

'I'm going in.'

'Good for you,' he says, without irony, and turns to lead us back.

As we arrive indoors, so do Leslie and the dog. That's it. I've accused Alasdair, he's behaving as if nothing's happened and I feel a complete prat. We make mugs of tea and, at Leslie's suggestion, toast a plate of crumpets. The label on the jam he puts out says Little Plum's Kitchen and there's a coloured-in drawing of Little Plum and Big Plum, presumably copied from the *Beano*. I study it carefully for something to do. Leslie says it's a present from one of his fans. 'Didn't I tell you?' he adds. 'I meant to. I thought it was a lovely idea.'

That gives us a few things to talk about. Comics we used to buy. The shows Leslie does, audiences in general, Alasdair's mother making marmalade and the smell of bitter oranges getting into every corner of the house. As the plates empty, we get closer. We don't mention funerals. We have a second mug of tea and decide on a plan for getting to Manchester. And all the time there are intermittent explosions outside which make Barney whine and tremble. We try to comfort him but he's inconsolable, lying hard up against Leslie's chair and ignoring his food bowl.

The door bell goes. It's Max. He says, 'Hi,' but stays where he is, in shadow on the step, his hat pulled low. I don't think he can see me any better than I can see him because he pulls the hat off and stands with it in front of his chest, like a gangster at prayer.

'Are you coming in, or what?'

'Actually, I was—'

We're caught off guard as Barney comes running towards us and aims for the street, dodging Max who grabs at his collar and drags him inside. The hat goes flying. I catch it and slam the door as Leslie and Alasdair dash out of the kitchen.

'Jesus,' Max says. 'What happened there?' Barney's cowering at his feet. He kneels and strokes him. 'All right boy, all right.'

'He's scared.' Leslie pats Max on the shoulder. 'Poor little chap.'

'He probably thinks the bangs are in here somewhere.' Alasdair says. Bravo. Thanks for the insight.

'Actually I was going to ask you,' Max says, 'if you'd keep him for tonight. I'll pick him up tomorrow, about seven. Is that all right? Only I've got a few things happening, you know. Be good to have the time. Only one more day, that's all. Pete can do Friday so the funeral's sorted.'

'Pete?'

'The dog-walker.'

'Great! That's great!' Leslie says. 'Isn't it, Mim?'

'Fine.'

Max stands up, then bends down again to say goodbye to Barney. 'Don't let him get out again.'

'I'll do my best.' I pass him the hat.

'We'll keep him close.'

The brim comes down. 'Ta-ta, then.'

'God bless, darling. Love to Jackie!'

He doesn't reply. A swirl of the coat and he's out of the door.

We spend the evening with Alasdair, having dinner in front of the television and watching *West Side Story* as loudly as we think the neighbours can bear, to mask the sound of battle. When we go upstairs, Barney comes with us. I won't allow him on the bed but he lies close to it, still trembling with the last, late fireworks. When I wake up, he's lying stretched between us. I leave him there until the alarm goes off.

After breakfast, Leslie says he wants to go out but he won't tell me why.

'What's the mystery?'

'Never you mind, Missus.'

'I hope I don't.'

When he's gone, I go out and pick up a few more rocket sticks. It's a grey day, too windy to enjoy the garden, so I tidy up the messy corners in the shed, bang in nails to hang bags on, stack plastic pots and seed trays and find a pair of secateurs I thought I'd lost. I was right about the dog. First, it was the sick dog-walker and then it was Guy Fawkes and in a few weeks it'll be taking Jackie on a winter holiday and then, in no time at all: Do you think you could you have him for the rest of his life while I spend the rest of my life sorting my life out? Poor old Barney, lying by the boiler on his blanket. As long as he's warm and full and far, far away from the dog track, I don't suppose he gives a stuff.

Leslie calls me from the back door. I walk up the path slowly, peeling off my gloves.

'Close your eyes.'

'Why?'

'Just do it.'

I close my eyes. There's a rustle and a thump.

'Open!'

It's a small tree in a pot. My first thought, before I say anything to Leslie, is to identify it. I find the label and twist it round. It's a white willow, salix alba. I look up. Leslie's grinning.

'What d'you reckon, Missus? Did I choose well?'

It's completely wrong for our garden. It'll be too big, too thirsty. In a few years it'll start to overwhelm everything else. Perhaps the tree isn't for us. Perhaps it's a present. 'What's it for?'

'You'll be surprised.'

'I am already.'

'Do you like it?'

'It's a lovely tree. Not for us, but it's a lovely tree. Who's it for?'

'Your dad.'

Like slow balls clunking together on grass, the facts converge. Leslie's bought this willow for our garden as a memorial to my father.

'We can't plant it. Not here.'

'Why not? Don't you like it? I thought you could put it in the lawn, right in the middle there.' He points. 'It'd be a feature, a lovely thing. The man at the garden centre says it's fabulous in the summer.'

'It's a big tree. We'd have no lawn left.'

He shakes the stem. 'It's a little fella. No size at all.'

'It'll grow. It'll be huge. Read the label, Leslie. Sixty feet, maybe more.'

'But how long's that going to take? Twenty years, thirty years?'

'Then it'll have to be cut down! That's not much of a memorial.'

'Memorial? I didn't say it was a memorial. I said it was for your dad, that's all. Something to remember him by. Something to make up for not going to the funeral. It's a gesture, Mim. Something living, something growing.'

'I can't have it in the garden, Leslie. You've never bought anything before. You know you haven't got a clue. Why didn't you ask me first? I could have told you this tree's no good.' Now *I* shake the stem. The poor tree's wishing it had never been sold. 'You'll have to take it back.' He sighs. I'm deliberately not citing Leslie's purpose in buying the tree, my non-attendance at the funeral or the idea that I might want to see a tribute to my father every time I go out with the compost bucket. Leslie's trying to be thoughtful, I know that. I'm trying not to be a baggage.

'What do you want instead?'

'Nothing. There's no room.'

'There's all that space in the lawn.'

'That's because it's a lawn.'

'But you could have a bed in the middle. That's what they do on gardening programmes. I've seen it. A nice bed in the middle with flowers in the spring. Suppose I got a blossom tree? Something with lots of white blossom?'

'We've got lots of blossom. We don't need any more.'

'But not in the middle.'

'Leslie.'

'What?'

'We've got a tiny lawn because we've got lots and lots of plants. I don't want anything in the middle of what's left.'

'And you don't want anything that reminds you of your father, do you?'

'No. I don't.'

'Not even a little thing?'

'Not even a little thing.'

'Moss?'

I shake my head.

'Have it your way then.'

'I'm sorry. It was a nice thought.'

'I'll take it back then. D'you want to come?'

So we go to the garden centre and have elevenses and buy a boxful of cyclamen in exchange for the tree, which is glad to be out of our reach for ever.

At seven, on the dot, Max arrives. I open the door. Next to him but barely up to his shoulder is a youngish woman wearing a coat of no particular colour and a scarf to match. Her face is small and the colour of raw shortcrust pastry, as is her hair.

Max says, 'This is Jackie.'

I say, 'Do come in,' in a posh voice and then add, 'please' to make up for it.

'Is Dad here?'

'He is. He's in the kitchen sorting the dog out. We don't let him near the door without his lead on since he—'

'Dad? Come and meet Jackie!' The woman's immobile, gazing at the floor in her dead leaf-mushroom-fog clothes. Leslie comes out of the kitchen with Barney and stops, rooted to the carpet.

'Jackie, this is my dad.'

Jackie nods.

'Hello there.' Leslie revives, gives the dog lead to Max and holds out his hand to her. She lifts hers in return but barely makes contact, slipping into and out of his fingers before he can grip.

I say, 'Are you coming in for a drink?'

Max puts his hand on the door. 'We won't, thanks.'

'Thank you anyway.' Jackie's voice isn't as indeterminate as her clothes. There's an interesting crack in it, as if it needs oil. Her face is small and oddly put together and there's a slightly stubborn purse to the mouth, although I imagine that the eyes could be submissive. None of the lines that are taking hold have been made by laughter. In fact she's severe. I'd cast her as a Puritan. She's moving from foot to foot now, almost hopping. She's suspicious of us, she wants to leave before we say or do something vulgar. Max bends to the side and puts his arm round her shoulders. 'We'll see you tomorrow then.'

I say, 'Absolutely. The more the merrier.'

Leslie opens the door and we all say goodbye and agree to meet outside the crematorium. As they walk down the path and turn away, I remember that I'm going to be ill. I cough loudly to suggest the first stages of a sudden, severe infection.

Leslie shuts the door. 'Strewth.'

I assume he's talking about Jackie and say, 'Wasn't she dismal?'

It's not Jackie. It's the cough. He demonstrates how I should have done it, alarming me as he whoops for breath. I tell him to stop, which he does, abruptly, and says, 'She was shy, that's all.'

'She's not shy, she's prim.' And so it goes on. I accuse, Leslie defends. What is Max doing with this woman? He said she played the viola so she can't be a Puritan through and through but it's impossible to think of her intoxicating an audience. *Mrs Pastry plays the viola, the timpani and pianola…* how does that body of hers pass music through to an instrument? She must play like an automaton: press on string there, bow here, count, bow, repeat. Will we be asked to watch her perform? No, she teaches… Is he sorry for her? He was kind tonight, whisking her away as soon as she started that hopping-rabbit routine. She wants to watch that – Barney might revert. I think this is funny and I want to tell Leslie but he's saying something about her being good for Max. '… a bit more serious than I thought. Level-headed. She'll help him settle down.' We're not going to agree. I keep the rabbit idea to myself.

Fifteen

It's Friday morning. Poppy calls to say that Rolf's recovering, she's coming back today to get more clothes and then staying in Manchester with him till he's allowed home. Were we thinking of visiting? Sunday, I say, when we've recovered from the funeral. What funeral? My father's. Oh, your *father's*. Good luck, darling.

Leslie hasn't heard from Constance, so the possible lunch is off. He's leaving early and eating at a pub somewhere on the way. As he's checking the map for the crematorium, he says, 'It's a long drive. Don't you want to keep me company? I could drop you off in Kingston and you could look at the shops. Wouldn't you like that?'

'I'll be fine. And you won't be lonely. You'll be busy getting there.'

'I hope I can find it.'

'Is it on the map?'

'Yeah.' He draws a little circle on the page and folds the book back on itself. 'Be easier if you were navigating.'

'I'm not coming, you know.' I stand behind his chair and put my arms round him. 'I'm really not coming.'

'Not even for Constance?'

'Not even for her.'

'What do I say if she asks?'

'What we agreed.'

'We never agreed.'

'Say I'm ill. Say I send her – say, if she wants to call, I'd be pleased.' I kiss the top of his head. 'I know you'll say I send her my love, so there's no point me telling you anything different.'

'I'll tell her what you want me to tell her. Anyway, if her husband's there, we might not be able to talk. The main thing is, the *good* thing is, I'll be able to see her. It's a shame you don't want to.' His back stiffens. He turns in the chair. 'I can't say I understand it, Mim, you not wanting to see her. Suppose it's your last chance?'

'That's silly.'

'You don't know. Look at Rolf.'

'If she wants to—'

'She'll ring. And if she doesn't?'

'Then she doesn't. She never answers your letters.'

'That's because she knows I write them on my own.' Leslie's stepped too far out of benevolence. 'I'd better go. I'll ring you when I get there so you know I'm safe.' He goes out to the hall and picks up his hat and coat. He's forgotten the map. I go back for it. 'Thanks. What are you going to do?'

'Potter about. I dunno.'

'Don't mope.'

'Why would I mope?'

'I should be home by five. If I'm going to be late, I'll call. You never know, Constance might want to go for a drink.'

'I'll see you when I see you.'

'I'll call. And don't forget. If Max rings, you're in bed, acting.'

My first thought is to make coffee and read the paper. I can do that any day but today it feels special, as if I'm bunking. Alasdair's in his room but I don't offer him anything. I make the coffee and have it with a croissant and marmalade. It takes me an hour or so to do the quick crossword and finish the *Guardian*, then I sit back to consider my options. Chores, the garden, shopping, a DVD, actually going to the pictures. Going anywhere. Reading a book...

'Hi. Shall I make us a coffee?' Alasdair's at the door.

'I've just had some. I didn't know you were in. You carry on.'

'Leslie's gone, has he?'

"Bout an hour ago.'

While I clear the table, he measures coffee and sugar into a mug and mixes in the milk, whisking it together as he pours on the boiling water. Then he licks the spoon, washes it, dries it and puts it back in the cutlery drawer. 'So what are you up to today?'

'I'm not sure.'

'D'you fancy a game of Scrabble?'

'Scrabble!'

'Why not?'

'What made you think of that?'

He rolls his eyes. 'I had a visitation from the letter G. Who cares! I just thought of it, that's all. Do you want to play?'

I do. It's exactly what I want to do, as long as he doesn't get personal. With the secret proviso that I'll withdraw at the first sign of subtext, I find the Scrabble board. He wins the first game. We make peanut butter sandwiches and play again, eating as we go. During the second game we start to talk.

After telling me that he's spoken to Poppy this morning and left a message with Aude, he says, 'You don't seem to have a lot of mates. Apart from the chosen few, I mean. You've not made friends with anyone new, these past years?'

Is this a simple question? I take it at face value although it sounds as if it might be leading elsewhere. 'No, not really. How about you?'

'I don't do too badly.'

'You're certainly out a lot.'

'I'm working, aren't I? I meet people… T.U.R.N.I.P… and I'm on my own. That makes a difference.' He writes down his score. 'Plenty of us on our own out there, hoping for a bit of camaraderie.'

'I don't go out much so… U.N.F.I.T… so no, I've not got many friends. They've snuffed it, or they've moved.' I pick up three As and a Q. 'Anyway, there's you lot and Leslie. He's really all the friend I need.'

'And you think I tried to spoil it,' he says, writing down my score.

Bugger! I was lulled! 'I don't want to talk about it. But yes, you did try to spoil it. He's disappointed in me. And hurt.' I tip all my letters into the box lid and pick out another seven. 'And angry.' I look up. 'It's your turn.'

'You decided not to go, it's nothing to do with me.'

'Be grateful Leslie doesn't know it was your idea. He'd have thrown you out!'

'No he wouldn't. He's an old softie. He didn't throw you out, did he?' When I don't reply, he makes a big show of moving his letters. 'Watch this, P.H.I.L.T.R.E. Philtre!'

'Very clever.'

If I was nineteen – thirty-nine? – I'd have thrown the board over by now and walked out. But I can't be that silly, even

174

though by staying I'm admitting my complicity. I've never been asked to justify myself like this, to inspect what I'm saying and doing. I'm seventy-one, for God's sake!

'By the way,' Alasdair says, 'what's the story about you not being there? Are you ill?' He winks at me. 'Of course you are.'

'Alasdair, you're being a pain. If you don't stop, I'm going out.'

'OK. Play on. Play on.' We do. The game's finished in silence and I win because I have to. As I go to fold the board he says, 'Best out of three?'

'No thanks. I think I'll have that walk.' I do the little bit of washing up we've made.

He stands by the table and leafs through the paper until I've finished, then as I'm drying my hands he says, 'I'm sorry, Mim. Have I said too much?'

'Yes, you have.'

'All from the best intentions, but I'm sorry. Pax?'

'Pax.'

'Enjoy your walk.' He gives me a thumbs-up and goes off, whistling.

I'm on my own. Is Alasdair on some kind of mission to turn me into a divorcee? He's got some bloody cheek, a lonely old man with no children. He hasn't even got a girlfriend! He could be envious of us, he could be meddling out of spite, he could genuinely be trying to make me, the pig's ear, into… what? I have no idea. He'll be gone in a few weeks anyway, and in the meantime, I absolutely refuse to be provoked again. That's it.

I'm putting my shoes on when the phone rings.

'Mum? It's Max. Where are you?' He's shouting.

'What do you mean, where am I?'

'Why aren't you here?'

I cough. It sounds good, more like Leslie's. 'I've got a bug.'

'Are you at home?'

'In bed.'

'So you're not coming?'

'No.'

'Is Dad coming?'

'Yes. Yes, he's coming.'

'Has he left yet?'

'Hours ago. Isn't he there?'

'No, that's why I'm ringing. He's not here. When did he leave?'

'Elevenish.'

'It's nearly two.'

'He left at eleven.'

'Did he know where to come?'

'I think so. He had a map.'

'I've tried his mobile. It's switched off.'

'Is it?'

'If he rings you, will you ring me?'

'Of course.'

'You're sure he's coming?'

'I'm sure.'

'I'll call you after. Let you know if he's turned up.'

'Please.'

'Bye.'

'Bye.'

Where is he? I can't go out now. I ring Leslie's mobile. Max is right. It's switched off. Alasdair's at the top of the stairs. 'Got a problem?'

'Leslie hasn't turned up for the funeral.'

'He'll have got lost.'

'Are you sure?'

'I'm sure.'

'What do I do?'

'He'll ring. Just wait.'

So I do, and of course Alasdair's right. Leslie gets to the crematorium in the middle of the service. He calls at the end to let me know he's arrived. He's brisk and cheerful. 'I got lost in the one-way. Couldn't read the map properly, silly sod. Anyway, Constance is here so I'm going to have a quick word. See you later. Be good.' And he's gone. I take my coat off the hanger and then put it back again. I've lost the urge for walking. I go upstairs instead, knock on Alasdair's door to tell him everything's all right – 'I know' – and sit at Leslie's desk, phone in hand. I don't have many friends, it's absolutely true. Is this a lack? Friends – it's almost *fiends*, isn't it? Fiends with an 'r'. Does that mean anything? It won't anagram. Firends, deifsnr, niferds. So, Mim, you don't seem to have many niferds. I've got lots and lots, you sad old bag.

I look at the black screen in front of me and reach for the switch. Am I still Leslie's madam? I pull my hand back. I don't want to start another fandango, not today. It's twenty to three. Now what? If this was an ordinary afternoon, I'd be in the garden or reading or out walking with Leslie. But that's silly. It *is* an ordinary afternoon. My father's being cremated, that's exceptional, in fact it's once-in-a-lifetime. And I've missed it. So what. The furnace isn't here, it's in Surrey. I can't see it, I can't smell it. If I'm not there (is the *Mona Lisa* still a masterpiece if it's on a desert island, blah, blah, blah) then isn't this just one of my ordinary days? So why am I wasting it? And I've just realized that cremated is created with an 'm'. M for Mim. That's me.

I decide to light the fire and read. Alasdair goes out soon after, standing by the door to tell me he'll be in late. Is he scared of coming too close in case I bite his little head off? By the time Leslie gets in, I'm sound asleep.

'Wakey-wakey, Missus.' I open my eyes in a groggy, post-anaesthetic sort of way, not knowing when it is or where I am. I can see Leslie, taking off his coat and poking at the fire. With a *pop* of remembering, I'm back. 'It's absolutely perishing out there,' he says. 'I'm starving. What shall we have?' He's cheerful. He's a sledgehammer of jolliness.

I stand up and stretch. 'So how was it?'

'Good. It was good. Can't believe I got lost, what a berk! Constance said she thought we weren't coming. She wishes you better.'

'How was she?'

'Beautiful. Plain black suit, no uniform. But she doesn't look any different. Same hair, face the same…'

'Was her husband there?'

'No. He couldn't get away.'

'And the rest of it?'

'Very successful. You'll be surprised. Wait till I tell you.'

'Tell me what?'

'What happened. You'll be surprised.'

I want to know, but I'm equally reluctant to be told. Right this minute, I'd be happy if Leslie had to go out again and I could go back to sleep. We decide on dinner, spaghetti for speed, and he tells me I'll have to wait for the details because he can't do two things at once. That suits me. He asks how my day went and I tell him I played Scrabble and read until I fell asleep.

'Bit of a waste,' he says.

'What should I have done?'

'Don't know. Something.'

'Like what?'

'Don't know. Something special.'

I don't answer. What is there to say?

We eat quickly with the TV on, then he takes the plates out and comes back. 'Right, Missus. Here we go.'

'You're making me nervous.'

He sits down opposite me on the armchair and leans forward, resting his forearms on his knees. 'You'll tell me if I'm going too fast?'

'I'll tell you. Just get on with it!'

'All right, keep your hair on. I missed the beginning but I was in time for the important bits. For instance. Number one. Are you ready? Your grandad – wait for it – your grandad. Was.' He sits back and lifts his hands with the index fingers pointing up to beat out the last two words. 'An. Actor.'

'*What*?' That's so ridiculously unlikely that I can't quite hear it. 'An actor? What do you mean, an actor? What sort of actor?'

'An actor actor. And your gran... she made costumes. Designed and sewed, the lot.'

'Who said this?'

'The vicar.'

'About my father's parents? You're sure that's who he was talking about?'

'Absolutely positively your father's parents.'

'Why didn't he tell me? Why didn't anybody tell me?'

'Because it was a secret. Because your dad never told a soul. Except near the end when he told Constance, and now we all know.'

'He always said his dad was in business.'

'Well he was, sort of.'

'Harry Shaw. Is that right?'

'Yup. Harry Shaw.'

'He never really made it then?'

'No. Small touring company. The usual thing. They put your dad in boarding school. I don't think he ever saw them – he more or less brought himself up. Anyway, there's more. Listen to this. Your dad told you his parents died before you were born, right?'

'Right.'

'Wrong. It was only your granny that died. Your dad put your grandad in a home. He was there for twenty years. Passed on in 1957.'

I work it out. I was twenty-two. Leslie comes to the sofa and puts his arm round me. 'He went senile. Your dad saw him on Sundays but he didn't want anyone else to know, so he pretended he was playing golf.'

'That's true. He played on Sundays.' I see him, stony-faced with his clubs over his shoulder, leaving the house. I would have gone to the home instead. I would have been happy to go.

'He said all this, the vicar?'

'I got the last bit after, from Constance. Do you want me to stop for a minute?'

'You mean there's more?'

'Yup. A bit.' He nods with his lips pulled in over his teeth.

'Go on.'

'Max caught me in the car park. He says there's a lot of money.'

'We know that.'

'I mean, up to your neck in it money.'

'How much?'

'I don't think they know yet but Constance says it's a lot apparently, and she wants to play fair by Max so she'll be giving him some. He asked me if we needed any. I said no.'

'Did you?'

'Well, we don't, do we?'

How extraordinary. Max is offering to give *us* money... Then I say, 'Anything else?'

'That's the lot, Missus. Isn't that enough? The vicar said a few things about your mum and Bernard and you. He said how your dad had worked hard for his family—'

'Crushed his family, more like.'

'Come on. The man's dead, he needs a bit of encouragement.'

The fire's burning low. I get up, shovel on some coal and wait for a spark to show through the cold, black mound. My father worked so hard at the illusion of our very proper domestic life. Harry Shaw didn't fit, he was disreputable and scrambled. Let him rot.

Leslie says. 'Are you all right?'

'I don't know.' I sit down again. 'I don't know.'

'I thought you'd love it, your grandad being an actor. What a story! What do you think?'

'I need a bit of time. It's hard to take in.'

'Constance says she'll write soon.'

'I'll believe it when I see it.' I have to do something, move about, bring myself back to earth. 'Do you want some ice-cream?'

181

'Have we got any?'

'Vanilla or pistachio.'

'I'll have both.'

After the ice-cream we make tea and watch some noisy special-effects drivel on the telly. Leslie's beside himself with pleasure at the day. He's seen his daughter, found a compatible ancestor and given me the shock of my life. When the fire's only a few red specks in the grate, I leave him to finish the film and go up to bed.

Looking back over my mother's life, I feel sorry. Sorry that she married my father, that he trundled over her, that I never bothered to ask her who she was or how she was or what she might have wanted. It's the sort of sorry that you feel when you see a dog shot off into space, the tragedy of the helpless, trusting patsy. With Harry, it's a different sort of sorry. There were no photographs, but I imagine a smallish man with brown hair and sharp features, like my father in silhouette. Never a tragedian, more of a comic, a man with wit, a man you could hold without delicacy. We'd have cherished each other, we'd have laughed like drains. And he lost his wife, forgot his lines, went on in the wrong wig, didn't recognize his son, didn't understand why he was being moved to the hospital-house, had no *here*, no *now* and all of that without a soul to cry to. I get out the red book and write:

Miriam? Is that you, Miriam?

Yes, Grandad.

Come here where I can see you. Where am I? I don't like it.

You're with me, Grandad. You're safe with me.

I hate this place. Will you cut the hair in my ears, darling?

Every time I sneeze it knocks me out…

I like it when you laugh, Grandad.

It's better to laugh than looking parsnips, as my mother used to say. My brain tells me what to do and I just move about. You've got some nice spinach there in your garden, girl. Lovely spinach. I always wanted a garden, more than anything I wanted a garden. If I'm not careful, I'll run away.

You're safe with me, Grandad.

Home's always fifty-fifty. Sometimes more, sometimes less. Take me home, Miriam. Get my coat and hat. Tell your father you want to take me home. He'll listen to you, he never listens to me.

I wish I could, Grandad. More than anything in the world, I wish I could take you home.

Sixteen

The first thing Leslie says when he wakes up is, 'We'd better tell Bernard about Harry.'

'Sod Bernard.'

I've got my back to him. He puts his arm over me. 'It's his grandad.'

'I'm not telling him anything. Harry's mine.'

'What about the money?'

'He'll find out soon enough.'

Leslie whistles into the back of my head. 'Poor old Barnyard.'

Poor old Barnyard. Quite so. This would be a good moment for me to show that I'm less petty than he is, less vengeful. But I can't do it and Harry wouldn't want me to. I stretch my legs down the bed. 'Shall we get up then?'

'If you want to. If it was up to me, I'd stay here.'

I get up.

When we've done the weekend shopping I ring Aude, hoping she'll answer the phone. She doesn't. Gully says, 'Mim, darling! What news on the Rialto?'

'Nothing much. Is Aude in?'

'I hear you've just flung your father into the cleansing flame.

What ho! *Death*! Not bloody likely. We must all laugh in the teeth of it, my darling!'

'I don't suppose Aude's there, is she?'

He bellows her name without taking the phone away from his mouth. I wait and then Aude says, 'Mim?'

'Hello.'

'How was the funeral? Did you go in the end?'

'No, I didn't. But Leslie did. And he came home with a story. Have you got a minute?'

'Hang on.' Voices and a door closing. 'Right. I'm all ears.'

I tell her everything.

She says, 'Max, offering you money? That's a good one.'

'Never mind the money! It's Harry, that's the thing.'

'Do you think your dad told anyone?'

'I've got no idea. I mean, they didn't even have him round for Christmas!'

'When my gran started dementing they had to shut her away. She ended up in a padded cell.'

'You never told me that!'

'Didn't I? Mum used to visit her and come home in floods. How terrible is that, your mother chucking herself against the wall? I'd sooner put my head in a bag, I would really. Are you sure you don't want any of that money? I can't quite believe Leslie turned it down without asking you first. It's your dad's money. It's not really up to Leslie to say you don't want it.'

This is so uncharacteristically biased of Aude that I'm stuck for a reply.

She backtracks immediately. 'I'm sure he had his reasons – he obviously thought he was doing the right thing. But you might need it, you never know.'

'I know…' She's right, I might. Why didn't Leslie come home and ask me before he told Max we weren't interested? If I'd been there I could have asked the vicar about Harry as well, while I had the chance…

Aude picks up my thought. 'If you'd been there—'

'It was Alasdair's idea, me not going. Did I tell you that?'

'Alasdair? God! You mean you didn't go because of him?'

'Well, yes and no. I mean, it was up to me in the end, but I felt that he sort of pushed me into it – did he ever try that on you?'

'Good Lord, no. No, never. I mean, he went on and on about Gully but that's different. He wanted the flat back the way it was. I can't blame him. So why do you think he told you not to go to the funeral?'

'Perhaps he was trying to stir things up.'

'What sort of things?'

'I don't know. Like when he said he thought I was in Leslie's shadow. And telling me not to go, he must have known that'd upset Leslie. I can't believe he didn't try to bulldoze you…'

'We were just a couple of old bats, rubbing along. I expect he's feeling lonely, living with you two, poor little gooseberry.' Pause. 'Gully and I are getting married, you know.'

She's probably thinks I'm going to hit the roof but I've been expecting her to say it and it's only a relief to know she's taking the first step on the short road back to the divorce court. I can't think of anything to offer by way of congratulations except an ill-delivered 'Good for you'.

'Living together like this, it's daft. We know each other so well, and it'll suit us both to put everything in joint names. For wills and things, you know. Anyway, I don't suppose you'll want to come but if you did, I'd love it if you could be my maid of honour. Will you think about it, sweet pea?'

'I suppose Gully'll be there?'

It's a lousy joke, and I picture her frowning as she tries to make sense of it. 'Oh ha-bloody-ha. Thirtieth of November.'

'That's a bit quick!'

'Two o'clock and lunch after. Will you think about it? And tell Leslie?'

'Of course I'll tell Leslie. And you know I'll come.'

'I know you will.'

I tell Leslie. He says, 'You never know, could be second time lucky.' I think I'll wear black.

It's a gardening afternoon. I'm dividing a crocosmia when Alasdair comes out in an Arctic number with a furry hood and stands behind me, watching. I haven't seen him since he went out yesterday afternoon, and I imagine he wants to ask me about the funeral. He says, 'Leslie tells me it all went well.'

'Apparently so.'

I can't concentrate on the garden with him there. I ask him if it's anything important. It's about Aude, he replies. Did I know she was getting married? I tell him yes, I know.

He'll be going to the wedding, he tells me. Are we going? I say we are. I'm leaning on the fork. I pick it up. 'So.'

He says, 'Cheerio then,' and walks off.

'I should have gone to the funeral,' I shout after him. 'So if you were thinking of suggesting that I don't have to go to the wedding, do me a favour and keep it to yourself.' He turns, Santa's little helper in his parka, and walks back to me. 'And I'm not in the mood for one of your—'

'You be angry if you like. I'm a big boy. I can take it.' He smiles. 'Actually I'm quite a small boy. I don't want to have to keep repeating this so I think I'm saying it for the last time. I gave you an idea. It wasn't up to me what you did with it. You could have gone to that funeral. You could have turned up in a wetsuit and played him out on a tambourine. The truth is you can do anything you bloody well like. And you should.'

To which I have no rejoinder. In the oddest way, I want to cheer. Alasdair grins at me and puts his hand out. He's right, it's up to me what I do now! I grab his hand and shake it.

Which is the exact moment that Leslie comes running out of the house with the phone in his hand to tell us that Rolf's just died.

Poppy's weeping so badly that any words she manages to sputter out come to nothing. I say, 'It's all right, Poppy,' even though it couldn't be worse, and then say it again and again until she can speak. It's all her fault, she says. She left him for twenty minutes because she hadn't had any breakfast or any lunch and she wanted a cup of coffee and when she got back they were running past her to the room, pushing her aside, because his heart was speeding up, faster and faster and faster, galloping away till it wore itself out and stopped. 'They did everything they could, I know they did. But if I hadn't have gone for that bloody coffee, Mim! If I hadn't gone, if I'd stayed there watching him I'd have spotted it! I know I would! I shouldn't have left him! Why did I leave him?' I tell her that the monitors would have picked up any problems with his heart long before she could have done. She says it all again, about leaving him for the cup of coffee, and I repeat that it would have made no difference. Leslie shakes his head and puts his arm round my shoulders.

Alasdair holds my elbow. We've all got our heads bowed. Leslie's in his brown moccasins, I'm wearing wellies, Alasdair's in green lace-ups.

I ask, 'Have you told the children?'

'Liz is coming down. Paul's trying to get a flight.'

'When will you be home?'

'Late tonight.'

'Ring us. We'll come round.'

'Rolf should be coming home tomorrow,' she says. That does it. I hand Leslie the phone and go indoors.

I like Rolf, I *liked* Rolf very much, even though he could be overbearing and opinionated. But I'm not crying for Rolf, not really, I'm crying for Poppy and for me. You think you've made all your important choices when you're young. By sixty, you think, maybe even fifty, it'll all be over, you'll have settled for what you've got, career or marriage or both, and by the time you're seventy – so old! – you'll be as flexible as stone pyjamas. But if you're still living with someone, then that's another thing entirely. They might go first and you might be left alone. More choices, and not the kind Alasdair's talking about. Do you keep on doing what you've been doing – which in Poppy's case means feeling thwarted and depressed – or do you try to make the best of the time you've got left? If Leslie goes before me, I might lock myself up, turn the house into a hermitage. Or I might bloom, like a shrub that's been pruned hard of old wood to let in light and air. He's calling me, wants to know if I'm all right. Actually I'm not. I'm trying on widow's weeds to see how they'll fit.

Aude has to be rung. When I tell her, she cries. She's crying for herself, she says, as much as she's crying for Rolf and Poppy. I know, I tell her, so am I. She says, We're all on our way out, soon there'll be no-one left. Nonsense, we've got weeks, I say. Weeks and weeks, ample time to get everything done. Why am I trying to make her laugh? I'm a graduate from the Leslie Lyons Buck Up school of mourning. I tell Aude we're seeing Poppy tonight, she says she'll go tomorrow. We tell each other to stay well.

Seventeen

Poppy's sober! The three of us got there at half-past ten to find her Sturmführer daughter and large, loud son-in-law organizing beds and bedding, so there was no harrowing reception in a darkened hall. Rolf wasn't even mentioned until we were sitting round the table having a cup of tea when Poppy told the story of his death again, and then everybody wept because it was suddenly real and we weren't all waiting for him to come home from the theatre after a late show. She's going to call us on Monday, when she's got the funeral date.

Now we're home and Leslie's in the bath. I'm cleansing my face. 'Could be a new life for her,' he says. 'You never know. She might sober up.'

'She hadn't touched a drop tonight.'

'There you go. A good start.'

'What d'you think we'll be like, when one of us dies? What would you be doing if it was me?'

'You won't be going first, Missus. Men go first. You'll be the merry widow.'

'But suppose I did?'

'I don't like talking about it, you know that. Neither of us is going anywhere.'

'I don't suppose Rolf thought he was either.' I wipe the cream off my face and look into the corner of the mirror to see why Leslie hasn't answered. He's disappearing into the water, that's why, making bubbles. I throw the cotton wool at his head and wait.

He stays under long enough to make me take a step towards the bath then comes up, shaking the water off his head and blinking. He finds the cotton wool, squeezes it out and throws it back at me. I miss the catch and leave it to make a puddle on the floor tiles. 'Pick that up, then,' he says. 'It's wet.'

'I will in a minute. Why won't you talk about dying?'

'Because it's morbid.'

'I've planned my funeral. Do you want to know what I've chosen?'

'No!' He reaches for the towel and gets out of the bath. 'That's sick, Mim. That's wishing it.'

'Why? If I go first, you'll be pleased I've bothered. It's in my wardrobe, in the shoe box on the top shelf. Left-hand side.'

'What's the point of that? I'd never have found it anyway.'

'I've told you. So now you know.'

'Look, I'm well, you're well. It's a terrible thing Rolf going like that so soon after your dad, and I know you're upset, my darling, *I'm* upset but we're as fit as fiddles and that's the end of it.' He picks up the cotton wool and puts it in the bin, then wipes the floor dry with a piece of lavatory paper. 'Like I said, Poppy might sober up, go to America. That'd be good.'

'What would you want me to do with my life?'

The towel's falling off his shoulders but he ignores it. 'Why are you talking like this?'

'We've just had two deaths. Can you honestly say it hasn't crossed your mind?'

'It hasn't crossed my mind. That's God's truth.'

'So what do you think you'd want me to do? Crack up? Be rel—'

'I'm not humouring you.' Leslie reaches for his dressing-gown.

I persevere. 'Be relieved? Get married again? Kill myself?'

'*Mim*! That's enough!' He pushes past me. 'Pack it in.' He slams the door behind him. He has never, in over forty years, slammed a door. I don't know why, but I'm pleased.

When I've finished in the bathroom I meet Alasdair outside the loo. 'You all right?' he whispers.

'I'm fine.'

'Only I heard a bit of noise there.'

I make an it-was-nothing face. 'Nighty-night,' I say, jittery enough to talk like a five-year-old. He says, 'Good night then,' and walks back to his room. How could I have forgotten that he was in the house – we all came upstairs together half an hour ago! It's a bit of a sitcom this, an ear at every keyhole.

Leslie's in bed, turned away from me with the duvet right up over his shoulder so that I can only see a fluff of white hair on the pillow and the corner of his book. Now I have to decide: I apologize or I stay silent and keep the row going. The minutes pass. I've opened my book but I'm staring at the page without reading a word. Why am I provoking him? I know what he wants, I know what he hates. I know he funnels everything through his good-nice-kind monitor, and that if I want to talk about anything he perceives as bad-nasty-mean, I haven't got a chance. So why am I pushing it? I remember a woman who said to me, apropos her marriage, How could I ever leave him? Do you know, every morning, before we get up, he cleans all our shoes and lines them up by the back door, then he brings me a cup of tea in bed before he leaves for work.

But still, you're talking about leaving, I said.

That's because he never makes me laugh – it's not like being beaten up or left with no money, is it?

Leslie makes me laugh, even when I don't want to. If I had to say why I could never leave, it'd be because he's never given me grounds. Unless ducking the truth counts. If I die first, he'll find out how he feels. I don't need to know in advance, I think I can guess. If he dies first, it'll be relief, despair… buy a ticket to somewhere and kill myself before I can use it. Why spoil whatever time we've got left by talking about it?

'Leslie?'

'Yes, Missus?'

'If you die, my heart'll break. So don't.'

He turns over and looks at me. 'Mine too. Will that do you?'

'That'll do me.'

Eighteen

We've bought the broadsheets and Rolf's got obituaries in two of them, both using the same photograph. He's smoking, his fair hair's parted, he looks as if he's about to tell us a good story and I'm going to miss him, even though he drove us all mad. The funeral's been arranged for next Friday afternoon, a week to the minute after my father's. There's no thought of me not going, in fact Poppy wants me to be one of the readers. It turns out that she was brought up to be an atheist and developed her 'private God' when she was in her twenties. He's the avuncular sort, available for prayer but fickle in delivery. Rolf was C of E and only went to church when he was invited – would he have wanted the whole palaver of a big service? Poppy says he loved funerals and reviewed them like theatre. 'Vicar stiff as deceased', was her favourite.

Max and Jackie are taking us to a restaurant tonight. I told Leslie we should wait until after Friday but he thinks it'll do us good to have a night out, even though a night out with those two is going to be as dreary as socks. Even if Max is getting a lot of money from Constance, he won't be seeing it for months so we can't be celebrating the windfall. Leslie says they might be getting engaged. Passé now, but then it always seemed a bit daft to me, even when it was the done thing. You want to get married or you don't. If you do, get on with it. If you're not sure, wait. Crazy to spend money on a ring and then risk having to give it back. I was years ahead of my time on premarital relations.

We've never been asked out by Max before and Leslie thinks Jackie's encouraging him, 'growing him up a bit'. I hardly think that going out to eat's a sign of maturity. My mother once told me – a single, exclusive disloyalty – that she had been in a restaurant with my father and that the waitress, 'a tiny thing', had brought them the dessert trolley. 'Your father chose a slice of the biggest, creamiest, most sumptuous strawberry cake I've ever seen,' she said. 'The poor girl couldn't keep all the layers together, putting it on the plate, but she did her best and it really didn't look too bad at all. Then she put it in front of your father and said, Will that be all right, sir? And he said, No, it won't, in that awful voice of his. So she had to take it away and cut him another slice with her poor little hands trembling so much it's a wonder she didn't drop the whole thing on the floor.'

'And then?' I asked.

'It was perfect. I couldn't breathe while she did it but it slid onto the plate without one crumb falling out of place. And she put it in front of him with a ghost – no more than that – of expectation.'

'Did he congratulate her?' I asked, knowing perfectly well that he didn't.

'No. He picked up the fork and ate it like a pig.'

This betrayal was said in a near whisper, even though my father was out. I was terribly shocked. Not because he'd been boorish, I was quite used to that, but because she'd told me the story and used the word *pig*. She'd unlocked the box. I'd under-rated her. She watched my father and made judgements, even though she could never defend herself or us. What did she think about when we were all asleep and he was lying there, the warder in the bed? She never made demands, never said, *When I was a girl, I wanted…* What? What did she want? When I think of her, she's barely there, as gently inconspicuous as a soap bubble.

We're in a very white Spanish restaurant, whitewashed walls, white linen, white chairs. Jackie's in a slightly browner version of what she was wearing the other night, like a mouse in a glass of milk. These clothes haven't been chosen especially for us, she's obviously worn them all day. I, on the other hand, have spent a good half-hour working my way through the wardrobe, going from Gloria Swanson to garden maintenance with a short stop at cabin crew. In the end, Leslie picked me out a jade jumper and a black skirt and sat on the bed until I'd put them on. He was right, it's perfectly pitched. As a situation, this is unique and unaccountably, I'm nervous. Does it matter so very much that I should make the right impression?

We hand in our coats and sit at the table. We comment on the weather and the decor: large inappropriate photographs of famous American film actors. Ivy trails down the walls from a gallery near the ceiling. I feel a leaf. It's real. The menus arrive and the waiter asks us what we'd like to drink. Leslie and I have martinis. Max and Jackie order a large bottle of water. Water? I keep quiet, Leslie keeps quiet. We choose our food, order wine for us but again, not for Max and Jackie. I'm assuming he wants to stay sober for her. I've never seen Max ask for water in my life.

'Well!' Leslie says. 'This is very nice!' He picks up his glass. 'Are we celebrating anything in particular?'

'Leslie!' I put my hand on his arm. 'That's not up to us to say.'

Jackie turns her head to Max without moving her torso, twisting her neck and raising one shoulder higher than the other, which makes her look like Charles Laughton swinging on the bells. Sadly, she doesn't have a speech impediment, which rather spoils the effect. 'Shall we tell them?' she says.

'I was going to wait.'

'Up to you.' She turns back and beams at us. It's a cliché that a smile can ginger up the least attractive face but Jackie's smile is a hosannah, a triumph, an all-conquering pushover of a smile.

I want to applaud it. I say, 'Why not now?' and beam back. We're in league, Jackie's smile and I.

Leslie says, 'Wait for what? Come on, darling. Spill the beans.'

Max brings Jackie's hand onto the table and holds it there. He may be sober, but he's not subdued. 'OK, if you want the big news early then pin back your ears. Ladies and gents, I have an announcement!' I look at Leslie, then back to Max and Jackie. Leslie's mouth is open. Max is mad-eyed, Jackie's smile has slipped into a nervous smirk and I'm still grinning, glass in hand.

'We are going to Madrid—'

'How marvellous,' Leslie says. 'Great place, we loved it. I'm sure you'll have a wonderful time.'

'— to live.'

'To live?' Leslie and I do it again, the chorus.

'How long for?' he says on his own.

'A year. At least. Maybe longer.'

'A year!' Leslie says. 'A whole year! What about the flat?'

My first thought, oddly, is what's going to happen to Barney.

Then I think, what if I never see Max again? And what if they have children and I never see them either?

'... so we're doing it up to rent out.'

'What about work?' I say. 'You don't speak Spanish, do you?'

'I'll learn, Mum.'

'I suppose you've told Charlie?'

'Of course I bloody well have.' The moody boy's back. 'Don't put your oar in. I'll find work, all right?' He turns to Jackie and says, 'I told you this was a mistake.' She shakes her head and squeezes his forearm. So it was her idea! She wants us to *bond*.

I'm conciliatory, smiling. 'What did he say?'

'He says he's going to retire. It was just the nudge he needed.'

'Isn't that marvellous!' says Leslie. 'The way things work out, you'd never believe it. Of course you'll find work in Spain. It won't be a problem, not there. We're glad you told us. It's great news!'

'Thank you, Leslie.' The little that Jackie says, in her funny, cracked voice, is always filtered through etiquette. If this was a play, by nine o'clock she'd be drunk, effing and blinding and flirting with the waiters. She refills their glasses, emptying the bottle and shaking out the last drops. 'I've got a job, you see, teaching music. That's why we're going. Max can teach English conversation while he's learning Spanish, there are plenty of opportunities for that. I can understand that you're worried. If I were a parent I would be too. But we're going to be very happy and successful there. Thank you both for giving us your blessing.'

I didn't think we had. Jackie's taken the Chair. Max is staring at her. So are we. She does the smile again and I say, 'Bravo. It sounds like a good plan.'

Leslie says, 'Fantastic! To Madrid!' and we all raise our glasses. 'And if there's anything we can do to help, you let us know.'

'Well,' Max says. 'Could you take care of Barney till we're settled? We'll come and get him as soon as we know where we're living. And if you'll keep an eye on the flat, I'll give the estate agents your number for emergencies. All right?'

'Of course it's all right. We'd love to have Barney.'

One waiter brings the starters, another the wine. 'So now we know the good news, let's all have a drink!' Leslie tastes the wine, nods his approval and waits for everybody's glasses to be filled.

'No thanks, Dad. Not tonight.'

'Thank you but no, Leslie.' Jackie puts her small fingers over the glass and then picks it up by the stem. 'May we have more water?'

Leslie flourishes the bottle and asks for two more. 'You don't drink then, Jackie? Is that right?'

'Yes, Leslie, that's right.'

We begin to eat. Jackie clears her throat and says, 'I'm so sorry about your father, Mim. It must have been awful for you to miss the funeral. Are you quite better now?'

I'd forgotten I was ill. Why didn't Leslie remind me? I build up to a cough and then stop. What's the point? 'It was a twenty-four-hour bug, that's all. Bad timing, awful timing.'

Leslie rescues me. 'I'm glad you met Constance, Jackie. She's a bit different from Max, eh?'

'Did Dad tell you about your grandad going senile?' Max says to me.

'Of course he did.'

'Locked up in a bin. What a life.'

200

I can't talk about him here. I don't reply.

Hello, Harry. What do you think of this girl?

She looks willing. Do the boy good to love.

'Were your parents on the stage, Leslie?'

'Noooo. My dad was a hack for a local paper. Mum was the editor's secretary.' He turns to me and puts his hand over mine, knife and all. 'When they were courting Dad wrote her little love stories – just short ones, a page or so – and put them on her desk. They'd be about him and her, what they'd do when they were married. Very sweet, the two of them, never had a cross word.'

'That's lovely, a lovely story. Don't you think so, Max?'

'It's news to me. You never told me that, Dad.'

I say, 'So how did you two get to know each other, then?'

Max pulls off a piece of bread and stares at me while he's chewing. Then he swallows and glances at Jackie, who nods. 'We met at an AA meeting,' he says, 'didn't we, Jacks?'

No chorus from us this time, not out loud, in any case.

'Not that AA,' Leslie says. 'You mean the other one.'

'Which other one?'

'The car one.'

'No,' says Max. 'Not that one. The other one.'

'Right. Well, that's a turn-up.' Leslie smiles at me. He knows perfectly well that Max didn't mean the car one. He's floundering.

'Unusual,' I say. 'Not common or garden.'

'We've known each other for three weeks,' says Jackie. 'That might seem like quite a whirlwind to you but when something's absolutely genuine you know you've got to believe in it.

Time loses its significance. Isn't that right, Mim? We have to trust. To believe.' Does she mean in Max? She's smiling again, her face radiant with love. Leslie's been silenced. It's up to me. I risk it.

'So you're—'

'Yup, we are.' Max is all bravado.

'When did you decide to go to—'

Jackie says, 'Six months ago.'

Max says, 'Three weeks for me.'

I want to get to the end of a sentence without trailing off but I can't think quite what to say. Do I ask why or how or applaud his – their – honesty, or sympathize…

Leslie's obviously in the same dilemma but he's quicker than any of us. He says, 'I think that's marvellous, I really do. Not that we noticed anything, darling. Of course we didn't. But if there's anything we can do to help then we're right behind you. Anything. That goes for you too, Jackie. It's lovely to see you both on the brink of a new life. What do you think, Mim? Aren't these kids fantastic?'

Before I can speak, Max says, 'I don't think I want to talk about this any more. You asked and I told you so can we drop it now?'

'Of course we can.' I'm relieved. I pick up my wine. 'To Madrid! *Salud!*' As I deliver the toast, I realize what I'm doing and freeze. Leslie laughs and pulls a toothy, horrified face. We all laugh, even Max. It isn't the slightest bit funny but we're all released by the noise.

During the rest of the meal, I find out that Jackie comes from Surrey, that her father's a policeman – short diversion to comment on the coincidence of Constance being in the Met –

her mother's a court clerk and they haven't met Max or been told about Spain. We don't mention Alcoholics Anonymous again but I assume her parents don't know about that either. Jackie's going to tell them she's leaving when she's actually left, 'when they can't do anything stop me'. How could they stop her? They'd do their best, that's all she'll say. I'm trying to imagine her drunk, pizzicato as a newt on her instrument. Does she get rowdy, or just cling to the viola and sob?

Max says, 'Bad news about your friend. Amazing really, two in a week. When's the funeral?'

'Who's funeral is that?' Jackie asks.

'A friend called Rolf,' I say. 'He died.'

'Oh, I'm sorry.' The opposite of the radiant smile is a face so deflated by bad news that it creases in the middle with a jerk. 'Was it sudden?'

'A heart attack.'

'Oh, dear.'

'Let's not dwell on it.' Leslie's emphatic. 'Bring us all down and to what end?'

It's a very fragile production, this dinner, like an egg-blowing contest.

At the end of the evening, when we're putting on our coats and waiting for Max to come back from the loo, Jackie says, 'Thank you both for coming. Max wasn't sure but I think it was important for us all to get together, don't you?' She's looking from one to the other of us, her face restored to its pallid, puffy doldrums.

'I enjoyed it.' And it's true, I did.

'So did I,' Leslie says.

Max comes back. We go to our cars and I kiss Jackie and then, because it seems like absolutely the right thing to do, I kiss Max. As he opens the door for me to get in, he says, 'Thanks, Mum.'

I say, 'Thank *you*.'

Leslie starts the engine. We pull out, passing them, and wave. We're all smiling. Leslie says, 'I told you she was a nice girl.'

'Strange.'

'Lovely smile.'

'Lovely.' After a while, I pat his leg and let my hand rest there. 'Bit of a surprise, though, wasn't it?'

'What?'

'The AA thing.'

'Certainly was. Mind you, plenty of people drink more than he does. Where's the line? Maybe he joined it like a club so he could meet girls. And what d'you know, he met Jackie!'

'You don't think he's in trouble?'

Leslie doesn't answer straight away. We pass a crowd of teenagers roaring along the pavement, their arms around each other. One of them spots me and does a cartoon grin with tombstone teeth and retracted lips, his head tilted. I grin back, the same. The car accelerates.

'Max is sorting himself out. He's a good kid.' Leslie puts the radio on. 'Nice evening, very nice.'

Nineteen

We want to thank Max for the dinner. I say I'll ring him, and
Leslie's pleased, 'It's nice to see you two getting along so well'.
Shall I mention the drinking? There's no point asking Leslie
what he thinks, he'd only take the same tack as last night – the
boy works, he's not on a park bench, he's in love, QED there's
nothing to worry about, Missus. I suppose I could talk to Charlie
and ask him if he knows about Madrid and if he really is retiring… Isn't it a fine thing, to see Max happy? Then again, I'll bet
AA doesn't applaud new members falling in love and zipping
off to Spain after three weeks. It's all whim, this, and of course,
we've ended up with the four-legged whim, as I always thought
we would.

I ring Max at work. 'Hi, Mum here.'

'Hi!'

'We had a lovely time with you and Jackie.'

'Isn't she fantastic?'

'Certainly is.' We're talking like ordinary people, people
with manners. I try another ordinary sentence. 'So how are the
plans going?'

'Great. We're seeing the estate agent later. Any chance of you
having Barney for a few days, while we show people round?'

'No problem.'

'I'll bring him over this evening.'

'Great. Stay for supper.'

'I won't, thanks. Not tonight.'

'Another time then. Is Charlie there?'

'Why?'

'I wanted to have a word about that interview. See if he's got any more gen.' I can hear Max breathe in through his teeth.

'Are you checking up?'

'Exactly. Do you know if he's heard anything?'

'I mean checking up on me.'

'Of course I'm not!'

'I told you. He knows I'm leaving.'

'So you did. Is he there? I'd still like to say hello.'

'He'll be back in after lunch. I'll tell him you rang. Forget the job. We haven't heard anything – it's a dead duck.'

'I'll see you later then. With Jackie?'

'I'll be on my own. See you.'

And that's that. No opportunity to talk to Charlie. I think I'm relieved.

I'm resting on the bed, reading the red book and looking at the ridiculous things I've written. Fairy stories! Conversations with dead people! Alasdair's gone. The woman in the flat he's renting had to vacate at speed because of some job or other and the agent said he could move in pronto if he wanted to. He left very quickly – just packed, said thank you and promised us a dinner as soon as he's settled in. Leslie helped him out with his tartan cases while I stood in the doorway and watched him go, two-thirds of a traffic light in his green jacket and red bobble hat. I should have been glad to see the back of him but I actually felt discarded, even though I never wanted him here in the first place. I turn to the next blank page intending to write something but lifting the pen is too much for me; it's a tree trunk. I put the book down and close my eyes…

… I'm on the Square Island of Bed, all alone, waving goodbye to my father as he digs down to the world below and to Rolf as he marches off, stage right. There's a plane for Max and Jackie and a car for Alasdair and a barrow for Aude as Gully drags her off up Dickie's meadow… I doze and dream about giant yellow hibiscus, up to my shoulder, wrapped in cellophane. The shop assistant says they'll cost a hundred and fifty pounds! I'll have them, I say, and wake up. I'm alone and cold. I get under the duvet.

All the goodbyes are piling in, little monsters. The night before I leave home, that's an unpleasant one. Me, the wild girl, throwing clothes into a case and my mother taking them all out again, folding and stroking as she puts them back. There's nothing I can say to make it better for her, so I'm cruel instead, telling her that I won't be back for weeks and weeks, months probably, certainly not until I've found a job as an actress.

You make the most of it, she says, true to form, enjoy yourself. My father, also true to form, stops talking to me the day I say I'm leaving and only starts again when the taxi driver's helping me out with the cases. *You're not getting a brass farthing from me, so don't come back here with your begging bowl.* He pushes my mother inside and closes the door. The taxi driver says, You're better off out of it, I reckon. Dead right, squire.

Was there ever a good goodbye? I run through them all, the

men, the friends, Constance, my mother, a dozen times my mother. Bad goodbyes, the lot. Was it always my fault? And why am I thinking about this today, when the recent gone have either died, which is nothing to do with me, or moved amicably round the corner? Now I'm hot. As I get up and put the book back in its drawer, the doorbell rings. And rings. Leslie must have gone out. I go downstairs, smoothing my hair, and open the door to a woman carrying a huge bouquet of yellow and white flowers, wrapped in cellophane. The card reads, *To Mim and Leslie with love and thanks, Alasdair.* What, no hibiscus?

Aude calls. She's going shopping and asks us to meet her at the patisserie for tea, 'Because,' as she says, 'we all need some sugar-love.' Leslie's game for it although his knees are sore today, and we walk up to the Broadway, holding hands as always, two old bods clinging to each other like Hansel and Gretel.

Leslie says, 'What time's Max coming?'

'This evening, that's all I know.'

'Nice to see Barney-boy again.'

'This AA thing—'

'What about it?'

'What do you think about him joining and then waltzing off?'

'There'll be one in Spain. There must be plenty of expats on the sauce, I reckon.'

'Are you saying you think he's got a problem? That's not what you said last night.'

'Maybe, maybe not. Maybe it's fate. Maybe he had to drink too much so he'd find Jackie and now they can be sober together. Sober and in love, isn't that nice?'

'Very funny. That's like being stabbed so you can meet a policeman.'

'Why not? These things happen all the time. Just think, all those years ago, if I hadn't gone to that wedding. But I did, and I met you. Suppose I'd stayed at home?' He squeezes my arm. 'If that couple hadn't stopped for a kiss at the exact moment I looked out of the window...'

I've heard this a thousand or more times but it's like a favourite song now, so I encourage him. 'Then what?'

'Then I wouldn't have felt like the loneliest bugger on earth and I wouldn't have changed into a suit and gone out and I wouldn't have seen you and I'd have wasted the last forty-one years talking to myself.'

'Instead of wasting them talking to me.'

When we're nearly at the Broadway, I ask, 'If you thought Max was drinking too much, then why didn't you say?'

'Why didn't you, Missus? Anyway, he's all right now.'

I can't answer. Why didn't I? Aude's waiting at the door of the café and starts to wave as soon as she sees us on the opposite corner, so we go through that awkward business of where you look while you make the approach. You can't stare at each other like Cathy and Heathcliff meeting on the moors but you can't gawp at the pavement either, as if you're avoiding potholes. I remind Leslie that we've got to have dental check-ups. Aude rummages in her shopping bags.

We leave our coats at a table and then go straight to the counter and make a lot of fuss choosing what we want to eat. I can't remember the last time I was so pleased to be in her company. While the tea comes, we talk about Rolf's funeral and Poppy's next move, then Leslie mentions Alasdair's new flat but

Aude's immediately uncomfortable – still guilty? – and I don't go into any detail. Her wedding plans go the same way: a doodle to sketch them out, nothing more.

Aude wipes the last smear of cream from her plate with her forefinger, sucks it clean and holds it up by her eye. She taps her cheekbone and says, 'You'll never guess what I'm doing after the wedding.' I think *getting divorced*. I can't imagine anything better and Leslie's silence suggests that he can't either. Aude gets impatient waiting for us to speak. 'I'm getting my eyes done!'

'Done?' I say. 'You mean that laser thing?'

'God no, sweetie. I don't want to see better. I want to *look* better!'

Leslie shakes his head. 'The knife?'

'You got it!' She lifts the skin underneath her eyes and pulls it taut. 'See? If you get rid of all that gubbins underneath and then—' she pulls at her eyelid, exposing her eyeball '– you cut the lid up and get rid of the fold—'

She drops everything back into place. 'And it just whips the years off. So what do you think?' she asks, smiling at me.

I stall. 'How much?'

'A few grand.'

'It's a lot.'

'It's a loan.'

'From who?'

'The bank.'

'Really? They'd give you money for that?'

'I said it was for work. Everybody's doing it. I heard some woman on TV say in twenty years it'll be like having your nails done.'

'But you're not working.'

'Not now. I bet I'll get jobs though. I'll look twenty years younger. Go on, tell me you think it's a fantastic idea.'

Leslie says, 'You're lovely as you are, you know that.'

'Thank you, sweetie.' She pulls up the skin again. 'But I'll be lovelier!'

Aude's doing this for Gully. When she was young, she was young-beautiful and in her altered, older way, she still is, so what's he saying to make her doubt it? I'm about to start my anti-surgery rant when Aude stands up. Out of the corner of his mouth, Leslie says, 'Don't look now, but…'

I turn round to see Gully pressing his nose against the shop window. He spots Aude coming towards him and heads for the door, reaching it at the same moment she does. She tries to push out as he's pushing in but the door only opens one way. He wins. She stumbles back as he strides through and grabs at her shoulder, stopping her from falling.

'I've found you!' he shouts. Then he sees us. 'What ho, Mim and Leslie! I must have cake to celebrate!'

Leslie pats his stomach. 'No more for me.'

'Nor me.'

'I will!' Aude pulls him to the counter. While they're away, we have a whispered summit and decide to leave as soon as he's finished eating. 'Got to keep stoking the avoirdupois!' he says, coming back. 'Can't say no to cake, never could.' He's become enormous, his belly hanging over his trousers. It's going to hit the floor soon and precede him like a snowplough. He sits down, as close to the table as he can get, and grins at us all. When we knew him before, his height compensated for his girth. Now his chin lies on his neck, echoing his belly, and he snuffles as he breathes. I try to imagine Aude kissing that little octopus mouth. Can she really be that desperate? He's talking, '… and what's so marvellous is that they've bought the bloody lot! The whole fucking shebang!'

'Is that a fact?' Leslie says. 'Well, I never.'

I don't know who's bought the shebang, or indeed what the shebang actually is, but Leslie appears to be on top of the situation, so I take his lead and smile and nod.

Gully puts a plump hand out to Aude. 'Had to come out and find you, dear. Couldn't keep it to myself.'

She hasn't been able to look at me since he arrived. Now she glances my way and says, 'It's a perfect wedding present, sweetie. Just perfect.'

His cake arrives. 'Ah! Merci bien, ma petite.'

'No problem.'

'Milles feuilles!' he says, mangling the French. 'Like Scheherazade, a thousand stories!'

They're hard enough to eat if you're fastidious. If you're Gully, the moment you put your fork in, the plate's a rubble of flaky pastry, cream and jam. It's an Act of God. He shovels it up, snorting. I can't watch.

Aude distracts us. 'I saw some youth on TV this morning, saying he wants his music to shock old grannies into coughing up their cornflakes. What do you think of that?'

Leslie shakes his head. 'I wouldn't know where to start.'

'If Granny keeps passing wind at your party,' I say, 'put her near the window where she won't cause offence. She can't help it, so there's no point shouting at her.'

'No! Who said that?'

'Local paper. God's truth.'

Gully's finished. He pushes the plate away. 'We'll use some of that money for your op. And then we'll go to Italy. I must show you the light.'

'And we must go.' I stand up.

'Our treat,' Leslie says.

'No way.' Aude edges out and comes to the corner. We hug. 'My treat, sweeties. And I'll ring you later.'

Gully stays where he is. 'Soon, dears. At the wedding. And you'll come to the restaurant to see the work?'

'Wouldn't miss it,' Leslie says.

When we're in the street, I ask Leslie what he's talking about. 'Some new chippy in Finsbury Park. They've bought his *oeuvre*.'

'All of it?'

'Twelve canvases. The fishy ones.'

It's dark already. The walk home's occupied with Gully's weight and Aude's surgery. When we're taking off our coats, I ask Leslie if he's ever wanted me to have a facelift. He beckons me to the hall mirror. 'Look at us,' he says, linking arms. I don't want to. I watch him, staring at himself, until he says, more firmly this time, '*Look*.' Reluctantly, I look. We're getting old. Or else we're no different, with wigs and plastic wrinkles and the channel that's been cut into the hall floor to make us shorter. He's not smiling, just moving his eyes from my reflection to his and back again.

'Did you think we'd end up like this?' he asks.

'I don't think we have. I think we've been through Hair and Make-up.'

'You've hardly changed. Not like me. Old man Methuselah.'

'How about this one.' I pull in my lips until they're slit-thin, set in barbed wire. My eyes go blank. I'm avaricious, brassy...

'The hard-boiled madam,' I say. 'What d'you think of her?'

Still gazing into the mirror, he reaches up and cups my face with his right hand. 'I never said you were hard-boiled. You know I didn't. You're still gorgeous.'

'You did, you know.' I let my features settle back. 'That's exactly what you said. You said I was perfect for the part.'

He strokes my cheek. 'Not because of how you look.'

'What made you think of *her*? Why not one of those gardening detectives? Or a *nun*?'

'Because I wanted something different, something with a twist... Make that posh ninny face. Go on, for me.'

'This won't work, Leslie. I know what you're trying to do.'

'Please?'

I say, 'I wish you'd stop being so bloody jolly,' but I do Posh Ninny as he asks. He laughs. 'See? You can do anything. That's you, Miriam Shaw. The star! Soft-boiled, hard-boiled, anything. Do the madam again, go on.'

'Shan't. Don't like her.' I hold up the skin at the corners of my eyes, copying Aude. Rather than improving things, it makes me look like an ageing Slav. I drop the skin again and watch it subside into place...

Still, we're holding up. We get sore joints, we take pills, we can't eat and drink the way we used to, I feel the cold more, we forget too much, we remember too much. But we're standing without help, we're not dementing like poor Harry Shaw, and there isn't much we miss when it comes to the world's doings.

Leslie runs his fingers through his hair and turns away. 'I'm surprised you're still here, Missus.'

'Why?'

'I look like your dad.'

214

'You do not!'

'I look old enough to *be* your dad, that's what I mean.'

'Only if you were at it in nappies.'

He flounces off. 'My best years, as a matter of fact.'

Max arrives. He leaves us the vet's details, bedding, toys, a case of food for starters, a packet of dog biscuits and the dog. As he and Jackie hope to leave by the end of next week, he says, there's not much point them taking Barney back for a day or two. I remind him that his uncle Bernard's in Spain, a fact I'd forgotten until this afternoon. He reminds me that he's only ever heard us describe Bernard as seven types of arse so why would he bother? Absolutely.

'Come and have a meal before you go?' Leslie says. 'With Jackie, of course.'

'I'll give you a bell. Let you know how things are going. Thanks for having the boy. Take care of him.'

'You bet!'

'Good luck with the flat,' I say. 'Make sure they've got references.'

'Of course they'll have references, Mum.' The withering face. 'That's what we're paying the agent for, right?'

'Glad you're doing it that way, darling.' Leslie pats his back. 'You don't want to go letting out to friends. Bad business, mixing things up.'

Max goes. No kisses. Just a hug for Barney.

Twenty

I'm at Rolf's wake, drinking too much. He's probably in the flames by now, melting like St Joan. Rolf's on fire. Isn't that peculiar? We had a full house for the funeral. His son read one of Rolf's poems, some early pontificating, written when he was thirteen: *Hold fast to the wheel, dig in your heel, death's a-stalking us, walking us to Elysium...* Doreen had the grace to stay away, guilty or not. Poppy told everyone no black, only bright colours and topped us all in lipstick pink. Leslie said, 'Wrong church. Mother of the bride,' but I think it's just the job. She's changing lives, she's marking it.

Alasdair's here. I thank him for the flowers but don't mention that I dreamed them an hour before they came. We talk about his flat and he asks me to come round soon and help him make decisions. What sort of decisions? Oh, colours, plates, that sort. I say I'd be pleased to and he wanders off, his attention caught by another guest. I don't want to talk to anyone else now. I get another drink and stand by the back door, looking out. It's a summer garden, drab now without evergreens. I'll offer to help her in the spring. We can plant new beds and bring in some trees to block out the neighbours, biggish trees, fast growers.

Rolf's on fire...

If there's a reckoning, he's standing there now, à la Powell and Pressburger, in front of the grand celestial jury, rows and rows of them, leaning forward, hungry for evidence. The judge lifts a colossal finger and points to a screen unfurling on the podium. The lights go down, the film starts. It's the story of Rolf's life, every minute of it, from the first birth cry to the leaving breath. The cameras, unbeknown to him, were everywhere. There's nothing he said or did that isn't playing, right now, in Technicolor, 3D and stereophonic sound. Rolf can't bear to watch. He closes his eyes and puts his hands over his ears. The judge, unperturbed, puts the film on *inside his head*. The jury applauds. We watch, I say 'we' because I'm standing next to Rolf now. I hook my fingers under my bra straps, face the jury and start my defence. Was malice proven? Did he do harm with the intention of hurting Poppy? I suggest that he was weak, that he was lonely, that he should have left her, yes indeed, but that he was trying to fulfil his role as a provider.

The prosecution, Felix Aylmer's twin, says that weakness and loneliness are so general a defence that they constitute no more than a common bleat.

True, I counter, but my client was ignorant for the best part of seventy-five years. One could almost say that he was asleep. If he'd woken up, if he'd seen how little time he had left, he would have snapped into action, taken his life in hand –

– But he didn't.

But he would have.

'Mim?' Leslie's standing next to me with a plate of food. 'Are you all right, Missus?'

'Yes…'

Actually, I'm still in court, saving Rolf from damnation but I

Twenty-one

Max and Jackie are leaving, and we've come to the flat with Barney to say goodbye. The whole place has been spruced up to such a degree that we gasp as we walk in, like people caught unawares on a makeover programme. If Jackie wasn't here, I might say, 'Haven't you spent too much?' or possibly, and worse, 'What a shame you couldn't make it look good while you were here.' Instead, I say, 'They're lucky tenants. It's fantastic.' Jackie apologizes for not being able to make us coffee, then we're led from room to room to make sure we've seen the full works. The walls are ivory, the curtains match the walls, the carpets are Jackie's trademark mushroom-fog. We marvel that they've found the time. A labour of love, Jackie says.

Back in the sitting-room, Leslie parks himself on the new cane chair, clearly anxious that he might crease the cushions. 'We'll miss you, darling. But you never know, we could come out for a week. What do you think about that? Shall we do that, Mim?'

Jackie says, 'You'd be very welcome, wouldn't they, Max?'

'When we're settled. Sure.'

'So when do you get there?' Leslie knows perfectly well, but he keeps asking. He's described the journey to me several times, the ferry, the drive, the places they'll stop.

'Couple of days, Dad. I told you.'

'So you did, darling. So you did.'

Max is different. It's in his eyes. They're still pouchy but there's a little more window, a little less veil. He talks to Leslie, spelling out the route again, and as he's speaking he puts his hand out to Jackie, not looking to see whether she'll take it, just knowing that she's there. When he was a baby and I cuddled him, heavy on my lap, he'd find my thumb and hold it.

It's time to go. The suitcases are lined up in the hall, topped with other bags and boxes. I take a knapsack, Leslie tries a suitcase and has to abandon it for something smaller, then we all troop down to the car where I stand guard while they bring down the rest. We stand in the street, not quite able to separate.

'Well!' Leslie says. 'Bon voyage! To your new life!' Who's going to make the first move? Leslie! Good for Leslie! He crosses the central space with his arms wide to hold Max while I cross the other way, being careful not to bump into him as we pass in the middle. I kiss Jackie's cheek. She allows the contact in the same way that a pillar box doesn't retreat from a letter. Civil acceptance, no embrace.

Now Leslie turns to face Jackie and I turn to face Max. It's Leslie and me again, on the move. We cross the centre space to change partners. Approaching Max, I stall. He's standing to attention and I echo him, putting my arms down at my sides. I've got less than a second to free them or we're going to meet like tin soldiers. I open my arms, he opens his. It's a brisk hug, with the slightest of kisses. As we separate, I catch myself gripping his jacket. I want to hold him close, but I can't. *I'm frightened of holding my son.* Frightened of what? That he'll push me away, that he'll cling on and cry, that he'll want something I can't give?

Jackie says, 'We'll write to you very soon.'

'And send pictures?' Leslie pleads.

Max strokes Barney. 'See you soon, chum.'

'Goodbye then, Mim. Goodbye, Leslie.'

'Goodbye, you two. Good luck.'

'Goodbye, darlings.'

Cheerio, toodle-pip. We're waving at the disappearing car. I have to pull Leslie's hand down. 'They've gone. They can't see you.'

He glares at me. 'I know.'

We turn for home with Barney at Leslie's side. We're quiet. After a while, he says, 'I'm going to miss him. I'm glad we've got Barney-boy.'

'It might not work out anyway. They could be home in a few months.'

'Don't get me wrong. I'm not wishing them back. I'm only saying it'll be strange not having him round the corner.'

'We could have a trip somewhere, as long as we go before I have to get busy in the garden. We haven't been abroad for years. What do you think? What about Paris?'

'We'll be in Spain soon.'

'Or Prague? We haven't done that. Or Dublin?'

'What about Barney?' Leslie stops to let him wee on a lamp post. 'We can't leave him in a kennel. When they want him back, then we can take him to Spain.'

'I've only got till March, then I'll have to be in the garden.'

'We'll be in Madrid in no time. Won't that be nice?'

*

Poppy spends the afternoon with us, or rather me, as Leslie disappears upstairs soon after she arrives. In the week since the funeral, she's come to a decision: she's going to live in Los Angeles for a year, with her son. When she talks about Rolf, which she does very little, it's with contempt. I try to summon his virtues – his intelligence, his self-possession, his grace, but she won't let me finish a single story that sets him in a good light. Doreen, she tells me, sent roses to the funeral, and a card reading, *To a dear old friend.* Poppy gave the roses to the caterer, who cried because it happened to be her birthday and she'd recently split up with her husband. 'So that all worked out very nicely, thank you.'

When I say that everybody's off somewhere, she says it's our turn next, 'The little duckies in search of a new pond.' God, I hope not. She leaves at six, for a night out at the theatre.

As we close the door, Leslie says, 'I've never seen anything like it! You'd think he'd been dead five years.' He walks down to the kitchen, not looking back to see if I'm following, still talking to himself. 'Not a fortnight gone. It's like Gertrude and What's-his-name.'

I'm close behind. 'She's not getting married again. Wrong play.'

He switches on the light and gets himself a glass of water. 'It's too soon, Mim. Too soon! I know they weren't that happy, but for God's sake, give the man a bit of respect!'

'That's funny, coming from you. I thought you'd be applauding.'

'Applauding what?'

'Her being cheerful. Are you all right?'

'I'm fine. I'm sorry for Rolf, that's all. And what about the ashes? I suppose she's thrown them away!' He's very pink. The water's trembling in the glass.

'Weren't you there when she told us?'

'Told us what?'

'She's burying them in the garden, under his favourite tree. Where they put the dog.'

'With a *dog*?'

'Rolf loved it. You know he did. It's a sweet thing to do.'

'It's sick. I'm going for a walk.'

'Are you sure you're all right?'

'Probably.'

'Take Barney?'

'With pleasure.'

When he's gone, I pour myself a glass of wine and sit down to drink it while I watch the end of the news. Leslie's rattled me. I know why he was angry – he's frightened that he'll be written off, a box of ashes scattered in a street.

At half-past six, I go back to the kitchen and pull out some pans to start dinner. At thirty-three minutes past, according to the cooker clock, the phone rings. I answer, not fully concentrating, standing in front of the fridge with my hand poised to pull out a plastic tub of olives. A man asks me if I'm Mrs Lyons. Yes, I say, pulling out the tub. I reach for sun-dried tomatoes. The man says he's ringing on behalf of my husband. Really? Why? I put the tomatoes on the counter. The man speaks more loudly, he's out of breath. 'I'm afraid your husband's been in a bit of an accident. Could you come down?'

'What do you mean, an *accident*? Who are you? Why can't Leslie talk to me himself? Let me talk to him, please.' Is this a joke?

'He was attacked. By some boys. I've rung for an ambulance. We're on The Avenue, do you know where I mean?'

I know The Avenue, of course I do, it's a couple of minutes away. I ask him to wait with Leslie, then I run upstairs for my coat and keys and run downstairs and then upstairs again for my bag, and then I run to the front door and remember I haven't locked the back door and run to do that, because burglars at this point would be ridiculous, and then I run three doors down the street and turn round, thinking that I should take the car, but as soon as I reach it I realize that I could waste minutes finding somewhere to park so I turn again and half run, half walk uphill to The Avenue with my breath burning my throat.

As I get closer, I hear the whooping of a siren and then an ambulance passes me and pulls in ahead, flashing that terrible blue light. A man's standing there, in his shirtsleeves, his arm raised to flag me in the dark. I croak, 'Where is he?'

'Here.' Behind him, on the pavement, there's a body. I didn't see it! He says something else but I'm not listening. Leslie's heard my voice, his hand is reaching out for me. He grunts my name. Why can't he get up? *Stay calm, don't babble, don't babble*. I kiss him. It's all right now, I say, you're all right, it's all right. He tries to move and opens his mouth to howl then clamps his teeth shut and crushes my hand so tightly that I'm the one who cries out. His cheek's swollen but there's no blood anywhere, then paramedics, a man and a woman, are kneeling with me, twice my size somehow, utterly comforting. You're all right now, I say to Leslie. The cavalry's here. They ask him his name and I tell them, then they ask him how he is and he manages, 'All right', then they ask me if I'm his wife and what my name is and all the time they're doing things to him. A mask goes over his face. One of them's explaining that it's painkilling gas and they tell me what it is but I'm too alarmed to listen. *Gas,*

gas, quick boys. No, Mim, shut up you're babbling. It might be a broken hip, the paramedic says. A broken hip? Fucking hell, what did they do to him, whack him with an iron bar?

They put him on a stretcher and he groans, but only once. I look up. There are doors open, curtains drawn back, people are watching. A woman comes across the road and offers us tea. A policeman thanks her and sends her away. As they wheel him to the ambulance, I pick up the folded coat that's been pillowing his head, realizing that it must belong to the man who rang me. He's talking to a policewoman. '… And then one of them punched him.'

I shake out the coat and hand it to him. 'I assume this is yours?'

He nods. 'Thanks. Is he all right, your husband?'

'Thanks to you.'

'And you are?' says the policewoman.

'Miriam Lyons.'

'And the victim, he's your husband?'

'Leslie Lyons.'

'I chased them.' The man's directing this at me. 'But I lost them. Crossing the road, a car came in between, they disappeared. Could have gone into a house, no way of knowing. I'm terribly sorry. Really tried to catch them up.' He doesn't look heroic. He's probably my age, a bit younger, greying, quite tall. 'I'm sure they didn't take anything. I shouted, you see, and they ran off. I had to get back to your husband.'

'Now then,' The policewoman opens her notebook again.

'May I ask your name?' I say to the Samaritan.

'Marriott. Roy Marriott.'

There's a paramedic at my shoulder. 'We'll be off in a minute, my love. Are you coming with?'

'I'm coming.'

I put out my hand to Mr Marriott. He's holding a dog lead. I look down. Oh, God, Barney. I've forgotten Barney. 'I can't come,' I shout. 'I've got a dog.'

'I'll take care of him.' Mr Marriott juggles coat, lead, wallet and gives me a card. 'Don't worry,' he says, 'he'll be fine. What's his name?'

'Barney. Barney Lyons.' Why did I say that?

'Someone'll be along to the hospital,' the policewoman says, dismissing me.

Leslie's still got the mask on. I sit next to him in the ambulance, squeezing his hand as we jolt over the bloody speed bumps. The paramedic tends him. I ask her name. It's Julie. Is he in a lot of pain, Julie? Only if he moves… My teeth are chattering. She unfolds a blanket and puts it round my shoulders. I love her. I love the way she's holding us together in the little world of this ambulance, keeping Leslie safe as she measures and logs and reassures. We're safe here in Julie's world. Then we're out in the night air, wheeling him through to A and E, and the smell and the commotion. Julie and Dave are by my side. I can't bear to lose them, they're who we know, they know what's happened to us. A nurse appears and they talk to her, handing us over like evacuees. Then they have to lift him from their stretcher to the casualty trolley. *This might hurt a bit, Leslie.* Before he can stop himself, he lets out a terrible wail and then it's over and he's flat and they're leaving, taking their stretcher and the gas. And the blanket round my shoulders, don't forget the blanket. Goodbye, Dave, goodbye, Julie! Thank you!

We're in luck, we're in a cubicle and we've been told it's a two- or three-hour wait until Leslie can see the doctor, that's all, only two or three hours. Do you need anything for the pain, Mr Lyons? No thank you. I'm all right.

We're alone.

'Hello, Missus.' It's an old man's voice, coming from high in his chest.

'Hello, my darling. Don't talk, not if you don't want to.'

'A little tap like that… I never… I mean, you don't…'

'What happened?'

'They asked me if I had any money.'

'And what did you do?'

'I told them to bugger off, that's what.' He breathes in noisily, as if he's remembered something important. 'Where's Barney?' He starts to lift himself up. 'Aaahhh, Jeeesus.'

'I'll get the nurse.'

'Don't!'

'Why not?'

'Don't need anything. Just sit, Mim, please!'

A nurse puts her head through the curtains. 'Everything all right?'

Leslie says, 'Fine.'

'Pain not too bad?'

'Fine.'

'If you're sure.'

I leave with her and ask if there's a chair I can use. We find one and I carry it back and sit down. 'Why don't you want anything for the pain?'

'Because I don't need it. Where's Barney?'

'He's safe, don't worry. That man, the one who helped you, he's got him.'

'What d'you mean, got him?'

'So I could come in the ambulance. He offered to keep him for me.'

'Who is he, this man? Barney'll be frightened half to death!'

'I could take him home and leave him on his own. Or stay with him and leave you. Take your pick.' *Come on, Mim, stop this*. 'He's a nice man, Leslie. He chased them off. And you've got a witness.'

'I don't know what Max is going to say.'

'What's Max got to do with it?'

'I could have lost Barney! I don't know what I was thinking, talking to them like that.'

'Like what?'

'Telling them to bugger off. They could have killed me!'

'Leslie, stop this.'

He's sweating, trying to keep still. 'I can't believe it. A little tap like that and I'm down!'

The curtains rustle and part. Another nurse appears, older, more senior I would guess. In this little cubicle, our second new world of the day, she's as bracing as a sea walk. After finding out who I am, she asks Leslie if he minds me staying. He doesn't. As she's cutting off his trousers, she asks him if he's fallen before. 'Never!' He's indignant. She asks him questions and examines him gently, then covers him with a blanket while she takes his blood pressure and then his blood – difficult this, for all three of us, in our various roles. Leslie does the 'almost an armful' joke and she has the grace to laugh. He's to have an X-ray, she'll arrange it and yes, this is most probably a broken hip: the rotation, the shortening… If he needs pain relief, then please ask. Can he have some tea or something? Not until we know when the op's going to be. Then *swish* and she's gone.

I put my hand on his. 'Are you all right?'

'You'll have to get my diary and see what bookings I've got. Tell them I can't make it for a week or two. Tell them I'll be in touch as soon as I'm out of here.'

'I'll tell them. But it's not going to be a week or two, is it? More like a month or two.'

He looks away. 'Are you sure we can trust Barney with this bloke?'

'Never mind the dog. Can't we talk about you?'

But he won't. After circling the Barney problem again, he dozes off. I close my eyes and think about hips. What do I know? People with broken hips get pneumonia and die, the artificial one isn't permanent, you'll be running a marathon in no time, they saw you through like a side of beef. And being in hospital means you're likely to catch an infection and die of that, long before whatever you came in with gets you. That's it, that's all I know.

A voice outside, 'The old boy's in number four.'

'Mr Lyons?' The curtains part again. Enter Police Constable Ballard, from scene one. She stands, looming over us. Nice face, polite enough, talking as if we're slightly deaf. Names and contact details please, which means I have to ferret in my bag and find the piece of paper with our mobile number. Like the nurse, she asks Leslie if he minds me staying – in the old days, you were told to shove off and have a cup of tea – then asks him to describe, in his own words, what happened when he was attacked. I say nothing, I know nothing.

Somewhere nearby, a man shouts, 'Get off me!' then he screams and we all fall silent. PC Ballard shifts her weight in case she's needed. A beat or two, silence, then she says, 'Mr

Marriott, the witness, believes that Mr Lyons fell because the two dogs were standing right behind him when he was hit.'

Two dogs? The youths had a bull terrier with them and he was trying to molest Barney when Leslie toppled backwards over them both. He doesn't know about the second dog, never saw it. Would he recognize the youths? One of them was in a rabbit suit, Constable and the other had a yellow sou'wester and a waxed moustache… Leslie's not sure, he'll do his best. CID will visit, possibly tomorrow. His daughter's in the Met, he says. Really? Constance Lyons, that's her name, perhaps you've heard of her. 'Fraid not, right then, thank you. She goes out, closing the curtains in front of her face.

Leslie tells me it makes sense that the dogs tripped him up because, he says again, he wouldn't have been downed by a little tap like that. A bruise is seeping into his cheek and the skin round his eye. I lean forward and touch the other side of his face. He takes my hand and kisses it, then holds it to his mouth. His lips are trembling. I'm not as frightened as I was. We've had the calamity, the turmoil in the dark, the flight from it. Now we're resident here and as far as I'm concerned, it's a question of endurance. Leslie's frightened – and why shouldn't he be? He's so frightened that he can't even allow himself to think about the state he's in. He kisses my hand again and lets it go. Back to Barney. We decide that I'll wait with Leslie until he's had his X-ray and been found a bed. Then I'll ring Mr Marriott. But I can't, it's already nine o'clock and I won't be away from here for hours! Revision: it'll have to wait till morning. I ask Leslie if he wants me to call Max. He says no, not while they're travelling, why worry them? I say I might tell Aude, then we lapse into silence.

Next on, top billing, the doctor. Young, harrassed. Again, Leslie's asked if he minds if I stay, which of course he doesn't. Suppose he *did* mind, then what? How many people leave here with their stories blown? I think the question should be blatant, a simple: 'Have you got something to hide?' The doctor's lifting back the blanket. He's going to move Leslie's leg. I might be wrong here, but perhaps this privacy business isn't about secrets. It's about being helpless. I excuse myself and go to the loo.

When I get back, Leslie's alone and asleep. I've bought a paper and a plastic cup of foul coffee and I sip at it, enjoying the warmth between my hands. His hair's matted, his skin's grey in this hide-nothing light. But he's alive. In Leslie's world, although he hasn't said it yet, he's the lucky one, he got away with it. Soon, by tomorrow, that's what he'll believe. And believing it makes him luckier. He has no choice in the direction his life is taking him. He can't walk on a broken bone, ergo: we're trapped. We could choose to go to a private hospital and that's it, the only other proper choice – unless he refuses to have any treatment at all, which is only an option if you're writing a paper on options and you need an unfeasible one to fill the space.

He wakes up. I stroke his arm. 'What did the doctor say?'

'It's definitely my hip.'

'Oh, Leslie…'

'Don't…'

I wait. 'Is there a bed?'

'He's sorting it out. Nice boy. He says I can have a cuppa and something to eat. Any chance of you getting me something?' I go back to the machines and get him a bar of chocolate and some grey tea. It's hard for him to get his mouth over the lip of the cup, but he manages, with help.

'Would you like me to read to you? They had an *Independent* left.'

'Good idea.'

So I read him the paper and we wait, and after a while we're taken to the X-ray department which means more pain for Leslie as he's positioned this way and that, and at no point does he complain, not even to me. Good news, there's a bed for him. And the operation's tomorrow morning at nine: more luck, no long wait. We walk and walk through the silent corridors, me and the nurse and the porter pushing Leslie's trolley, until I'm reminded of that poem about Toomes the butler, leading the feckless dinner party down to hell. It's not quite dark on the ward, in that hospital way, nicely designed to keep you from deep sleep. There's more pain for him, being transferred to the bed. As we kiss goodbye I whisper that I'll be back in the morning, as soon as I've dealt with Barney. He whispers not to waste my time, they'll be operating. I say I'll ring. We kiss again then I'm back in the corridor, in the lift, in the foyer phoning for a taxi.

'Everything OK?' The driver says. He's very young, Spanish, oddly enough.

'I hope so. I hope everything's OK.'

'For you, God makes miracle. I promise.' He looks at me in the rear-view mirror and our eyes meet. I have to look away.

Twenty-two

The lights are on and I'm wary, then I remember that I left too quickly to think of lights, and anyway it's nearly half-past one. I don't want to go upstairs on my own. Why don't I sleep on the sofa? Because I'll get a stiff neck and a sore back and it's a miserable thing to do, an admission of dread.

I go to bed. It's cold without him, even with the electric blanket on. I kiss my hand and put it on his pillow. Goodnight, Leslie. *Goodnight, Missus.*

Unbelievably, sleep.

I ring the hospital as soon as I wake up. He's 'comfortable', the nurse tells me. The operation's set for nine and yes, of course I can visit this evening.

'Would you be kind enough to pass on a message?'

'Sure.'

'Please give him all my love and tell him I'll be in later. And tell him I said to break a leg.'

'Pardon?'

I plough on. 'Tell him I said to break a leg.'

'Right… Oh!… Oh, I see.'

That'll go better second house, says Harry Shaw, unbidden. He stays with me as I shower and wash my hair. It's an adjournment for Leslie, not half a lifetime as it was for Harry. But today? Today he'll be cracked open like a crab shell. I point the hairdryer at the mirror and tell the little shits who knocked him over to put their hands up.

By seven, I'm ready. On any ordinary morning, we'd still be in bed so there's no precedent for filling this time up. It's too early to ring anyone, so I have breakfast and watch TV for a while, flipping between the two news programmes, then I wipe down the kitchen and make a list of the things I need to take tonight. After I've gathered them, wrapped them and packed them in a bag, it's still only eight o'clock and here I am, standing in the bedroom with my hands at my sides, rudderless. I look through the window at the garden. Boots on.

For the next hour, as I pick up and cut off and sweep, I think: how shall we be, Leslie? When you're limping about and I'm playing nurse? If we hadn't had that row about Poppy, mightn't you have postponed the walk? If Max hadn't left Barney here, if Poppy had been kinder about Rolf, if I'd be kinder to Leslie, if those boys had been properly brought up, and if and if and if… *Bigger fleas have little fleas upon their backs to bite 'em, and little fleas have smaller fleas and so ad infinitum…*

He'll hate having to rely on me. There's no precedent, except for the odd virus, and even then he'd stagger down as soon as he was well enough. This is Leslie truly in need, me having to tend him, him on edge, me worse… the worst nurse… I'll have to take his lead and play it down. Stay perky. At nine, I go indoors, take off my coat and boots and head upstairs. Leslie's diary on his desk. I find the list of retirement homes, with their numbers and contact names. The phone's resting on my left hand, poised for dialling, when it rings. I squeak with fright.

It's only Alasdair. He's off to buy some stuff for the flat and hopes I can tag along. I tell him about Leslie. He offers to come round instead, help in any way he can.

'I can't think of anything you can do, but thanks for the offer.'

'Would you not like a bit of company?'

I think about it. There's an all-day wait before I can go to the hospital. If I pick Barney up now and get the shopping I need, then what? 'Yes, actually. I would. Come for an egg. Twelve-ish?'

I phone the six homes. Everyone I speak to is appalled at the story and wants to know where they can send their get-well cards. *We do love him, we'll miss him, he cheers us all up.* I hear six of these accolades, all from the heart, and promise to ring with news of his recovery. I've never seen him do this work but I've watched him here, rehearsing and it's true, he's a big fizzy life force. Big, fizzy Leslie, out for the count. Next call, Mr Marriott.

'Hello, it's Mrs Lyons here. From last night.'

'Good morning to you. How's your husband?'

'He's got a broken hip. They're operating this morning. Listen, thank you for everything. You've been ridiculously kind. I hope Barney hasn't been too much of a nuisance.'

'Not in any way. He's a lovely dog, very well behaved.'

'I was wondering if I might come round and pick him up?'

'Whenever you like. You've got the address.'

'I'll come now.'

When he answers the door, I'm surprised. He's older than I remember from last night, more substantial. His face is heavily

235

creased and bright-blue-eyed, framed with a lot of grey hair and short sideburns. He says, 'Mrs Lyons?' and shakes my hand with skin as rough and dry as pumice before standing aside to let me in. There's the pungent smell of paint, a ladder leaning on the bare wall with tins stacked beside it, no carpet on the floor or stairs. He opens the first door we come to and says, 'Look who I've got for you, Barney Lyons!'

And here he is, the boy. I sit on the nearest chair and nuzzle his face, unreasonably pleased to see him again.

Mr Marriott sits opposite me, very still and four-square. I can't imagine him running after the thugs. He says, 'Any news from the police?'

'No. Fat chance.'

'I wish I'd got a better look. They were too quick for me.'

'Leslie was very lucky. If you hadn't been there…'

'Well, I was.' It's not immodest, not curt, just gently honest. We've got a bond, Mr Marriott and me, but it's not sturdy enough to support any overenthusiastic feelings. He confirms it by adding, 'They've got the hang of it now, mending hips. I'm sure he's in good hands.'

'As long as they're clean!' We don't laugh because it isn't funny, in fact it's only a reminder that Leslie's taken up residence in a Petri dish. I change the subject. 'You're decorating, then?'

'Top to bottom, or rather bottom to top. It should be finished by Christmas, that's the plan.' He's staring at me. His eyes really are quite odd, too blue, too sharp, like cutting tools. I look round. It's finished in here, reeking of new paint. We're on crisp loose covers, green and white. Walls milky, curtains pale green, Indian rugs on sanded floors. And he's wearing black espadrilles! I'd have put my money on slippers…

'It's lovely, very fresh.'

'I'm pleased with it.' He leans over to pat Barney, who's moved across to sit on his foot. I glance at my watch. 'Leslie's op might be finished soon. I'd better go home, I suppose, in case there's a message. May I have Barney's lead?'

He gets up slowly, like one piece of furniture leaving another. I follow him out. 'If you ever need a hand with Barney,' he says, 'you've only got to ask. With all this going on, the last thing you want to worry about's the dog.'

'That's very kind, thank you.'

'I mean it. I've had dogs all my life so it's only a pleasure.'

'I may well take you up on it.'

'As I said, any time.'

Barney's on the lead, we're by the front door, his hand's on the latch. He says, 'I know this might sound a bit, well – but I seem to know your face. We haven't met before, have we?'

I shake my head. He turns to stare at me. I'm standing in a strange man's hall, nobody knows I'm here, Barney's no Rin Tin Tin and for all I know Roy Marriott likes to kill elderly women and stuff them under the floorboards. In fact, that might be why he's redecorating, to cover his tracks after an opportune visit from a lonely neighbour wanting help with a tricky lid. I'm thinking that I might have to be rude and insist that he opens the door when he says, 'The Curfew! That's right, isn't it? Weren't you in The Curfew?'

Of course, I'm being a chump. He's recognized me, but more than that, he knows where from. Even though he's blocking the door, I'm flattered that he's got the film right. And I owe him one.

'Yes, I was.' I say it as diffidently as I can but the old

237

exhilaration begins to bubble in my chest because I'm ashamed to say I've never got over it, the pleasure, however occasional it is, of being properly recognized. Barney pulls at the lead, he wants to go out but I hold him back. We're nearly at my name…

'Which means you're…' He points at me. '… Miriam Shaw! Well, I never! I can't believe it! I'm so happy to meet you.' He puts his hand out and I grasp it. We're newly acquainted, we have to start again. 'I know you've got to get home, but won't you stay for a quick coffee?'

'Why not?'

Off comes the lead and we tread carefully past the tins and the ladder and make our way to the perfectly decorated kitchen, where I sit while he puts on the kettle, slowly, and gets out the biscuit tin. I'm Mim, I say, he's Roy, no ceremony. They went to the pictures twice a week, Roy and his wife, Bonnie. Never missed a visit. Catholic tastes but were more than fond of British film in the sixties, they had a very soft spot for that. 'Don't you get fed up with being recognized?' he says.

'It's rare. People tend to say things like, No wait, I've seen you before, I know I have. Weren't you on the telly when it was black and white? To which I say, I think you've confused me with a woman on Z *Cars*. That shuts them up.'

'You've hardly changed. They should be ashamed.'

'I'm forty years older. They should be congratulated.'

'Why haven't I seen you in anything since *The Curfew*?'

'Because I retired.'

He's shocked. Can't believe they'd let me. There's no *they*, I tell him, it's not one man or ten men, it's an industry. But didn't I keep trying? No, Roy. I didn't. And what about you? And he tells me that his wife died five years ago. For the first four, he went a bit mad. Locked himself away, drank too much. Then last Christmas, he had a row with his daughter because his grandchildren were too frightened to visit him in what they'd started to call The Horrible House. He spent a day without a drink and looked at himself and at the rooms and decided they were right. If he had the choice, he wouldn't be visiting himself either.

'So what did you do?'

'Stopped drinking, started to see a counsellor and bought a job lot of paint.'

'Really? All that, so quickly?'

'No time to spare, not one day.'

I drink my coffee and refuse a custard cream.

'Bring Barney tomorrow,' he says. 'When you visit your husband.'

'You'll be decorating.'

'I'll stop.'

'Thanks, Roy.'

'No thanks needed, Mim. It's my pleasure.'

When I get in and let Barney off his lead, he snuffles about, running from room to room and then back to me. Is he trying to find Leslie? I explain that Leslie's in hospital but he'll soon be home, and it seems to work, at least for the dog, because he bolts down a tin of food, lies on his blanket and goes straight to sleep. The only message on the answering machine is from Aude. I'm immediately guilty that I haven't told her the news and then grateful that I wasn't in – she sounds rather too upbeat, as if she's acting tough. I can't face ringing her now though, not if it's a Gully saga. I try the hospital. Leslie's not back from theatre yet, another few hours at least.

Alasdair's coming to lunch. I take six eggs out of the fridge and put them in a bowl, then put two back. Leslie isn't here. Scrambled? Fried? Whatever Alasdair wants, I don't care. I'm drained of impetus, unable to make a choice so I sit at the table, a choice of sorts, and think about Roy Marriott losing himself for five years after his wife's death. Five years! And he only came through it because his daughter cared enough to bully him back. She must be a good daughter. Lucky old Roy…

When do I tell Max? And Constance? I don't have to tell her, Max will. She might visit but I doubt it. Leslie's having a perfectly common operation. He isn't ill. Unless he gets an infection… always possible, an infection… I *should* have told Aude, that was naughty. I'll ring her, and Poppy and Max, as soon as I know how Leslie is. I'm hot. I realize I've still got my coat on. As I go to hang it up, the doorbell rings and I see two silhouettes through the glass. Is it Mormons? It turns out to be Alasdair and Aude.

'Why didn't you tell me?' She's quite cross. 'I'd have come straightaway, you know that!'

I apologize, say I haven't had time, was about to when the bell rang.

Alasdair holds up a carrier. 'We've bought lunch.' I put the eggs away and while we put out the food, deli things, I tell them the story, becoming almost as absorbed in the reliving of it as I was in the event. Details come back to me that I had no conscious memory of: the gap in PC Ballard's front teeth, the sound as Leslie's trousers were cut and ripped away, his varicose veins, the chrome support at the side of the trolley… I don't mention these things, or the others, they just float in while I'm talking. Now and then Alasdair and Aude stand still, with a hand on a plate or pulling at cellophane. At the end – I stop when he's safely on the ward – I say, 'And he never once complained. Not once.'

'Old soldiers never do,' says Aude.

'He wasn't in the army.'

'You know what I mean, sweetie. He's an old soldier, an old pro.'

'Brave man,' Alasdair says in his soft drawl, 'and very lucky, as it happens, not having to wait all night to be seen. I've spent whole lifetimes in casualty.'

'Why?' I'm feeling less anxious now. It's actually pleasant to have them here, a tranquilliser. And the food's good. I fill my plate, pull a chunk off the French bread and pile on the butter.

'Well,' Alasdair counts it off on his fingers. 'I was always in punch-ups, loads of those. Latterly, a car crash, scenery collapsing, badly infected cut, champagne cork in my eye. I think that's it.'

'That's enough, isn't it? Nothing lately though, not since I've known you.'

'I'm having a jammy patch. And this man who took Barney, what sort of fellow is he?'

'Nice man. Widower. Lives in Alexandra Park Road. He's offered to take care of Barney while I'm at the hospital. Isn't that kind?' Telling them that Roy recognized me doesn't seem quite the thing to do, so I don't do it. 'And he's decorating his house,' I say, to fill the space. They nod, quite seriously. Ah. They're thinking that in the aftermath of the shock, I'm feeling inappropriately interested in this kindly widowed neighbour who's inappropriately concerned about the dog, and that it's all going to end messily as soon as Leslie gets out of hospital. If I say anything, if I even make a joke, I'll make it worse.

Aude puts down her fork. 'I've got to ask you something. Alasdair's heard all this, but I know he won't mind hearing it again. Will you?'

He makes a *what choice?* face and helps himself to more pâté. I wait.

'Gully's gone back to Italy.'

'Has he?' I'm genuinely surprised. If the whole point of the remarriage was to get at Aude's money, he's skipped off too soon.

'His ex, you know, the last wife, she's been on the phone every day, every bloody day, nagging at him to come back.'

'And he says?'

'He's got a new life now but he's always there for her if she's in trouble, blah, blah. Well, last night she stabbed herself.'

'To death?'

'No, worse luck. So Gully's gone haring off to see what he can do, the old sweetie.'

'And you've got to decide what, exactly?'

'Whether to wait here or go out and do what I can to help.'

Alasdair's chewing, his eyes are vacant. When I ask him what he thinks, the bottom lip comes up, he lifts his shoulders, lifts his hands, shakes his head. 'I sink she will follow 'im, whatevair we say, so we might as well say *allez-vous-en.*'

Aude says, 'I sink you are a swine,' and looks at me defiantly, waiting for a harangue but I've got nothing to add. Alasdair's summed it up. She'll go and play the martyr while Gully plays triangles and the ex plays suicidal gestures and they'll all have a sensationally miserable time. 'I'll end up going, I know I will,' she says, deflated. 'There's no point me being here if I'm going to spend the time worrying about not being there. I'll be better off worrying with him than without him, that's the crux of it. If I'm there, we'll be together, we'll help her together. If I'm here —'

'There are situations,' Alasdair says, interrupting the gabble, 'that can't be changed unless one of the parties crosses the line.'

'What do you mean, the line?'

'Out of one state into another.'

'Don't talk in riddles, not now.'

'It's not a riddle at all. As long as you want whatever you're getting from Gully, you'll follow him wherever he goes. If you stop wanting it, you'll stop following. Dead simple. That'll be forty quid. You can pop it in the saucer.' I laugh. Aude doesn't. Alasdair reaches across the table and takes her hand. 'I'm not being unkind, it's how it is.'

'I know,' she says, dropping her head. 'And I still want it.'

Alasdair isn't being unkind. He seems to want the best for us all, from high, high up in his unbreachable tree. So what is it that disturbs me? I'm looking at him now, instructing Aude in the manners of separation. He's in emerald green and yellow, gaudy as a parrot, but I can't actually see him. He's always mulishly himself but it's a camouflaged self, a spokesman sent down from the summit. And when he talks about his past, I always get the feeling that I'm being shown photographs, with captions. Here, now, he's doing his best for Aude, sympathetic about Leslie, but what about *his* life? Doesn't he have problems? I'm not sure why this should be particularly acute today, but it is.

Eventually, after coffee, they leave. 'I'll visit Leslie before I go to Italy,' Aude says, when she thinks Alasdair's out of earshot.

'*Sotto voce, signora,*' he says from the street.

Twenty-three

Alasdair comes back later to take me back to the hospital. He drops me outside the main door and I make my way through the smokers to the information desk where they direct me upstairs. I think of a friend who once had to attend a fracture clinic that had been placed on the second floor, in a building with no lift.

There's a lift here. I get into it and steel myself, hating the smell of the place and the pain and the fear, the whole purpose of the building: to put you through it by piercing and plucking and pumping until you decide to right yourself or die. There are signs leading to the ward but they run out at a point where there are several doors, a staircase and a lift. I go back to the first sign and try again, as if a small boy might unexpectedly appear, holding an arrow. No small boy. I'm still lost. I start to push open one of the doors, see a woman's face through the glass panel and step back as she pushes through. She's obviously a doctor, stethoscope, blue pyjamas. I tell her that the signs peter out and that they should send the management out on trial runs because it's bad enough having to come here at all without the added excitement of getting lost and wandering round corridors when you could be visiting your husband.

That's why they do it, she says. For the excitement. Then she tells me to go through the door I was trying to open and keep walking, then turn left and left again. I thank her and she wishes me good luck. When I finally arrive, I have to wait for several minutes at the desk because there's only one nurse and she's on the phone.

When I ask her for Mr Lyons, she smiles. 'Mr Lyons? Oh, *yes.*' I assume she's been charmed. He's in a four-bed ward, dozing in the far right-hand corner. There are three other patients: a young man reading a book, an old man flat on his back, staring at the ceiling and the third, next to Leslie, a man on his side, his face hidden by the sheet. The first two turn to me with that blank, bedridden look and then turn away again. I'm of no interest, neither friend nor staff. Leslie's got a bag of blood hanging up beside him. I've seen this often enough but this time it jolts me. And there's another bag, filled with what I assume must be urine, hanging on a short stand nearer to me. I manoeuvre in and touch his face. He wakes up, a bit snoozy but definitely present. He's in a white hospital gown, smelling of whatever it is that makes up the scent in here.

'Hello, Missus.'

He reaches up and I bend to kiss him. 'How are you feeling?'

'Top hole.'

'Are you not in pain?'

'I've had an epidural – can't feel my leg at all, can't move it or anything. And I've got tubes all over – I'm like a bloody telephone exchange. There's another one down that side.' He points. 'That's where it's draining off.'

I sit on the green leatherette chair, getting in as near as I can. 'So what did they do to you?'

'She's put in a screw.'

'What sort of screw?'

'It's a screw, that's all I can tell you.'

'How long does she think you'll be in?'

'Six days.'

'And then you'll be able to walk?'

'I might be out of bed tomorrow.'

'That's good news, isn't it? And they didn't have to knock you out or give you a new hip. It's all gone very well, considering.' We try to smile at each other but it's weak, no more than a reflex. He looks at the ceiling. I look at the blood bag and follow down the tube feeding into his elbow. 'I saw Aude and Alasdair today. They both send you their love. They were horrified, couldn't believe it. She says she'll visit you tomorrow, before she goes to Italy. Gully's ex is there, trying to top herself, so Aude's going to give her a hand.'

He shakes his head. 'Shame she didn't top Gully while she was at it. Where's Barney?'

'I've left him at home. I won't be staying long tonight. You need to rest.'

'Was that man all right?'

'Roy? Very nice. Says he'll have Barney every day if I want. I'll probably take him up on it. Have you eaten anything since the op?'

'I'm not sure.'

'You can't have forgotten—'

'Leaving him with a stranger, it's not good. Have you told Max?'

'Not yet. I will, now I've seen you. And this man's very nice. I've had a chat with him.'

'I don't like it. You'd better ask Max what he thinks.'

A nurse comes in, writing on a clipboard. We watch her, wondering if she's coming to see us but no, she goes to the reading man and closes the green curtains round his bed.

Leslie pulls at his sheet. 'Did you get a taxi?'

'Alasdair brought me.'

'Where is he? Is he here?'

'He's waiting at the pub. He thought you might not feel up to too many visitors.'

'Tell him thanks from me. Are you all right in the house on your own?'

'Of course I am. You must be exhausted. Why don't I let you sleep? I'll stay all afternoon tomorrow.'

'You can't leave Barney that long.'

'Of course I can!'

'Come and see me, that's all I want. An hour'll do.'

I get up and trip over the canvas bag. 'Look, I nearly forgot. I've got all your bits and pieces here.' I take out his things and put them where he tells me.

'I can't have the mobile.'

'No, of course, sorry. So what can I bring you?'

'Chocolate, that'd be nice. Thanks, Missus.' I reach him without knocking anything over. As we kiss goodbye, he puts his hand on my head and holds me to him. 'I'm going to be all right.'

'You are, my darling.'

'Sleep well. I miss you.'

'You too. I miss you too.'

'Give Barney a hug.'

'I will.' I blow a kiss from the door. The two men who watched me come in, watch me go out. The third man hasn't stirred.

After I've told Alasdair how Leslie is, he says, 'So when's your son coming to visit?'

'I haven't told him yet.'

'Haven't you?' He turns to me, amazed. 'Why on earth not?'

'Because he's in a car, on his way to Madrid.'

'But he'll want to know, won't he?'

'If it was a heart attack…'

'This is a serious operation, Mim!'

'I know, I know, I know. I'll ring him.'

Traffic lights. Pulling away. 'So why's he going to Madrid?'

I explain about Jackie and the job and the flat. '… And that's why we've got Barney.'

'And what about your daughter?'

'What about her?'

'Are you not telling her either?'

I can't answer him immediately, the question's too big. Constance has never given us her phone number but Max would ring her if I asked him to. And what if I tell Leslie that I've done that, and then she doesn't respond? And then there's the whole police thing: the CID are going to come to the hospital and ask Leslie questions. Wouldn't he hope that if Constance knew about the mugging, she might put a little pressure on the local force? Or would she tell him, as I would, that it's pointless, that these youths will get away with it because they're like piranhas, darting back into their anonymous mob? I have some photographs of individual piranhas here, Mr Lyons, perhaps you'd like to see if you can identify the one that tried to chew your leg?

'What are you thinking?'

'I'm not sure what to do.'

'It's not up to you. It's up to them. Stop censoring the news.'

'Could you possibly shut the fuck up?'

He double-parks at the door. 'I've no idea why but I'm volunteering myself to be your taxi for the rest of the week.'

'You can't—'

'I can and I am and there's an end to it. And tomorrow, if you don't think it'll be too much, I'll come up for a minute and see Leslie.'

'He'd love that. Do you want something to eat?'

'Not tonight. Tomorrow, maybe?'

'Thanks for taking me. Could we be there for two o'clock?'

'Al cars, at your service.'

The night is young. So young, in fact, that it's only twenty past six. I walk Barney to the end of the road, grateful to the commuters for keeping me company as they plod home in the dark. Even though people get set upon everywhere in this and every other city, I've never felt vulnerable myself, not until Leslie's attack. Now I'm all antennae: the feet behind, the boys crossing the road, the car door opening, the obscuring hedge, the man coming towards me… I reach the corner and turn for home, finding myself a short distance behind a large woman with a briefcase who stops quite suddenly and wheels round, obviously expecting me to have criminal intentions. I freeze and smile sheepishly. Barney sits down, possibly expecting a ticking off. She says, 'Good evening,' in a voice so modulated it makes me think of Margaret Thatcher, and then carries on as if nothing out of the ordinary's occurred, which of course may be true for her. She might have long adopted a policy of preferring to look down a gun barrel rather than being shot in the back. I trail her to my gate, curbing the impulse to call 'And a very good evening to you' as she disappears round the corner.

When I've made myself some dinner, beans on toast because I can't be bothered to cook, I phone Max, rehearsing out loud as I walk up and down the hall:

'Your father's had an accident, he's in hospital.' No, too bald.

'Your father's been mugged but he's absolutely fine.' That's ridiculous.

'Your father says not to worry, and whatever you do don't interrupt your journey but he's in hospital. He fell over. Well, he was pushed and *then* he fell, tripped actually, over two dogs, and broke his hip. They've mended it with a screw. He'll be in for six days.' That's the one, informative but not alarming.

I ring Max's mobile, running through my lines as I wait to be connected. When he answers, there's so much racket in the background that he can't hear what I'm saying so he shouts that they'll find a parking place. I read the paper and wait for him to call me back which he does eventually, from a lay-by. My script's successful until I mention the broken hip, at which point Max starts to have two conversations, one with me and one with Jackie. I can't hear exactly what she's saying but she's persistent. He tells her to be quiet. He asks me to explain again, more slowly. I tell him the little I know and all the time, Jackie's talking. I catch 'can't' and 'expecting me', little crescendos in the flow. She's not sympathetic, she's bristling. Max tells her to put a sock in it and says he'll ring me for the address tomorrow, when they arrive, and in the meantime, regards to Dad. Oh, and have I told Constance?

I don't have her number.

He'll call her but it'll have to be tomorrow. Jackie gets closer to the phone. 'Give Leslie my best wishes, won't you, Mim?'

I put the phone down. I've done it. I didn't want to but I've done it. Alasdair should be pleased. And now it's half-past seven. I ring a sober Poppy. She can't believe it, she says, not Leslie!

'Dear God, are none of us safe? When can I see him?' I suggest that she visits him tomorrow, after five. 'Then I'll come to you afterwards,' she says, 'and bring supper. No arguments. Tell Alasdair to join us.' We say goodbye, with me promising to call her if I need the slightest, tiny thing.

I leave a message for Alasdair, then I stand in the hall for a moment, uncertain which direction to take. Leslie and I spend most of our evenings doing nothing in particular and might be accused of sloth but it's companionable sloth, usually well earned. This evening, I can't settle. I decide to watch TV and end up staring at some crap hospital drama and fiddling with my hair. If the staff at Leslie's hospital are engaging in this amount of sex and personal crisis, I can't imagine how they have the time to bother with post-operative old men. During an ad break, I go upstairs for a fleece and as I walk past the chest of drawers I get out the red book, not with any particular intention to write but rather because it feels like an ally in the empty house. Barney trails me and then, when we're downstairs again, he goes to the front door, looking back to make sure I've got the message. I get my boots and put him on his lead to make sure he doesn't wander onto the beds, then we walk round the back lawn until he wees against the apple tree. There's very little noise out here, in fact we could almost be in the country. How would it feel, to be in a rural garden, alone? Tonight I'm glad I'm not, in a rural garden, that is. I'm alone, though, of that there's no denying.

'So what happened to him, Barney?' I sound very loud. 'Would you know that dog, if you saw him again?' He responds, coming to me for attention. I stroke his head and ask him if he's finished. He has, he says, quite finished. We go in. I give him biscuits and make myself some hot chocolate, taking two mugs out, measuring the milk wrongly. Is this what happens after your husband dies, that you go on laying two places? I tell Barney what I've done: talking to the dog is better than talking to yourself. He listens, then lopes off ahead of me to the sitting room and waits by the sofa.

They're still in uproar on the ward. Somebody's rallied, a nurse is sobbing in the sluice, the surgeon's got the shakes and slices clumsily through a rubber artery. The blood gushes up. The surgeon has inoperable tremors, he's botched it, the patient dies, his career's on the skids and his wife, the sobbing nurse, has started an affair with the gynaecologist. If I hadn't retired, I could be doing this nonsense. Miriam Lyons, the old girl in bed seven, irascible, heroic, teaching the doctors a thing or two about life…

I turn the volume down and pick up the red book and the pen. Barney's still sitting by me. I pat the sofa and he jumps up, settling on Leslie's side with his head on my knee.

Open the book. What to write?

Hello, Mim, my little sweetheart.
Hello, Grandad.
That man of yours, he's going to need a bit of looking after. Here, where do cows go on holiday?
I don't know, Grandad. Where do cows go on holiday?
Moozambique. Get it? Moozambique… Guess what I had for tea?

Moosli?

No, peas on toast.

That's nice. Where are you now, Grandad?

I'm with the holy goats, that's where. Put me there and left me bare and nobody wanted to know me.

The phone rings. I jerk so violently that I scrawl a line across the page.

'Mim?'

'Aude? What's the matter?'

'I'm so sorry, sweetie. I must have frightened you.'

'You did.'

'How's Leslie?'

'He's doing well.'

'Good, that's marvellous. When's he coming out?'

'Six days, or so they tell me.'

'You must be very relieved. Listen, Gully's ex has discharged herself from hospital and turned up at his hotel. She's screaming the place down. I've got to go out first thing. Will you apologize to Leslie? I'll see him as soon as I get back.'

'Of course.'

'Are you coping?'

'Absolutely.'

'Must go, sweet pea. *Arrivederci.*'

'*Arrivederci.*'

I take up the red book, bring down the spare-room duvet, investigate the video shelves, make more hot chocolate and curl up on the sofa with Barney to watch *The Ladykillers*. At midnight, we go to bed.

*

I don't sleep nearly as well as I did last night. I feel as if I've been strapped to a chair and put in front of a revolving door that's spewing people out at me, *whooosh and whooosh and whooosh*… What do I say to Constance if she rings? If I imagine it, I freeze. So I put myself in her shoes. How would she feel hearing *my* voice? If I'm her, listening to me, I freeze too. Mother-and-daughter love, two women with nothing in common but a little scrap of DNA… *whooosh*… if things don't work out for Max, what's he going to do? I see him, blind drunk on the floor, with Barney howling because he hasn't been fed… *whooosh*… Will Leslie be able to get upstairs? Will he be able to work again? I don't want him hanging round here every day… *Whoosh*… Poppy… *whoosh*… Aude… *whooosh*… *whooosh*. No more dossing in front of the television. Tomorrow night I'm going to do something purposeful, get so tired I can't stay awake… How do I thank Roy?… *whoosh*…

Twenty-four

After breakfast, even though it's starting to rain, I take Barney for a good run round the park. When I get back there's a call from an old acquaintance of Leslie's, another entertainer from the homes. I tell him all's well. 'Ah, that's great,' says Jimmy. 'He hasn't changed, you know, not since we first met. How many people can you say that about?'

While I shower and wash my hair, I think about Jimmy and wonder if that's a good thing to say about a person, that they haven't changed? And is it true of Leslie? Or of me, as Roy said? Imagine a different Leslie, the cup half empty... nagging Max, looking for trouble... I unwind the dryer lead and bend to plug it in, grunting with the effort. Good morning, naked face! Hello to you, mottled, slumpy skin and thin grey roots! I yank away with the brush, exposing even more grey hair... I must get my streaks done... *No matter what I look like, I'm still me inside,* that's what we chorus, but perhaps they should be running abreast, the inner and the outer. If I slapped my soul up on the bathroom wall and asked a stranger to identify its age... What would it look like, my old soul?

I find Roy Marriott's card.

'I've been hoping you'd ring,' he says. 'How's your husband?'

'They've put a screw in, that's all I know, but everything seems to have gone well. He might even be getting up.'

'They don't like leaving you in bed, not these days. Were you wanting me to have that lovely dog of yours?'

'Only if it's convenient.'

Of course it's convenient. He asks me if I'd like to have a sandwich, nothing grand, cheese and pickle. It's a deal, I say, sounds perfect.

I ring Alasdair and ask him if he'd mind picking me up at Roy's. A1 cars never discriminate, he tells me. A fare's a fare. He'll be there at half-past one.

OK. Or is it? Something's not quite right. I remember that Leslie wants chocolate and decide to go to the bank while I'm out so that I can offer Alasdair cash for petrol. He won't take it but I'll feel better if I offer. And why not buy Roy a little something to say thank you?

Ah, there now, it's guilt – that's the nasty bird-trapped-in-the-gut feeling that's not letting me settle. If Leslie were here, I wouldn't be having lunch with Roy. If Leslie were here, I'd never have met Roy but that's not the point. The point is that my husband's in hospital, and instead of reading improving literature or initialling handkerchiefs as I wait piously by the ward door, I'm eating cheese and pickle with a man he doesn't even trust to look after the dog. I consider cancelling lunch but then, as I bend to put on my shoes, I catch sight of myself in the long mirror and laugh.

Very silly, Mim.

I buy Leslie half a dozen bars of chocolate and get Roy a pot of jasmine on a hoop. The phone rings as I'm taking off the price. It's Jackie.

'We've arrived, Mim! After a very long two days. My goodness, it's such a long way, over hill and down dale.'

'Well done you!'

'Max is asleep but I thought I'd ring and ask you if you wanted him to come home, to help you with Leslie?'

'You mean he's asked you to ring?'

'No. He's asleep.'

'Does he *want* to come home?'

'I don't think so. I just wondered if you wanted him to. To help with Leslie.'

'Well, no. There's no need. Leslie's being well cared for. He's fine.'

She waits a little too long. 'We're well too. We're a bit tired, that's all. Happy of course, but tired.'

Have they come a cropper? Already? 'You must both be exhausted. Well, thank you for ringing, Jackie. Please say hello to Max and don't worry, everything's under control. Perhaps you could ask him to ring me later, after five, say?'

'I certainly will, Mim. After five. Please pass on my sincere good wishes to Leslie for a speedy recovery.'

'I certainly will, Jackie.'

Roy's made the sandwiches. They're on a square plate, covered with cling film. He puts a bowl of water down for Barney, in his deliberate way, and I hand over a rattling box of dog biscuits and the jasmine hoop which Roy sniffs and positions carefully on the window sill. Did he tell me that he used to be a florist? No, he didn't. I ask him to say more, but he doesn't seem to want to so I drop it.

While he makes tea I look round the kitchen and compliment

him on the custard-yellow paint. Not his choice, he says, his daughter's, the most cheerful colour she could find. She's a wonder and a marvel, his good-luck charm. He points out the noticeboard that I'm steering clear of in case he thinks I'm snooping and there she is, the blessed Stevie, surrounded by children and smiling at me as if we've been friends for years. 'She's lovely,' I say.

'Inside and out,' says Roy. 'You'll have to meet her.' The sandwich is perfect, thick bread and strong cheese. We eat opposite each other, smiling.

'Was Leslie an actor too?' he asks.

'An entertainer,' I tell him. 'Singing, dancing, a bit of stand-up, not that they called it that in those days.'

Roy taps his forehead and says he thinks he saw him once, at the Palladium. 'In the fifties, isn't that right? Leslie "Oooh You Beast" Lyons.'

'That's him, that's Leslie.' And I tell Roy about a visit to John Lewis when the sales girl shouted, Oooh, you beast and the security guard came running. Oh, it's *you*, the guard said when he saw Leslie, and then he held out his notebook for an autograph. 'It wasn't the best of monikers,' I say. 'We've tried to obliterate it.'

'So does he still perform?'

'He couldn't stand the touring so when he married me, he stopped. There were London shows, a few, then he gave up altogether to write for other people. And he did well at that, for a while.'

'So he still writes?'

'Oh no, Roy, no. The writing dried up. TV's so hard to crack. He goes to retirement homes now. He sings. He makes them laugh.'

'This is going to hit him hard then, not working.'

'I expect it is…'

'And you. I can't get over it, meeting you like this. I've got it on tape, you know, *The Curfew*. I watched it again last night. Marvellous, it really is.'

'It's a good film, I have to agree.'

'We saw it at the Rex, as was. Very unusual film for us, a bit arty, but we'd already seen the double bill at the Odeon so we took pot luck. Bonnie cried, you know, all the way home.'

'Did she?'

'Such a sad ending. Still not sure I get it. Do you think he finds her?'

'I don't know. I'd like to think not. For her sake.'

'Me too.'

It's one-thirty. I pick up my things and go to the front door. Alasdair's in the car, waiting. Roy follows me out, watching as I get in the car. Then he knocks on the window and waves. At Alasdair.

I wind down my window. Roy says, 'I don't believe it! You two know each other then?'

Alasdair leans across me. 'Roy, isn't it? How are things?'

'Good, thanks. Very good. How about you?'

'I'm well. Good to see you.' He sits back and starts the engine. 'Take care of yourself.'

'I will. What a turn-up. See you later.'

We wave, we drive away.

'How do you know him?' I ask.

'He's a client of mine, your dog man.'

'No! When?'

'I don't know, a year or so. I can't really talk about it, Mim. You'll have to ask Roy.'

259

'Sure, of course.'

'So how was Max?'

'He was still on the road but I think he got the gist of it. Jackie rang this morning, while he was asleep, and offered him up, a sort of oblation to Leslie's leg.'

He laughs. 'That's going well then.'

'Max has a gift for being querulous. Perhaps he's met his match.'

And then we're quiet, listening to the jazz Alasdair's put on, Miles Davis, he tells me. I think about Roy. Why did he visit Alasdair? Needing advice, comfort of some sort, psychic information. *Roy?* He really doesn't seem the type – but then I don't think I do, either.

A seaside town. Swanage. It's August 1960, eight years before I make *The Curfew*. There's a board on the pavement. Portento, it says, fortune teller to the famous. I go inside. In the hall, a bead curtain covers an open doorway. There's a television on. I say, Hello? And then nearer to the curtain, Is anybody there? A scraggy old man pushes through the beads, cigarette hanging from his mouth, a strand of curtain draped across his ear. I say, I'd like a reading. The room's very gloomy, light from the screen and a red-shaded lamp. On a small round table there's a bottle of beer, a half-eaten cheese sandwich and a full ashtray; next to them, a crystal ball and an outsize pack of cards. He tells me to sit but keeps his eye on the screen where a race is about to start. He watches, shouting at the riders and eating the rest of the sandwich. Bollocks to 'em, he says at the end and turns to me. What d'you want then? Cards, palms or crystal? A quid for one, two-fifty the lot. I ask for the lot. He turns off the television, finishes his beer and puts the ashtray on the floor, then lays his hands over the crystal. They're fine hands, long-fingered. The nails are surprisingly clean. We sit in silence, leaning towards each other. He takes a handkerchief out of his pocket and wipes his face. *What do you really want?* he says. I can't answer. My eyes are hot with tears. Shall we have a look at your cards then? He shuffles and splits the deck into three. Put them back for me, he says, any order you like. He moves the crystal ball aside and deals the cards into a pattern, turning the pictures with a flourish.

There's a man here, if you understand what I'm saying. You on the boards, are you?

Sort of.

Should do more. Got talent there. Shame to waste it. Not my place to say but there we are. Not easy for you, if you understand what I'm saying. I'll take your hands now, palms up, lay them here on mine, that's the ticket.

He peers at my fingers, tells me that I'll make old bones. There's glamour here, oh yes, and fame and fortune, have they come your way or are you still on the lookout, if you understand me?

I'm still on the lookout.

They'll be there for you, all your life, that's what I want to say. If you want it, that is, if you understand me. He puts my hands down, very gently, on the table and pats them twice. There we are then. It's been a pleasure.

And I'm out in the street, buying fudge that I eat until I'm sick. So is this what Alasdair does? Two-fifty the lot?

Alasdair says that he'll give me a bit of time alone with Leslie before he comes up. I pass on instructions about how to find the ward and get in the lift, no less tight-chested than I was yesterday. Leslie's chatting to the man in the next bed who looks very unwell, a watercolour in green and grey. I'm introduced, seized by the idea that his hand will come off as I shake it. 'This is Nat,' Leslie says. 'You'll never believe it, but he's a sound man.'

'Was,' says Nat, making almost no sound at all.

'I was telling him about you.'

'Very nice to meet you,' says Nat.

'You too.' We smile at each other. He closes his eyes. I wait a second or two but they stay shut so I turn to Leslie and whisper, 'Your blood transfusion's gone. That must be a relief.'

'No need to whisper, he drops off all the time.' He points to both sides of the mattress. 'I've still got two in. Have a butcher's at the drain and tell me what's going on.'

I look down. Whatever this is in the container, there's blood in it. 'It's filling up nicely.' I don't mention the blood.

'They're taking it out tomorrow. And getting me up.'

'That's good.' I kiss him, take my coat off and sit on the green chair. 'So. What's new?'

'They sent a detective to see me.'

'Did they? When?'

'Last night. I couldn't tell him much. They were white, no glasses, hoods up, ordinary. He said I'm lucky to be alive.'

After a lifetime of wearing them like garlands, my ethics have done a bunk. 'I want those boys locked up, the little shits.'

'Me too. The bloke said they'd do what they could, i.e. no bloody chance.'

I take his hand and hold it to my lips. He turns the palm in and cups my cheek.

'Are you hurting?'

He shakes his head then whispers, 'Have you clocked bunny boy over there?'

There's a new occupant in the opposite bed, a man in his eighties clutching a large toy rabbit. He's staring at me. I smile and he waves with the tops of his fingers, like a child out of a car window. I turn back to Leslie and we exchange raised eyebrows. 'Jimmy Hughes rang,' I say after a pause. 'Wanted to know how you were.'

'Little Jimmy! That was nice.'

'He says in all the time he's known you, you haven't changed a bit.'

'Did he say that? Aah, little Jimmy.'

'Don't you mind, though? Not being any different?'

'Of course I don't. He means I'm still fabulous. Why should I mind?'

'Why should you mind.' It's a statement, not a question. 'I've got your chocolate. Would you like some?' I take out the bars and lay them on the bed for him. 'I spoke to Max and he sends his love. And Jackie rang this morning to see if we wanted him home.'

'Did she? That was nice of her.' He chooses what he wants and pushes the rest at me. 'Bung that in the locker, would you? He can't come back, not when he's just got there. Did you tell him about Barney?'

'I couldn't, he was on a main road. It was hard enough trying to tell him about you. I'll do it tonight.'

He unwraps the paper, snaps off a square of chocolate and hands it to me. 'But you'll explain, you promise?'

'I promise. I can't believe you're so worried about it.'

'I'll feel better if Max knows, that's all. I suppose you've told Constance?'

'Max is ringing her. She'll be in touch, I'm sure.'

'Course she will. Soon as she knows. She'll want to talk to that CID bloke, chase him up.'

'How's the food?'

'I haven't been hungry.'

'I could cook you something and bring it in. Would you like that?'

'Maybe. Let's see how I am tomorrow.'

Alasdair arrives. I leave him by the bed and use my loo excuse to find a nurse. There are two at the desk, a man and a woman, talking over an open file. I wait. Eventually, the woman turns to me. She's in her forties, long brown hair, clear skin, big eyes. I like her immediately. I introduce myself.

'Oh, yes, *Leslie*,' she replies, in a voice you'd want to hear on the radio, 'I'm his nurse, my name's Fay.'

'Hello, Fay. I was wondering – there's a lot of blood in the container by his bed. Is that normal?'

'Absolutely. It's only the wound draining off. He's not very happy, I know, but don't worry. It's never easy on the second day. He's uncomfortable because his epidural's gone and he's wearing those tight stockings, and he's probably told you the catheter keeps pulling, but we'll take that out as soon as he's up. And the drain comes out tomorrow. He'll feel much better when he's walking about.'

Why hasn't Leslie told *me* that he isn't happy? What stockings? Fay's waiting in case I've got any more questions. 'Thanks,' I say. 'It's kind of you to explain.'

She smiles and walks off. I go back to the bed. I can't say anything in front of Alasdair but I'm alert, watching to see if Leslie touches the catheter or looks distressed. We talk about

Alasdair's flat, hospital food, Aude and Gully. After a while, Alasdair says, 'It's time you two were alone now. I'll wait for you downstairs, Mim.' He embraces Leslie, who closes his eyes for a moment and drops the entertaining face.

'You're tired,' I say. 'I'll go too.'

We leave him almost asleep. I wave from the doorway but he doesn't see.

It's only half-past three, so I ring Roy on the mobile to say I'm early but he tells me to go straight there and see the raised bed he's building opposite the back door. Alasdair and I don't say much in the car, except to comment on Leslie's luck in finding a decent hospital with enough nurses and no blood up the walls.

'If you get a good one, you'll be mended,' Alasdair says. 'If you get a bad one, you might as well toddle past the ward and go straight to the mortuary. And everybody's got a story. Me, I'd sooner take my chances and stay at home.'

'Even if you were dying?'

'Especially if I was dying.'

Roy asks about Leslie, repeats his astonishment at my knowing Alasdair and shows me the old bricks he's using. He has good planting plans; a nice eye for colour. I check my watch and it's five o'clock. 'I'd better go,' I say. A friend's bringing dinner.'

He takes his coat out of the cupboard. 'It's dark. I'll drive you.'

'Barney needs the walk.'

'Then I'll walk with you.' When we're halfway home, Roy says, 'Alasdair's amazing, isn't he?'

'He's a good friend.'

'I'm sure, but that's not what I mean. I went to see him when I was trying to get myself out of it, you know, the horrible house and all that. I'd been told he might be able to talk to Bonnie. And he did!'

'What do you mean?'

'She was in the room, right there, and Alasdair was crying – not his tears, he said, they were hers, he was feeling what she was feeling. She said all the things she'd wanted to say… things she was sorry about and silly things he couldn't have guessed. I tell you, Mim. That man's got the gift.'

'It sounds extraordinary.'

'It was. I'm surprised you've never asked him.'

'He's a friend…'

'Sing for your supper.'

'Exactly. How many times have you been?'

'A couple now.'

'Did your wife—?'

'No, she didn't turn up the second time. We talked about how I was coping and Alasdair told me a few things I needed to hear.'

For the rest of the walk, we work out a plan for tomorrow. I'll take Barney round at the usual time, then Roy can walk me back and come in for dinner. He's nearly finished painting the house, he says. I'll have to have the grand tour.

There are messages: Max and Charlie. Charlie says he's just heard about Leslie and would I ring him. Max says he wants the address of the hospital and he'll ring back this evening.

I feed Barney and pour myself a glass of wine. Then I set the table and tart up my face and all the time I'm thinking, I'm thinking… this must be telepathy, what Alasdair's doing… If he can talk to people who've died, then why didn't he offer to talk to Rolf, or my father? Does he get told what's going to happen to us? If he does, then maybe he knew about the mugging! Or perhaps it's selective, he's allowed to know some things and not others. Does he think I'll have no-one to shadow – that I'll be out in the open, on my own? He's harassing me because I've got so little time… Cut! If the gods have to summon a third to fill the quota, then let it be my brother. Leslie's staying here!

And this *gift*? If it's true, I'd describe it as a curse, being available to the next world. Imagine it, you're dead, wandering the streets, looking for a sympathetic ear. You find a phone box, not a red one but something lucent, crystal or mother-of-pearl. Inside, there are cards pinned to the wall – not *Miss Butterfly, needs mounting*, but ALASDAIR. *I always get through… let your Spirit be willing*. There's a receiver but it's transparent, and the line isn't attached to anything, it's free-floating, like a hair in water. When you're in the box, you think *Alasdair*, very, very hard and then the line straightens and points to the floor, earth, down here somewhere. As he connects, a little screen on the wall shows him talking to… Yes, your beloved! You speak into the receiver, bursting with loss, desperate to be heard. Alasdair listens. Oh yes, he says, I understand…

You try to make your message unique, something you've shared that has the authority of accuracy – how about that day last week, when the tank flooded? You were there, you saw it, you wanted to help but your hands kept passing through the bucket… the white freesias by your photograph… lemons… *Sergeant Pepper*…

I can't buy it. This place I'm inventing, it's no more than a jumble of heaven-films. Wherever I end up, if indeed I end up anywhere, it won't be full of infinite staircases and glittery dissolves. It's more likely to be a suburb with the dead coming in on the tube.

Charlie calls. He says he couldn't wait for me to ring back. 'It's outrageous, I can't believe it. What did they take?'

'Nothing.'

'All that for *nothing*! The poor darling. I want to visit.' I give him the details, then he says, 'So Max isn't coming back to see his dad? That's not so good.'

'There's no need.'

'Spain'll be a bit different. Mind you, it's not the best place if you've just sobered up. I'm not saying anything out of turn here, I assume?'

'Not at all.'

'He's worked hard, don't get me wrong, but he's no chicken – how old?'

'Forty.'

'Exactly. It's time for him to move on, try something new. I've never met this Jackie. What's she like? Is she a pretty girl?'

'Not particularly. So you're retiring. Is that right?'

'In January, fifty years to the week.'

'And what'll you do with yourself?'

'I'm going to sculpt, dear girl. I've built a studio in the garden and I'll be hiding myself away in there.'

'I didn't know you could sculpt!'

'I don't know if I can either, but I'll die trying.' His other phone starts ringing. 'Hold on, would you?' I wait. He's arguing, demanding more money than the contract offers. 'You know where I stand,' he says at the end. 'Call me back.' There's a rustling and then 'effing hell' and then 'Mim?'

'Yes, Charlie?'

'Actually, I've got something here you might be interested in.' He's silky again, on the make.

'What's that, Charlie?'

'It's a job—'

'No, Charlie.'

'Shall I tell you what it is?'

'Why are you putting me up for things?'

'I'm not. This came along, that's all. You're wanted again, Mim – you should enjoy it! I'll tell them you're a bit preoccupied, shall I? Maybe another time…'

'If you want.'

'It's an ad. For posh soup.'

'No ads.'

'As you wish, as you wish.'

'Sorry, but there it is.'

'No worries. Love to Leslie. God bless now.'

'Bye, Charlie.'

The phone rings again. It's Max, who tells me that Constance is probably going to write to the hospital and that Madrid's great, they're great, everything couldn't be greater. He wants to know how Leslie is and says that's great too. He'll ring again soon. Then Poppy arrives, with Alasdair close behind. She's bought a complete Indian takeaway, two carriers full. We clatter about unpacking while she tells us that Leslie's furious he's missing the dinner but glad she's here to keep me company; Alasdair puts out the bottles he's bought and polishes glasses and lights the candles; I put on Chet Baker and find the napkins and fleetingly, we're not three people in their seventies having a curry, we're flatmates celebrating payday.

'I'm drooling,' says Poppy, fishing about in the cutlery drawer. 'My body is *craving* spicy food.' She dispenses spoons into the tinfoil dishes, counting as she goes. 'Let's *eat!*' I'm half expecting her to refuse the lager but she tucks into everything on the table, an elated woman, free to come and go as she chooses. Which, of course, she was whenever Rolf was away, although she chose to be restrained by the very idea of him being in the world. Unlike Leslie, I'm not outraged because she's pitchforked their marriage over her shoulder but there's definitely an imbalance now, a surfeit of jollity.

As the beers loosen us up, I tell them about the posh soup ad.

'I'll do it,' says Poppy. 'Give them my number.'

'But you're going to America next week.'

'I'll change my flight.'

'OK, I'll ring him on Monday.'

We refill our plates. As Alasdair opens more lager, I say, 'I asked Roy about his reading or consultation or whatever you call it.'

'Did you now?'

'He thinks you've got the gift.'

Poppy's leaning forward, fork in hand. 'What gift? Who's Roy? What are you on about?'

I explain. She's confused. She looks at Alasdair. 'Have you been talking to Rolf behind my back?'

'No, my dear. Why would I do that?'

I've been a fool, mentioning this in front of Poppy. 'I don't think that's how it works,' I say. 'Is it, Alasdair?'

'Well, how *does* it work then?' When Poppy's not confident of her ground she gets a little ugly, as if we're being clever dicks, deliberately vague, possibly even laughing at her. 'I thought it was all faked anyway,' she says, 'this spooky-wooky lark. Do you mean you actually get messages? Proper messages?'

'Sometimes,' he says, picking up his lager.

'I want one! Let's do it now! *Get Rolf!*'

'You can't ask Alasdair like that.'

'Why not?'

We watch him draining the glass. He lowers it slowly, looking at Poppy. 'It's not on demand. I don't put in a chitty, a requisition: Rolf, here, now. If they want to talk to me and I'm in a proper frame of mind, then I might be lucky. Right now, I'm in a state you might think of as call waiting.' He tears off some nan bread. 'So you're off to America,' he says, wiping his plate. 'That's fantastic.'

Poppy ignores him and lifts her glass to me. 'And here's to good old Roy,' she says. 'Isn't this a bit of a dress rehearsal?'

'What for?'

'When Leslie's gone.' It takes me a second to understand what she means. This isn't ugly Poppy, this is full-on monster. I'm so shocked, I can't think of a single thing to say. I put my hand to my open mouth. She drinks and wipes the froth from her top lip.

'I've had enough,' says Alasdair, pushing away his plate. The CD ends. All we can hear is the boiler cutting in and the dog snuffling.

'I'll clear away.' We've eaten almost everything. Alasdair starts to stack the tinfoil while I collect the plates.

'I've buggered everything up,' Poppy says. 'I'm sorry.'

I shake my head. 'It's my fault. I shouldn't have said anything in the first place.'

'I'm sorry too.' Alasdair folds his napkin, corner to corner, twice, before putting it tidily on the table. 'I can't quite remember why, but I'm sure it'll come to me in a minute.'

Coffee and ice-cream and mouths washed out with soap.

As Poppy leaves, she rolls down her window and shouts, 'Call your agent, won't you? About that job?'

'First thing Monday.'

Alasdair walks me down the road and back again with Barney. We hardly speak, except to praise the curry. He says he'll see me tomorrow, outside Roy's house, one-thirty. I say good night and thank you. And then I sit on the sofa, my hands folded in my lap, until I'm calm enough to go upstairs.

Twenty-five

On Saturday morning, incredibly, I get another call from Charlie. 'Are you absolutely dead set against this soup ad? What's the harm?'

'Actually Charlie, I was going to ring you. Do you remember Poppy Lamb?'

'Who?'

'Poppy Lamb. Actress friend of mine. Did a lot of theatre?'

'Vaguely. Can't say I do.'

'I told her I'd put her in touch with you. She might be exactly what they're looking for.'

'They're interested in you.'

'If they met her—'

'You.'

'I've got a lot on my plate.'

'I know. But Leslie'd want you to ring, wouldn't he? If you won't do it for me, do it for him. Do it for Leslie.'

There's toast in the toaster, the kettle's nearly boiling. 'No, Charlie. Not for Leslie, not for you. I'm not interested.'

'All right, all right. Your choice. God bless.'

'Bye.'

I butter the toast so roughly that it breaks up under the knife, leaving me with clumps and holes. The phone rings again. I put on the answering machine in case it's Charlie and listen while I eat, holding the plate under my chin to catch the greasy crumbs.

From the first word I know her... it's Fay. 'This is a message for Mrs Lyo—'

I interrupt, pretending to be out of breath. 'So sorry, just walked in. Is everything all right?'

'Mrs Lyons?'

'Yes?'

'I'm calling from the hospital, the orthopaedic unit.'

'Hello, Fay.'

'Hello, Mrs Lyons.' There's no reason for her to ring me unless there's a problem. In a wink, I'm in disorder. I remember a gag about a telegram, *Bad news, details to follow*... 'I wanted to have a word, to give you an update on your husband. He's rather unwell this morning...'

Oh, no, don't do this.

'... A bit breathless and we're a little concerned so we've called the doctor, who's seen him and thinks it's probably a blood clot that's travelled from Leslie's leg to his lungs. So we've started treatment, some drugs into a drip and some oxygen to help him breathe. He's all right in himself but he said he'd like us to call you to let you know—'

Too many words and I don't like any of them. I interrupt her. 'Can I come in now?'

'It might be a good idea, if you'd like to.'

'I'm coming.'

Alasdair says that he'll be round in five minutes and Roy says he'll be waiting for Barney by the door. Running from room to room – it's like the night of the mugging – I gather what I'll need. Alasdair arrives. He's very calm. I put on Barney's lead and we drive round the corner to Roy's. He's calm too. 'You leave him with me,' he says. 'Off you go and don't worry.' In the ambulance I was quiet but now I'm talking gibberish, asking Alasdair where he went to school and why he left Scotland and he answers me properly, which is kind because if he were to try to bring me back to the present, in the car, driving to Leslie's blood clot, I'm not sure what I'd say. We're at the hospital quite quickly, but there's no parking space so Alasdair says he'll wait for one and follow me. I get out of the car, dread stacking up with every step as I go through the automatic doors and get into the stinking lift, belly fluttering, chest taut.

The desk's busy with doctors and nurses. I spot Fay but she's on the phone and I don't want to talk to anyone else, so I go and stand in front of her with my accommodating face. She sees me and mouths, 'I'll be with you in a minute,' then goes back to her call, her face grave. Is she asking me to wait because Leslie's dead? In a minute, when she puts the phone down, she'll lead me to the room where they break the news… I listen more intently… 'He's not very well at all,' she's saying. 'He's being moved into a side ward. Yes, today.' Side ward? Isn't that where they take you when you're on your way out? She puts the phone down and smiles at me. 'Hello,' she says, 'I wanted to explain what we're doing before you go in. The drip's there to give him the drugs he needs and the oxygen's to help him breathe.'

'I know,' I reply, 'you've told me that.'

'And he'll be having an X-ray soon,' she says, 'and a scan. You can stay with him, if you like.'

'Are you moving him?'

'No. Not at this stage.'

'So he's going to be all right?'

'Well, it's a serious complication but everybody responds differently to treatment. He's fit and well for his age and that's to his advantage.'

But he might die, that's what you're not telling me, Fay. To my own surprise, I think of the children and whether we should all be gathering round the bed, the family Lyons, assembling in grief. 'We have a son and daughter. Should I tell them?'

'Yes, that's a good idea.' I haven't got the mobile, it's the one thing I've forgotten. I haven't got Max's number either. I'll have to wait till I get home. She takes me to the bed. He's propped up. His eyes are closed, his skin's like candle wax and he's struggling to breathe, even with the oxygen. The noise is harrowing, a spaceman cast away from the mother ship, breathing his last.

'Look who's here, Leslie!' says Fay.

He opens his eyes. They're alone on his face, stranded over the mask. I put my hand over his. 'Don't try to speak. I'm here. You just keep breathing.' He grunts and coughs and closes his eyes again. I put my coat over the back of the green chair and sit down while Fay checks Nat in the next bed. He looks much worse today, if it's possible to look worse when you're already on the brink, almost decomposing. He's not asleep, he's unconscious. I don't know how I know that, but there's something in Leslie's face, pale and pinched as it is, that still declares consciousness. Perhaps Nat's the one who's off to the side ward. On her way back to us, Fay looks at the doorway, her eyebrows raised in query. I turn and see Alasdair, absurd in here in his red check trousers and his bright green jacket. I apologize for forgetting to mention him. It's all right, she says, he can stay. He gets a chair and sits next to me. 'Hi, Leslie,' he says. 'Alasdair here.'

276

Leslie opens his eyes and lifts a hand two inches from the bed. Drops it down. He might be asleep so I whisper, 'Did you find a parking space?' and then, 'Of course you did, or you wouldn't be here. Sorry.'

'What happens now?'

'They'll do a scan and take X-rays. She says I can go with him so there's no point you waiting. I could be here for hours.'

'I'll stay a while.'

And we're quiet again. I was never in a film that felt as much like a film as this. A woman sits by a hospital bed, staring at her husband. He's too ill to be thinking about anything but the next gulp of air, she's so frightened by the noise that she's leaped out of herself and settled on the ceiling where she waits…

Leslie lifts his mask and splutters, 'Barney!' I explain that I've spoken to Max and I'll be ringing him again tonight and that Barney's actually thriving. I turn to Alasdair for corroboration but he's staring wide-eyed at Nat.

'I think he's being moved,' I whisper, 'to a side ward.'

'Ah,' he says. 'Excuse me a moment.'

He leaves us and a minute later, he's back with a nurse. She goes to Nat's bed and touches his neck then pulls the curtains shut. Alasdair sits down again. 'What's happened?' I ask.

'He passed, that's all.'

'How did you know? He didn't make any noise.'

'I just knew.'

The nurse comes out and gives Alasdair an odd look before she fetches Fay who walks towards us, thinks better of it and does a sharp turn towards the curtains, shaking her head. I'm as confused as Fay but before I can ask Alasdair any more, Leslie's being collected for X-ray.

'I'll be here for hours yet,' I say to Alasdair. 'So I'll get a taxi home.'

'Ring me if you need to,' he says. And I want to ask, Does that mean you think I will – need you? But I don't because I don't want to know, which is feeble but true. When he's gone, I remember that I haven't got his number with me either.

There's plenty of time, during the rest of this awful day, to think about how he saw Nat dying but I don't, even though the bed's newly made when we come back to the ward. At lunchtime, I walk down to the café and buy a sandwich and a coffee and a paper that I never open. Fay says goodbye because she's off for the next three days and Leslie's new nurse, Gregor, comes in to take readings. He's tall, straightforward, a bit of a naval officer and he has to stoop a little to tell me that the news has come through – it's definitely a blood clot. 'You might want to go home and rest,' he says. 'Why don't you do that? Come back in the morning?'

I don't want to say, But what if he gets worse?, not in front of Leslie, so I say, 'And if there's anything to report?'

'I'll let you know.'

'Do you promise?'

'I'll let you know.'

Leslie lifts the mask and I kiss him, as quickly as I can. I remember a television programme with a woman who said that she'd climbed onto the bed next to her dying husband, to hold him in her arms, but the nurses made her get down because it wasn't safe or proper or some other pitiless bylaw. Shall I start a campaign for bigger beds? I want to stay here, next to him, where I can hear him breathe. But Leslie isn't dying, Mim, that's what you have to think.

When I get to Roy's it's nearly seven. He's welcoming and eager
to know how Leslie is. I tell him, and say that I've got a taxi
waiting.

'Why don't you leave Barney with me?'

'I think I'd like the company. Can I bring him back
tomorrow?'

'Of course you can. He's a lovely dog, no trouble at all.'

'I'm really grateful. You're being very kind.'

'Your Leslie, he's going to get well. This isn't a disease he's got,
it's the knock-on from his hip. They'll sort that out in no time.'

'I'm sorry about dinner tonight. Will you come round when
he's better?'

'Of course I will.' He picks up Barney's lead and gets him from
the kitchen. 'We had a good long walk this afternoon, didn't we,
boy? And he's been fed.'

'Thanks, Roy.' I hold out my hand then, on impulse, reach
forward and kiss his cheek. 'I'll ring you in the morning, when
I've spoken to the hospital.'

The house isn't right. It's dark and empty, not just unin-
habited for the day but *empty*, as if I've been given the keys to
a holiday cottage. Standing in the hall, I'm overwhelmed by
the simple tasks of doing lights and curtains and listening to the
answering machine, so I leave everything as it is and sit in the
curry smell in the kitchen, with Barney at my feet. I've still got
my jacket on, but I don't move for some time, not until the
phone rings.

It's Alasdair. 'How's Leslie?'

'The same.'

'Do you fancy a bit of company?'

I'm about to say no, I only want to sleep but on the other hand, being here alone… 'Yes, please.'

'I'll come straight round.'

I listen to the messages: Poppy, apologizing, Aude in Italy, complaining and leaving me her hotel number, two homes asking after Leslie.

When Alasdair arrives, we look in the fridge and dig out bacon, tomatoes and mushrooms on the edge of slime. He cuts the bread, faultless slices, two each. I don't ask about Nat Holloway, not yet, but we talk about the hospital and Leslie while the bacon sizzles and the smell of last night's curry is gradually overwhelmed by the burning fat. We're eating when the phone rings. I've left it in the hall and I dash out, tripping over Barney.

'Hello?' There's a delay. Oh, no. I get ready for the worst, holding my breath.

'Mum?'

'*Max*! I was going to ring you. Listen, your father's got a blood clot in his lung. He's not in very good shape.'

'You'll have to shout,' he shouts. 'I can't really hear you. There's a lot of noise in here.'

He's drunk! 'Where are you? What's going on?'

'It's over. Miss Violetta has found something bettah.'

'Did you hear what I said about your father?'

'Got a clot?'

'That's right. He's got a clot.' I'm shrieking now. 'It's serious. Do you understand?'

'Do *you* understand? My heart is *breaking*.'

'*Max!*'

'I rang Constance,' he says defiantly. I might have set fire to the house, Mummy but I saved the cat.

'Ring me when you're sober. I can't talk to you now. Ring me tomorrow.'

'If I'm still here.'

'Wherever you are. Ring me.' I hang up.

Alasdair's sitting with his chin on his hand, watching me come through the door. 'Everything OK?'

'Max.'

'Ah.'

'Jackie's dumped him and he's rat-arsed.' I sit down. 'Sorry, you shouldn't have had to hear all that.'

'You sounded pretty pissed off, Mummy Mim.'

'He doesn't give two stuffs about Leslie. It makes me mad.'

'What about your daughter?'

'He says he's told her. God knows.' I attack the bacon, stripping off the rind and picking it up to chew. 'They make me sick, both of them. How ill does he have to be?'

'I daresay they've got a point of view.'

'And what's that supposed to mean?'

'I think it takes a bit of history to give your parents the chop. What about your dad, eh? You couldn't bear to be in the same room.'

'My father did nothing for me, not once in his life, not ever. Leslie adores those children. He gave them everything.'

'So have you ever asked them what the problem is?'

'They were born like that, Alasdair. That's who they are.'

'You don't really think that.'

'You've got no idea. No children and no idea.'

'Yes, Mummy Mim.'

'Stop it.'

'Do you want my bacon rind?'

'No.' I put down my fork. 'I've got to go to the lavatory.' I don't need to go at all but Alasdair's back in his pulpit, fulminating at me, the ignorant sinner. He's got a point, of course – Alasdair always has a point. The children can't have been born entirely devoid of loyalty, but have we – have *I* – contributed to their retreat? I can't deal with this now. There's a book of cartoons to hand and I leaf through it for a minute or two, then flush the loo, just to demonstrate that I've been. I'm calmer now. As I sit back at the table, I say, 'Why don't you tell me about Nat.'

'Who's Nat?'

'The man who died in front of you today.'

Alasdair sighs, picks up his mug and looks at me over the rim. 'What do you want to know?'

'What you saw.'

'Hard to describe, really. He left, that's about it.'

'But how did you *know*.'

'He didn't sit up and float off in his pyjamas, if that's what you're thinking. That only happens in the movies. It's more like a feeling… You know when you see something out of the corner of your eye? Well it's a bit like that… *plus* a feeling… imprinted with seeing a shadow, but not really. Is that clear?'

'Not in the least.'

'A slip of a shadow, or the other way round, a shadow slipping away, that's it.'

'And what do you think the person – what did Nat – feel when that was happening?'

'I have no idea. I've been told lots of different things. I suppose it depends who you are and how you die and what you're expecting to find when you get there.'

'Is Leslie going to die?'

He puts down the mug. If he says Yes, I won't believe it. If he says No, I won't believe that either. What he says is, 'I can't answer that.'

'Give me a reading.'

'What, now?'

'Yes.'

'Why?'

'Because you might be able to tell me what's going to happen.'

'I don't work with friends, Mim. You know that.'

'This is different, isn't it? Please?'

Alasdair rubs his lips with his middle finger and stares at me, then heaves himself up in the chair. 'I'm not saying I'll get anything, and even if I do, there's no guarantee it'll be about Leslie. Do you understand that?'

'I understand.'

'And I'm not going to do this as if you were a client. I'll just see if I can get anything on Leslie, OK?'

'OK.'

We clear the table and sit down again. Barney gets off his blanket and lies heavily on my feet. 'May I have one of your rings?' Alasdair asks. I take off my wedding ring, the easiest. He holds it between his hands and closes his eyes. 'I need to tune in.'

What am I doing? Leslie would be outraged! I didn't even tell him about Portento... I think I should stop this right now. A huge mistake, big apologies. But what about Nat Holloway? When Alasdair said what he'd seen, I pictured my death bed. That's what frightens me, not where I'm going afterwards. It'll all be over. *I'll* be over. But not if I'm going somewhere else...

'There's a man here, in a suit. Quite smart, but old-fashioned. Harry, is it?' Alasdair opens his eyes so wide that he startles me.

He's rubbing my ring between his finger and thumb. 'Yes, he says his name's Harry. Does that mean anything to you?'

'Yes,' I whisper. 'It does.'

'Harry wants you to know he's glad he's found you.' Alasdair listens, his head slightly tilted. 'He's sorry he didn't help you when you were young. He says his son was mad as a two-bob watch, keeping you away. Does that make sense to you, Mim, what he's saying?'

'It does, it does.'

'And Harry wants you to know he's watching over Leslie. He's been there all along.'

'Where?'

'He's describing the ward. That big bucket, he says, by Leslie's bed. The one with the blood in it. You were worried about that, you asked the nurse. Leslie's going to be all right, that's what he says.'

'Is he?'

Alasdair nods. He's talking to a man who's been dead for fifty years or more. And I want to believe him! I blow my nose.

Closing his eyes, Alasdair puts his fingertips together, high like a church roof, and then lowers his head slightly as if he's examining something on his lap. 'What's this book?' he says. 'A book with red writing on the front. No, it's a red cover.'

'I jot things down, that's all. How do you know about my book? No-one knows about my book.'

'I'm being shown a book. Harry's showing me a book, that's all I can tell you.'

'Is he *sure* about Leslie?'

'He was sure… He's gone now.'

'Oh.'

Silence. The fingertip roof. 'And Spain... is that to do with Max? No, not Max. Something to do with Spain. A man... a Spanish man?' He looks at me, wanting information.

A man who's involved with Max? I can't think of anything else. Oh, Bernard! 'My brother?' I say, so pleased to be helpful. 'He lives there. That must be who it is.'

'It's not your brother. I can't get any more on that. Except it isn't Spain, it's a man who's got connections there...'

'It must be Max.' I'm too noisy, too normal, I'm going to drive the spirits away. I lower my voice. 'Is he in trouble?'

'I'm sorry, my dear. I can't get anything else. But you've got your answer as far as Leslie's concerned. He's going to be all right.' He smiles and hands me back the ring. 'Good news, eh?'

'Good news.' We consider each other. I have no idea what I should be saying or doing at this point. 'What normally happens when you've finished?'

'People say thank you. That's quite common.'

I snap, 'Thank you,' and immediately regret it. 'How *did* you know those things?'

'I'm glad we found out about Leslie.'

'And did I not mention Harry to you?'

'Not that I know of. Who is he?'

'My grandfather, Harry Shaw. I never met him. My father had him put in a home – it was his big secret. I only found out at my father's funeral, or rather, Leslie did.' I push Barney off my feet and get up. 'Really, Alasdair, that was extraordinary. I'll ring the hospital and see how he is.'

The switchboard takes a long time to answer, and then the nurse who answers for the ward takes a long time to find the person who's looking after Leslie and while I'm waiting, Alasdair does the washing-up and puts everything away. A woman comes to the phone, a staff nurse. 'I'm afraid there's no change,' she says.

'No change?'

'He's no worse, Mrs Lyons. He's as comfortable as we can make him.'

I tell Alasdair, who says, 'We'll have to resign ourselves to a bit of a wait then. Are you all right? About tonight?'

'I think I'm a bit dazed, actually. I wasn't expecting you to say anything quite so… unexpected. But thanks.'

On which note, he goes home, telling me to call him in the morning. I'm glad I asked for the reading, but even so I'm feeling – not wrong-footed exactly – but uneasy, trying to reconcile Alasdair's abracadabra with the world I think I know. The banal interpretation: he read my mind, he caught a glimpse of the red book, Leslie mentioned Harry in passing. Or Harry's really watching, in which case, *where is he*? I'm out of my depth and Barney needs to go out, so I get dressed for the cold and we dawdle round the garden in the light from the conservatory. There's work to be done out here, jobs I haven't been attending to… The messenger might like sticking his nose in, but I can't help being encouraged by the message: Leslie should be out of danger soon.

Bed, the worst place. I'm trying to read myself to sleep but it's not working: no sand in the eyes, not so much as a grain of it. I need a more boring book. Barney's on the bed – he's too big but we've both realized that I'm not going to make him sleep downstairs – and he's having a doggy tizz, turning twice on the spot and then settling back exactly where he was. Is Harry here, watching me? Does he follow me about?… I say, 'Hello, Harry,' to the ceiling, assuming that he'll be elevated if he's in here at all, then I get up, nearly smothering the dog with the duvet, and fetch the red book and a pen. With a fleece round my shoulders and Leslie's pillows added to mine, I get back into bed. There, settled. I open the book. The last entry's a talk with Harry – peas on toast and the holy goats. I'm not writing a play, Grandad, whatever you might say. No play, no novel, nothing laborious, nothing that might look as if I'm trying to compete with Leslie. I take the lid off the pen and press it onto the base.

Leslie, I miss you. Alasdair asked Harry who says you're going to be all right.

Am I writing to Leslie then? Not about Alasdair, I'm not! A pretend letter? An As If letter – as if he'd listen if I said,

I'm sorry about our children, Leslie. Alasdair says we should ask them why they've turned out as they have, why they don't like us. You'd have said that's nonsense, of course they like us. I said they were born that way, but Alasdair knows better, and he's right. Constance has been meticulous in her cutting-off, no surgeon ever did better with a leg. And now Max is a jilted drunk. Isn't there a point when you begin to behave according to your proper nature? Or can your parents really twist that so totally out of true that nothing of your original self remains? Unless they offer you the opposite to butt up against – did Constance use our inconsistency to polish up her self-possession?
    This is tosh. I wasn't polished by my father, I was made miserable. Max was loveable once. Constance was serious, nothing more. So what did I do wrong? More than once, the belittling.

Wanting them to be cute, to be toy stars. Is that enough? Or letting them down, being too noisy, too lazy. And then the opposite, expecting them to behave like soldiers on parade – be this, be that, be whatever I want, whenever I say.

Who are you? What do you want? Did I ever ask them that?

And Leslie – why did you always confuse love with giving in? Not that you made any rules to break. Love me, my children. You'll never hear me raise my voice, you'll never hear me say no! Mummy says no. Mummy gets cross. Look, she even gets cross with me!

But, Daddy, says Constance, that's not how the world works. I want laws.

And, Mummy, says Constance, you only care about yourself. You make me sick.

I put down the pen and cup my eyes in my hands. I hate Alasdair. He drives me to think. Ho ho, very funny. I tell Harry we're going downstairs now, to find a book that'll send me off. Tonight I just want to sleep. The collected works of Dr Spock, that should do it.

Twenty-six

I ring the hospital as soon as I wake up. The nurse – a voice I don't recognize or like – says she's only just come on and doesn't know how Leslie is. Hang on. I wait. She comes back. 'No change.'

'I'm coming in soon, if that's all right?'

'Up to you.'

'Give him my love, would you? And tell him I'll be there sometime this morning?'

'OK.' And she hangs up. Why isn't he better? The drugs should be working by now. It's too early to call Alasdair, so I have breakfast and try to read the Sunday paper. Then, as I'm picking up the phone, it rings. 'Is this all right?' Poppy says, without introducing herself. 'I thought nine was a good time so I waited. In case you were having a lie-in.'

'I've been up for ages.'

'How's Leslie?'

'Not very good.' And I tell her, and of course she feels even worse about what she said and she's quiet for a moment. Then she asks whether I mentioned her name to Charlie.

'I did, but they're after me for some reason. Sorry.'

'*Que sera*, long odds. Why wouldn't he want you? You're perfect.'

'For what?'

'Whatever it is he wants you for. Are you going to follow it up?'

'Not till Leslie's better. If at all.'

'No, of course you're not.'

'When are you off?'

'Wednesday. Wednesday afternoon.'

'I might not see you before you go.'

'It's quite hectic. I'll call you later, see how Leslie is.'

And that's probably that.

Roy's daughter opens the door, I recognize her immediately from the photograph. She's in her thirties, small with short, thick, fair hair sloping off from a side parting and a full-of-beans face.

'I'm Stevie,' she says. 'And you must be Miriam. And Barney!' She shakes my hand and stands aside as Roy comes up the hall.

'Have you got a minute to come in?' he says.

'A minute. Alasdair's picking me up.'

'Dad's told me about your husband,' Stevie says, leading us into the sitting-room. 'Toe-rags.'

We sit down. Roy's next to me on the sofa. He puts his paint-stained hand on mine and says, 'They'll find a way to help him through it, you'll see.'

Kindness is the unendurable offering. My eyes brim but Stevie rescues us. 'Dad gave me that film of yours. I saw it last night. You were brilliant!'

'Thanks. I'm glad you—'

'That bastard, locking you up. Sorry, Dad! Anyway, locking you up like that – he's in a soap now, isn't he? – I wanted to kill him! Dad says that was your last film. I can't believe it!'

'I had children and…'

'Didn't you want to go back though? After?'

'Stevie!' Roy's rebuke isn't harsh but she says, 'Whoops, I'm being gobby.'

'It doesn't matter. I'm really pleased you liked it.'

'Well, I did. And you're fantastic.'

I smile at her and stand up to look out at the street. Alasdair's there, singing and tapping on the steering wheel. 'I'd better go. Thanks again, Roy. Shall I call you from the hospital?'

'I'm taking your Barney to madam's here for lunch' – he points back at Stevie with his thumb – 'but I'll be back by four at the latest.'

Before I can say a formal goodbye to Stevie, she puts her arms round me and hugs me tightly. 'Your husband'll be all right, I'm sure he will, and I'm sorry if I said too much.' Perfect daughter and her perfect dad. If I'd been given a choice of father, he'd definitely have got the job.

Alasdair's listening to Jerry Lee Lewis. He turns it off as I get in. I turn it back on. 'Leave it. It'll buck me up.'

'How're you doing?'

'Well enough. How about you?'

'Aye, blooming.'

I consider saying something about last night and decide against it, then I consider telling him that Roy and Stevie love *The Curfew* and decide against that too. There's no more conversation until we're in view of the hospital. Then, 'I've been wanting to ask you,' I say, 'how come you're so free these days?'

'What makes you think I'm free?'

'Because you're always ferrying me about.'

'Ah. I've got a job next week. But I'm all yours till Tuesday.'

'Lucky me.'

'Funny how things turn out.' He pulls up at the main door. 'I'm off to do a bit of shopping for the flat but you've got my number, I presume, so you let me know when you want picking up. Understood? And I'll pop in to the ward and say hello to Leslie. You be brave now, he's getting better.'

Alasdair's talking to me as if I'm being dropped off at school – from having no father at all, I seem to be gathering a small flock. I get out of the car and lean through the open door. 'If you're shopping, why don't I get a cab?'

'Because I want to play taxis.'

'Are you sure?'

'Go and bother Leslie.' He gives me a thumbs-up and pulls the door shut. I blow him a kiss and watch as he drives away.

I want to see Leslie, of course I do, but I can't quite face the ward, not yet. I stand in reception, choosing between a seat here in the deserted foyer or a cup of coffee in the café but of course it's Sunday morning and it's closed. Rolled-down shutters, high ceiling, grey tables, it's as convivial as a boiler room. I get coffee from the machine and sit down, choosing a table well away from the few others that are occupied. The paper's in my bag in case Leslie wants me to read to him. I fish out the magazine, put on my specs and peer over the rims to see who else is patient-shy. There's a bald man, my age, holding his chin and staring at the floor, a couple talking quietly, hands linked on the table, a woman in a black beret, reading. A blonde in a black coat, writing, one hand supporting her head… she picks up a bottle of water from the table and takes the top off, still looking at what she's written… she lifts her head to drink…

It's Constance.

I turn away, put everything in my bag, get out of the chair as quietly as I can and hurry to the lift, heart hammering. But what if she's seen me? What if she follows me upstairs? I'll hide here… wait near the doors…

'Hello, Mum.'

Oh, God, too late. Slap-bang cornered and I turn round before I can control my face, my dismay. 'Hello! Where did you spring from?'

'I was in there.' She points. 'With you.'

'No!' She's too thin… What do I say next? Is this how she stares at criminals? 'I didn't see you! Have you been up to your father?'

'Not yet. How is he?'

I step forward, an inch only, unsure whether to reach out. I can't shake hands with her, I can't hold her. I can't do anything. She makes no move at all. I step back, the whole inch. 'Don't know. I mean, not since I rang this morning. He was the same then, the same as yesterday, that is. Are you off duty?'

'I am.'

'You've lost weight.' *No, no, no!* Don't say that! 'But it suits you. You look well.'

The couple from the café appear, wanting to use the lift. We stand aside and watch as the doors open and close, neither of us making a move to get in.

'So what happened exactly?' she says. 'Max tells me he was mugged.'

'He was. Two boys. He was walking Barney, that's Max's grey-hound – we're looking after him – and the boys had a dog as well and Leslie fell over them, the dogs that is. I'm not explaining very well, am I? Anyway, they didn't get anything but your poor father broke his hip. And now he's got this blood clot in his lung so it's all rather difficult.' I'm so unnerved by having to tell her this story that I recount most of it looking at the lift buttons. Off-duty or not, this is a policewoman. Anyone watching us would assume – what? That we barely know each other. We're not even tiptoeing into the shallows of our separation; we've still got our shoes on and the tide's going out.

'And no luck finding them?' she says.

'None at all.'

'I'm afraid to say that's the usual outcome.'

'So we were told.'

'I might ask around a bit, see what I can find out. Do you want to go up first? I can wait down here.'

'No, no. I'm going to be with him all day. Why don't you go? He'll be so pleased.'

The bald man arrives. He presses the lift button and we all look at the doors.

'We might as well go up together then,' she says.

'Why not.' In the lift, the bald man rubs his eyes and yawns. Nobody speaks. I study her back, her expensive coat. She frightens me. Do I still look like the person she keeps in her mind's eye, the mother she hates? Or am I someone she has to bat away, an ageing stranger? Once, Constance, we were *one inside the other*. The lift bumps to a stop. 'It's a bit of a warren in here,' I tell her. 'They don't make it easy to find your way. But I expect you're in and out of hospitals all the time, if telly programmes are anything to go by.' We push through a set of swing doors. I indicate a right turn. 'CID came to see your father. Are you CID now?'

'Yes, I am actually.'

I don't know what you do, day-to-day, I don't know the man you live with, if you've got a garden, how you look in uniform. Who are your friends? Have you told them why we never see each other? I want to apologize. I want to stop now, here in the corridor, and tell you that I'm sorry. But I don't. I keep walking. As we come into the ward, we see a nurse at the desk, fussing with a thick file stuffed with papers. She's young, with eyes tucked in under snake-lids.

'Good morning. I'm Mrs Lyons, Leslie's wife.'

She looks through me, no, *at* me, as in Whaddyawant, and says nothing.

'I think we might have spoken a couple of hours ago. Is Leslie—' I dry up, silenced by her scowl. Find a voice. 'How is he?'

'Like I told you, no change.' And she doesn't care and never will, and she's doing this job because she was too fierce for the Paras.

'I'll go straight through, then.'

A shrug. 'Sure.'

He's asleep. Does he sleep all day when I'm not here? They've taken away the mask and put plastic pipes up his nose. It's a relief not to see the paradox of the suffocating oxygen mask, and the drip's gone too. I walk round the bed. They've taken the drain out. I feel as if I'm introducing Constance to an exhibit. We stand by the bed and whisper. Her hair smells of shampoo or conditioner, it's aromatic, a patch of sweetness in the antiseptic. I tell her that I have to find someone who knows how Leslie's getting on and leave her in the green chair, watching him.

Gregor! I can just see him through a crack in the office door. I knock. He answers, inviting me in. Leslie's still very poorly, he says, but they've taken out the drip because his blood's less likely to develop another clot now. They're going to inject him instead. 'But the *other* nurse' – I say this carefully, not wanting to sound as if I think she's got a heart like a swinging brick – 'the *other* nurse tells me he's no better.'

'Not at the moment, no. But he's no worse, either.'

'But if he's no better, doesn't that mean…'

Gregor's hands are very capable, practised hands, well shaped. He picks up a pen and balances it between two fingers. 'It means we can't be sure of the outcome,' he says, 'not at this point. But he's fit and well for his age and that's—'

'To his advantage?'

'That's right, Mrs Lyons. That's absolutely right.'

'Thank you, Gregor.'

'You're very welcome.'

Leslie's awake, alone, waving at me. 'Guess who's been in!'

'Hello, darling. Constance. Has she gone already?'

'To the loo, be back in a minute. Did you ask her to come?'

'No, Max told her you were ill.'

'*That* ill?'

'No, just ill.'

Talking exhausts him and he stops, putting the back of his hand over his mouth and then dropping it to his chest as he falls asleep. His lids are grey, the skin below his eyes looks as if it's been pressed flat by a sooty thumb, his cheeks are hanging off the bone. I've never seen him with such a face, not in my worst imaginings. Turn *this* into a knees-up, Leslie Lyons…

After a while, Constance comes back. Her make-up's freshened but she's still red-eyed and tight about the mouth. Leslie surfaces again. 'There's my girl,' he whispers, 'get another chair.' She sits down and he takes her hand. This is a portrait: the beloved daughter, half the way home, the son missing, believed drunk. They're talking, he's asking her how *she* is! I can't hear what she answers, her back's to me and she's talking too quietly, but he smiles and says, 'If I was really ill, I would…'

After five, maybe ten minutes, Leslie goes back to sleep and releases her. I expect her to say goodbye to me and leave, but she asks if we could go back to the canteen.

Together?

Together.

On the way down, she doesn't speak. I talk about Leslie's treatment, then I'm quiet until we've dealt with the machine and got two coffees. There are more people now but she leads us to a corner and pulls me out a chair. I'm going to be interviewed, that's my first thought. Guilty as charged, that's my second. I take my jacket off and sit with it on my lap, waiting.

'I didn't realize it was that serious,' she starts. 'He looked so well at the funeral.'

'Did he? Yes, he did. Of course he did.'

'So what's the prognosis?' she asks.

'They can't be sure. Not yet.'

'Are you – on your own?'

'I've got good friends,' I say.

She nods. 'I never flap, you know—'

'I know.'

'But this is quite…'

'… alarming?'

'It is, it's alarming. I'll come back tomorrow. I'm not sure when, but I'll definitely be here.'

'He'd love that.'

As if prompted by a whistle, we both pick up our plastic cups and drink.

'You weren't able to come to the funeral?' she says.

'I was ill. I'm sorry I didn't see you.'

She tenses her neck. 'The thing is, Mum…' How odd that sounds. Here I am imagining her in the dock, giving evidence – effortless gravitas, even sitting in this café. And then she calls me Mum and hey presto, she's six. 'I know it's been a long time.' She waits, expecting me to interrupt.

I'm watching you, Constance. I'm listening. I'm not going to speak until you've said everything you want to say, and even then I'm only going to tell you that you're right. Whatever you say, you're right. And you're beautiful…

'I wanted to explain about your father's money,' she says solemnly. 'I did try, you know, but he absolutely wouldn't change his mind – it's the only argument we ever had. Mrs Wilmott's share, that was a different matter. I think she was very kind to him over the years, and it seemed perfectly proper to reward her for that. And I'm aware that you saw him infrequently—'

'Twice a year. Calls every Sunday.'

'Whereas I went quite often. And Max never went at all. But I daresay you both had your reasons, and I'm not here to sit in judgement.'

Don't be pompous. Please. Not when I'm trying so hard to see the best of you.

'So when the executors have sorted everything out, I'm giving a third of my inheritance to Max and the other third to you.'

'I don't want the money, Constance. Please keep it. Split it with Max if you must,' I hold up my hands, 'but not me.'

'Why not? You must have a use for it.'

'We're quite comfortable.'

'Have a holiday. Or a cruise. Wouldn't that be nice, when Dad's recuperating?'

'Your father loathes cruises. He'll be much happier convalescing at home. The money's yours. Your grandfather wanted you to have it because he loved you.' She sighs and bends her head. I pull back her hair, like I used to, so that I can see her face. 'Why's it so important? That I take it?'

'Because I want to be fair.'

My hand falls away. 'He didn't like me and he didn't want to give me anything. Which is why I don't want anything from him. Do you see?'

CID and child-Constance flicker across her face. She reaches into her handbag and pulls out a large envelope. There's no ring on her wedding finger, but perhaps that's politic, particularly if you're a professional, a detective. 'I've got something for you,' she tells me.

'Is this from him?'

'No.'

She hands it to me but I put it down, between us. 'It's not a cheque, is it?'

She shakes her head. 'Did Dad tell you what we found out? About your grandfather?' I nod. 'It must have been a bit of a shock, getting news like that. I take it you'd never been told.'

'Never.' I look at the table. 'So what's this?'

'Grandad gave me a bag of papers—'

'Evidence?'

Almost a smile. 'I found this.' She picks up the envelope and hands it to me again. 'Open it.' Carefully, in case it's something

I don't want to see, I lift the flap and see the top of a yellowed newspaper cutting. I look up, wanting reassurance. She nods. 'Go on.'

I slide the cutting out, wondering if it relates to me. It's an old typeface, very hard to read – am I so ancient that my reviews are crumbling? Hold on, while I find my glasses. Ah, it's not me. I begin to hope... the headline: A *Thrilling Night Out*. A grainy photograph, actors in costume, Shakespeare – looks like Lear. Scan the page, the names...

Mr Harry Shaw, a very personable Gloucester.

I peer at the faces.

Constance says, 'Second from the left. You could get it blown up, you'd see him more clearly. Was I right to bring this for you?'

'You were very right. Thank you.'

'I expect you're sorry not to have met him.'

'Very.' I'm still studying the photograph, trying to absorb it.

She nods. 'I'd better go. I'm working this afternoon.'

I put Harry back in his envelope and drop him into my bag. At the main doors, I say, 'So you might come tomorrow?'

'I'll try.' She gives me a card. 'Here are my numbers. You'll call me...?'

'Of course. But he'll be all right, I'm sure he will.' I manage a tight smile.

Then she's through the door and gone, a swing from the black coat, a blonde on the run. I sit down on the nearest chair and have another look at Harry.

The day looms. There's a knack to this, surviving the hours. When I get back to the ward, Leslie's still asleep, so I read the paper until he wakes up. He's happy, he's seen Constance. He wants to know if she's told me anything but I say No, nothing she didn't tell you, then I read to him. A nurse encourages him to move a little in the bed. His food arrives and I help him eat.

Then I go down to the café – it's open now – but I can't face sitting in there again so I find a pub and have a Guinness and a cheese baguette. Up to the ward, no change. The failed Para walks past with another nurse and whispers, 'That's a tough cookie,' wagging her head at me. *You don't know the half of it, dearie…*

I go on reading. I watch him. I doze. Sometimes we talk, not for long because it tires him out and he gets breathless, but at one point he says, 'Don't believe everything they tell you.'

'Everything who tells me?'

'About me, how I am. I'm not dying.'

'You're not dying! Of course you're not! Nobody thinks that.' I kiss his hand and hold it to my face. He moves a finger, to stroke my cheek. When he's peaceful again, I walk round the corridors to stretch my back, noting landmarks so I don't get lost. I examine the other visitors and watch a new patient settle into Nat's bed. The nurses come to inject Leslie in the stomach, test his oxygen levels and empty his catheter. No change, Mrs Lyons, not yet. I pop in to see Gregor, before he leaves. 'We've taken some blood,' he says, 'and we're waiting for the results.' I ask if I can call later. Of course I can, any time.

Day over, Mim, I'm not doing the evening shift. It's dark outside and Leslie's asleep, and I might as well have a proper meal and a rest before I start again tomorrow. This is my new life: Alasdair, Roy, the green chair, Alasdair, Roy. And this is Leslie's new life, a pin in his leg, plastic piping up his nose, all

Twenty-seven

I get a taxi because I don't want to talk to Alasdair, then I ring
him and lie, pretending that I couldn't get through, that his
phone was up the creek. He knows I'm making it up, he knows
I know he knows, but he doesn't try to catch me out, he simply
asks how things are and tells me to ring in the morning, or later
if I want to talk. I stop to buy emergency rations and keep the
taxi waiting at Roy's, then we're home, me and Barney boy.

I need to think. Sitting by that bed should allow for hours of
reflection but the opposite's true, all I do is hold steady as Leslie
breathes and the other patients talk to each other and to me and
the trolley comes with pills and then food and they're checking
this and doing that – it's difficult enough to read the paper,
rumination's out of the question. Athough there was a moment
of grief today, when I was looking at his face, a pinhole in the
parapet, nothing more…

I make dinner and watch TV for half an hour while I eat.
Then I lie down flat on the sofa and pick up the envelope with
Harry's cutting that I've put close by me on the coffee table. The
phone rings. Why do I never remember to bring it in? Shouting,
'Wait! Wait!' I struggle up and dash to the kitchen.

'Hi, Mum. It's Max.' Charitably, I assume that he's rung to see how his father is or because he's heard from Constance and he's anxious now, considering a flight home. I think all that in the gap before he says, 'I'm not having a very good time here.'

'Your father's still very ill.' I press on with my end of the conversation, whether he's interested or not. It's a bad line as well, and he's drunk. 'Constance came to see him today. Has she rung you?'

'No. How is he then?'

'There's no improvement.'

'What a bummer.'

'He can't breathe without oxygen.'

'Shit.'

Last night, Max, I was guilty. I wanted to make amends. I wished you a different childhood with a mother who didn't try to turn you into a pet rat, dressed to do tricks in your dear little sailor suit. How is it that tonight –

'I'm coming home.'

'Really?'

'I can't keep paying out for hotels now I'm by myself. So what I was thinking is that I could stay with you for a few weeks while I get another flat. Then I can see Dad, give you a hand...'

'No!'

'Why not?'

'Because I don't want you living here.'

'For God's sake. Why not?'

'It's not convenient, Max. Not at the moment.'

'So what do you want me to do? I can't stay here, don't you understand? Nobody bloody well speaks English and if they do I haven't got a clue what they're talking about and Jackie's left me and you don't give a shit. Thank you very much. I haven't even got a home to go to any more. Fucking hell, Mum. Give me a break.'

'Max.'

'What?'

'Listen to me! Your father's very ill.'

'Exactly! That's why I've got to come home! But where am I supposed to *sleep*?'

'Haven't you got any friends?'

'Not with a room.'

'A floor?'

'Suppose I stay for two days? Two days, that's all. I'll sort something out. I'll ask Charlie. I'll tell them to get out of my flat. Two days?'

While he's talking, I'm looking through the address book. Aude! If I could get a key… 'Max?'

'Yeah?'

'I've had an idea. Ring me in half an hour.'

The rumination's going west. Aude's at the hotel, a stroke of luck. When I tell her how Leslie is, she says she wants to come back and help me out. There's no need, I say, but I do want to ask her a big favour. Anything, sweet pea, anything at all. I explain about Max, '… and of course it's ended in disaster and he wants to come home but he's rented his flat out. Is yours going to be empty for a week or two?'

'Mim, I'm selling up! We're going to Lucca. Gully wants to grow olives.'

'In Italy?'

'It's exciting, isn't it?'

The parallel with Max is so unambiguous that I'm amazed

she hasn't seen it. 'Wouldn't you be better off renting yours out for a bit? You might—'

'Not likely. North London, dreary, dreary. Anyway, of course Max can stay at the flat, sweetie. No point trying to sell till after Christmas, is there? The keys are with Hermione, upstairs. I'll give her your number and say Max'll be picking them up in a day or two, is that right? You'll have to show him how to work the central heating.'

'Please don't sell up, not until you're sure. What happens if you get olive pest?'

'I don't think I'll ever want to come back. Why don't you and Leslie visit, as soon as he's better? It's so beautiful here. You'll love it.'

'I miss you.'

'I miss you too.'

'I'll make sure Max pays his way.'

'I'll ring tomorrow to see how Leslie is.'

I lie down again and pick up Harry's cutting. The phone rings.

'Is that Mim?'

'Yes.'

'It's Jackie. You know, Jackie of Max and Jackie.'

'Hello, Jackie.' Stretching my legs the length of the sofa, I give myself an agonising cramp in the foot.

'I hope this isn't an awkward moment—'

'Not at all.' My face is screwed up with pain, I'm kneading my instep.

'I've been thinking about Leslie and wanting to ask you how he is.'

'He's – all right, Jackie. Thank you.'

'Is he in hospital?'

'Yes, he is. And how are you?'

'It's very nice here. Mim?'

'Yes, Jackie?'

'Have you spoken to Max at all?'

'He told me you'd split up. Is that right?'

'Yes, that's absolutely right. I did try. I tried all the way there, in the car, but I'm afraid it wasn't enough. And I didn't want you to think badly of me because I know you'll be wondering if there's something I could have done to stop him, but… there wasn't. And I did my very best, I can promise you that.'

'I'm sure you did, Jackie. Please don't blame yourself.'

'We're very different, Max and I, and I don't think either of us understood exactly *how* different until we were actually travelling. A small space like that, it snowballs with a vengeance. I don't want to sound as if I'm criticizing him. You don't think that, do you? But he went his own way and there wasn't anything I could do. I told him, I said your parents are going to think I've let you down.'

'We'd never think that.' My foot's stopped hurting. I stand and wiggle it about.

'Thanks.' Pause. 'Mim?'

'Yes, Jackie?'

'I also wanted to say… I wondered… well, when I've got a proper home, you could both come and stay. It's lovely here. Leslie could convalesce in the sunshine.'

'That's very kind, Jackie. Thank you.' We wish each other well and say we'll keep in touch, but it's goodbye to another passing encounter, a well-mannered weed in my life's garden.

I'm not going to bother to lie down again, not if I'm going to

307

be interrupted. This time it's the door. Alasdair, in an enormous mac, a brown tarpaulin. Is he preparing for a storm at sea?

'Cakes and wine,' he tells me, holding up a plastic bag. 'I assume you've had your veg. I won't stay if you'd rather be be alone, but I was passing and I thought I'd offer you the option. Of me.' He hands over the bag and takes his coat off.

'You smell like a tyre.'

'I bought it today. Do you not like it?'

The phone rings. I give Alasdair back the bag and tell him to go in the kitchen.

It's Max, ringing back early. 'Not quite half an hour,' he says, 'but I'm going nuts here.'

'Aude's away and she says you can have her flat for a few weeks.'

'Where is it?'

'Crouch End.'

'No tube.'

'I'll tell her you don't want it, shall I?'

'I was thinking about getting to work, that's all. I'll manage. Thanks for sorting it out.'

'No problem. Are you all right?'

'I'll live.'

'Leave a message, tell me when you're due in.'

'Will do.'

'Take care, Max.'

'Say hello to Dad.'

Alasdair's opening the wine. 'I won't stay long.' I turn on the answering machine then turn it off again, just in case, and we take a tray into the sitting room.

'So?' Alasdair says, balancing his plate on his knee. 'Tell me what's happened to you, every second of it since this morning.'

'Did you buy what you wanted for the flat?'

'Aye, most of it. Leslie's no better, then?'

'Not when I left.' The cake's on its way to my mouth, dropping little flakes of chocolate as it climbs. 'He says I'm not to believe them, that he's not going to die…' And up comes the cake, closer to my mouth and then… I let it fall, on my lap, on the floor, wherever it lands. Alasdair comes to the sofa and sits with his hand on my back while I weep. When it's over, he takes the cake from my skirt, gets up without speaking and goes to the kitchen while I go to the bathroom, followed by an agitated Barney, and splash cold water on my face. I'm unrecognizable, swollen-mouthed and puffy-eyed with damp hair. I put on my jeans and go back downstairs. Alasdair's made tea and put what's left of the cake on a new plate.

Before I can speak, he says, 'Don't you go apologizing. That's been brewing up for quite a while.'

'Today was a bit… much. And now I look like a frog, sorry.'

'Blonde frogs, they're à la mode.'

'Actually, I don't cry easily, not as a rule.'

'Neither do I – well, not as often as I'd like. I envy you.'

I blow my nose. 'What about when your wife went off with the drummer?'

'Not one drop. Only glad to see the back of her. What do you call a drummer without a girlfriend?'

'Don't know.'

'Homeless.'

I laugh, snottily.

'I'm not trying to cheer you up.'

'Just as well.'

Apart from the mac, his clothes are subdued tonight, black trousers, pink jumper – probably new. He sits back in the chair. 'I was quite tearful as a boy. There was nobody I could talk to about the things I was seeing… I did try a few times but—'

'When did you first find out? That you were, you know…'

'There wasn't a big clash of cymbals – oh my word, I must be psychic. I just saw things and then they'd turn up.'

'What sort of things?'

'Dad having a bit of an accident at work, my friend Paul getting a new bike, nothing dramatic, *things*. And I'd know if women were pregnant, that happened quite a lot. But my auntie Evelyn, she was a bit of a breakthrough. She died very young, breast cancer and the rest, thirty at most. Plenty of tears about that, although I had to keep them to myself… So I'm sitting up in bed one night, reading, and she's there! Hello, Auntie Evelyn! We had a little talk and she said I had to be careful for my mum, stop her getting low. And I should give people messages if anything came through. I asked her if she wanted me to give a message to Uncle Rory but she said he'd only get upset and tell me I was a bad boy for making things up. She never came back, but I don't think she needed to. She'd done her job, as it were. Are you going to eat that cake?'

'I can't taste anything, I'm too bunged up.' I pass him the plate. 'So why didn't you take it up properly?'

'I did for a while. Then it all got a bit too much, the stories. I like it the way it is, a bit of this and a bit of that. I'm not a great one for doing the same thing twice.'

'Did you know Leslie was going to get mugged?'

'No, of course I didn't.'

'What about Gully pushing you out of the flat?'

'Well I had a feeling there – but you don't need to be psychic to know that man's going to play the royal prawn, now do you?'

'Why couldn't you warn Leslie about the mugging? Why not stop a drama before it starts?'

'Not up to me. I can't tell you what I don't know.'

'So who decides?'

'No idea. I'm the go-between, I don't know anyone at HQ. Look, I'm not selling insurance here. You think what you like.' The big smile. 'I'll tell you what, though – why don't you try the hospital? I've got a feeling Leslie's turned a corner.'

'Alasdair…'

'Really, I mean it.'

And of course he has. The staff nurse says his oxygen levels have improved slightly, and when I ask whether I should come in early tomorrow, she says there'll be no need. The afternoon will be fine.

'See?' Alasdair says as he puts on his stinking tyre-coat. 'Everything can go back to normal now.' He grins. 'If that's what you want?'

Twenty-eight

I take Barney round the garden and then lie on the sofa, unin-
terrupted, as I've wanted to do since I got home. I close my
swollen eyes and settle into the cushions. *Normal.* What's
Alasdair getting at? We're not going to be *normal.* We've got
stairs to deal with, hospital visits, driving, the bath… What
about work? I picture Leslie fretting, limping round his room.
Me, cheering him along, checking the floor for obstacles,
watching for setbacks. To be normal means living in small
ways, every day like every other, no risk, not moving the air too
much. For nearly forty years I've troubled the air no more than
a terracotta pot. But I *did* stir the air, oh yes! I blew myself right
out of the door and there was no way back, not once I'd said
goodbye.

Scene: the premiere of my first film. I send my parents an
invitation, they don't reply. I telephone. My mother answers.

I'm sorry, Miriam. Your father says I'm not to come.

Let me talk to him.

I'm sorry, dear.

I put the phone down, cowed by my father's intimidation.
Away from there, I'm free of him; anywhere near and I'm seven
again with my voice torn out.

Scene: my first spring fete as local celebrity, a church hall, west London. Tea at the high table, properly set for the vicar and me, not paper cups with the hoi polloi. I sashay from stall to stall, best suit, heels, hat, gloves. They need to make me look as if I'm special so that they can feel specially blessed by my being there – even though I'm pretty much a nobody unless you happen to like the cinema – and I play the game because I so enjoy the tarantara.

Scene: the day before the fete, when I can't think how to start my opening address, I ring my new friend, Aude. 'Easy,' she says. 'Try this. Ladies and gentlemen, thank you so much for coming. Fork out or fuck off.'

And now Aude's gone and Poppy's going and Rolf's dead and my father too. My life with Leslie will never be the same again and soon we'll be gone and what'll be left of us? Max and Constance…

The wind's been whipped up into a tornado and we've all been lifted off our feet and set down somewhere, groping for signs. The sofa's not comfortable any more. I get up, turn off the lights and wake Barney. We go up to bed with the red book. I want to talk to Harry.

Come on, girl, let old doctor twitnuts put that smile back on your face. Nothing to moan about. Have as much milk and sugar as you want.

I've made a mess of things, Grandad.

Nothing that can't be put right.

It's much too late.

Ah, not a po emptied, not a bed made and the fleet's in…

Why did my father want to lock you up?

Can't answer. No allowing for wickedness. He was always a difficult boy. Unkind, even to his mother.

I can't see the point of anything. Not if it all turns out like this.

Sometimes I look to the right and I see goodness. Sometimes I look to the left and I see badness. You're whining, sweetheart. It doesn't suit you.

He's right. I an whining. I'm finding it very difficult to make the distinction between accepting that this is it and being grateful for what I've got. Is it too late for me to ask for something different? Barney puts his head on my leg and looks at me, blinking, his big eyes soft with affection. 'It's all right for you, mate,' I say, stroking his head. 'You've been rescued. What about the rest of us?'

Twenty-nine

I'm up at seven to put on the washing and take Barney round the block. While I'm having breakfast, I suddenly remember that I haven't checked Leslie's emails since the mugging. There are only two messages, one from a friend in Australia and one from… antonio.west@… *Antonio West?*

My Antonio? Mr Maggoty-Screen? I read on, sucking the words up in one go and then recapitulating more slowly, several times over.

Hi Leslie, intrigued by your idea. Will ring you when I've sounded this out. All best to you and Ms Shaw.

Sent on Wednesday, the night of the mugging. What 'idea'?

What's Leslie done?

Check the outbox, stupid! Nothing there… click… check Deleted… nothing there either.

He's hidden it.

I stand by the computer, rattling with anger and curiosity. Has he sent Antonio the brothel series? I open every document, but there's nothing that could possibly be of interest except the brothel, the bloody brothel. Oh, God. *How could Leslie do this?* I

315

go through his desk and the cardboard files looking for a printout or anything else that might give me a clue. There's nothing. I could wait till later this morning and see if Charlie's still got Antonio's number or wait even longer and confront Leslie when I visit, but at this point I'd sooner walk to Antonio's – even if he lives in Cardiff – and get him out of bed. I decide to send him an email.

Dear Antonio, thank you for your reply. Leslie's had an accident and is in hospital but I, Mim, am at home. Please reply *the minute* you get this.

Delete.

Dear Antonio, Leslie's in hospital but I'd very much like to talk to you! Any chance of a call this morning? With best wishes, Miriam Shaw.

Send.

I've forgotten to give him the phone number. I send a PS. Now what? I suppose I ought to ring Constance and tell her about Leslie so I can leave the line clear. I find her card and tap in the number quickly. With any luck, I'll get her voicemail. No, damn, it's the real thing. *Don't think about it, Mim, just say the first thing that comes into your head.*

'Hello, Mum here. I thought you'd like to know that your father's a little better.'

'That's very good news,' she says in her blonde voice. 'What does better actually mean?'

'His oxygen levels are improving.'

316

'Excellent. I'll be free at four o'clock. I thought I might visit for half an hour. Will you be there?'

'I should be.'

'I'll see you later then.'

For a moment, I want to cheer. Good Mummy Mim! Then I remember that I'm also the brothel queen, the bawd. I'm as angry now as when I first discovered Leslie's script. After everything I've said... Did Leslie not understand me at all?

The phone rings.

'Hello?'

'Ms Shaw? This is Antonio West.'

I sit down on the stairs with one hand draped over the bannisters. 'Hello, Antonio.' He asks about Leslie. I tell him, not everything, but enough. He's very sympathetic, he was robbed himself, at knifepoint. When there's nothing more we can say about mugging, he says how sorry he is that we weren't able to work together on the advert.

'But,' he says, 'this proposal of Leslie's—'

'Yes?'

'I've had quite a bit of interest.'

'I'm sure you have.'

'And there's particular interest in you, making a comeback.'

'That's very gratifying, Antonio, but I'm afraid Leslie's led you astray – I'm not making any comeback. You'll have to find someone else to play the madam.'

'The madam? I don't think Leslie mentioned her – is she significant?'

'It's a brothel! Of course she's significant!'

'I don't remember a brothel either—'

'So what are we talking about?'

'Leslie's email. It's such a brilliant idea! *The Curfew* for the twenty-first century. A sequel, with you playing the original character, as she is now.'

I seem to have made my way downstairs and now I'm standing by the washing machine. I can't quite grasp what Antonio's saying. Bending down, I open the door to empty out the clothes. They're dry. I've forgotten to turn it on. I mumble, 'Excuse me a minute,' close the door again, pull the switch out and wait for the water to gush before I put the phone back to my ear. 'The washing,' I explain. 'What was that you were saying?'

'*The Curfew*. A sequel—'

'Yes, that's what I thought you said.'

Roy's in overalls, wiping his hands on a rag that he stuffs in his pocket. I give him the lead and he takes Barney. 'Do you fancy coming in?'

'I won't if you don't mind. Alasdair should be here any second.'

'I'm hoping you'll have a meal with me,' he says, 'when Leslie's up to it. And Stevie, of course. She wouldn't miss that. We'd be tickled to bits.'

'We'll make a date.' Alasdair draws up, waving. We wave back. 'I might not need to drop Barney off tomorrow, not if I only go in for a couple of hours.'

'Tell me later. And say hello to Leslie from me. Tell him he was great at the Palladium.'

Leslie doesn't know that I've been spending time in this man's house. He's already jealous about Barney. If he thought Roy had been looking after his wife as well as his dog, he'd be distraught. And why should he know? There are times when you have to keep quiet about minutiae, times when the important thing is to stick to fundamentals. If Leslie's more alert today, then perhaps I'll explain a little about who Roy is and what it is about him that I like. Roy, the horse chestnut. A big tree, a trunk you can lean on. Resurrection Roy, born again in the horrible house, made it pretty, made himself well. You'll like him, Leslie, no you will, you really will. He's been so kind. Why do we have to have dinner there? Because he wants us to be friends. Yes, I think we could be. No, I'm not rehearsing for the Merry Widow. Is that what you think? That he's a rival? Well, you're wrong. You'll always be my best tree, Leslie. You're a silver birch. My silver birch.

I don't mention Antonio to Alasdair. In fact, I'm not going to mention him to anyone, because the moment I do I'll be bombarded with opinions and anyway, I'm not sure that I'm certain in my own mind about what I've done.

Alasdair's had a haircut so we laugh about that and then he reminds me that this is his last day as my driver. He's off up north to do a telly. I tell him I'll get taxis. 'I never use the car if Leslie's out. It's a quirk – I like to know he's at home in case I break down or hit something.'

'What could he do from home?'

'It's not what he could *do*, it's that he's there. Otherwise I'd feel stranded, out on a limb. Silly, but there it is.'

When he drops me at the main door, he says, 'I'll be back on Sunday. But I don't think you'll need me any more.'

'Who says?'

'Does it matter?'

'You've been… thank you.'

'So have you.'

Leslie's tubes are still up his nose and he looks as gaunt as he did yesterday but he smiles when he sees me. There are things for me to report: Max leaving Spain, Aude staying in Italy, Constance wanting to visit at four, but I save all that. I ask how he is and he tells me, with difficulty but at least he's talking, that he's going to be allowed into the chair tomorrow, while they make the bed.

'That's marvellous. You're going to be back on your feet in no time.'

'I'll do my best.'

'I checked the emails this morning.'

'Did you?'

'There was an odd one.'

'Was there?'

'From Antonio West.'

'Ah, yes.' I don't know how you'd direct a man who looks as ill as this to add guilt to his face but there it is, culpability laid bare. 'So?'

'What do you think he says?'

Leslie stares at me and shakes his head.

'He says it's brilliant.'

'*Does he?*'

'Why didn't you tell me what you were doing?'

'You wouldn't have liked it.'

'I emailed him back. I thought you'd sent him the brothel play—'

And now there's hurt, nestling in with the guilt. 'Course I didn't.'

'I know. He told me.'

'So you spoke to him?'

'I spoke to him.'

'And?'

'He says there's quite a bit of interest—'

'Is there?'

'… And they want to arrange a meeting, when you're better.'

He smiles. 'Perfect.'

'Do you really think I can do it?'

'Did it before. Do it again. Never know where this could lead, Missus. So what did you say to him?'

'I said yes.'

Thirty

*So, Grandad. Things have changed. There's been a storm, a
tornado.*

*I'm no bigger than a raindrop, falling on a leaf, pitter patter,
pitter pat. Is that any use to you?*

Was I right to say yes?

Yes, darling, yes.

But will Leslie want me to? He didn't before.

*Before was way, way back. What about him thinking up the
bawdy house?*

That's true, but I didn't like it, not one bit.

*You stay happy, that's his wish. He never locked the door. As for
you, having a proper life – it's all right to do it, you know. It was
always all right to do it. If you'd have asked me then, I'd have told
you the same. How's your garden growing? White lilies in mine
and dahlias aplenty. I'm moving on from vegetables.*

I wish you were here, Grandad.

And how do you know I'm not?

Leslie's coming back this afternoon. I prepare the house,
moving hazards, changing sheets and cleaning up the mess.
There isn't much in the garden to cut but I manage a small vase

for the kitchen table. Then I make him a card – 'Hip Hip Hooray! Leslie's home today!' under a cack-handed drawing of Barney banging a drum – and put it next to the bottle of champagne that Roy dropped in last night.

I get a taxi to the hospital to pick him up. Yesterday, the doctor told us that it's going to take time for him to really pull through, and when we're out on the street by ourselves, away from the nurses, I can see that he looks older, more bent, more frail. On the journey home, we talk about Antonio: he'll be coming to lunch soon with his producer friend. Leslie's thrilled, of course, and can't stop smiling idiotically. I'm smiling too – ol' brown eyes is back. Who knows, I could even get asked to open another fete. It's strange to imagine working again but I'm coming round to it, there's always the possibility that I'll be dead before they can find anyone to cough up the money.

Alasdair thinks it's all going to happen but then, of course, he would. I'll be seventy-two next week. We're having a birthday dinner and Constance says that she might well come.

I've promised to behave.